TRACKING EVIL

TONY MAXWELL

Maxwell, Tony, 1943-
Tracking Evil
Print ISBN: 978-0-9938127-7-4

Published in 2020 by
BRATONMAX
P O Box 146, Red Deer,
Alberta, Canada T4N 5E7

Cover by Streetlight Graphics

CHAPTER 1

NDLULAMITHI

'THIS IS HOW I WOULD like you to remember me and this country that I love so much,' Theunis Meyer said to his young son Andre, as they sat in the front seat of his old Ford *bakkie* looking out over a waterhole in the Kruger National Park. 'Son, I do not have the words to tell you how sorry I am for the way things have turned out for our family. But I want you to know, our decision to get a divorce is the hardest thing your mother and I have ever done.'

Theunis paused, staring out at the bush-fringed edges around the waterhole shimmering in the midday heat wave. 'You see, when your mother and I met nearly twenty years ago, we fell deeply in love. But, as the years went by, our differences in outlook grew. I am a simple Afrikaner farmer with family roots going back to before the Great Trek. Your mother, on the other hand, was born in England. She's far better educated than I am and most deserving of the finer things in life, which, no matter how hard I've tried, I've not been able to give her.'

He turned in his seat and looked directly at his son. 'I had hoped that once we had enough money for the deposit on the farm, things would be different. Our lives would be better. Unfortunately, I never realized just how badly the isolation would affect her; cut off as she was from her few friends and the simple pleasures of Hoedspruit, little as they are.'

Choking back the lump in his throat, Andre, in an effort to change the subject, asked his father, 'Is this where you first saw that elephant?'

'Ah, yes… Ndlulamithi. In the Tsonga language it means taller than the trees,' his father replied pausing in reflection. 'Yes, this is where I first saw him. He appeared out of the tree-line over there with his distinctive shambling gait and the most spectacular set of tusks I've ever seen. He was closely followed by his two safari elephants which ran ahead and drove off the four old buffalo bulls and a sprinkling of zebra and wildebeest gathered around the water's edge. Elephants, you see, don't always like to share waterholes.'

'Dad, what are safari elephants?' Andre asked, hoping to keep the conversation going in this new direction.

'Bull elephants are, by their very nature, solitary creatures; they only spend time with females during the breeding season. However, younger males, which I call safari elephants, occasionally attach themselves to older, more experienced bulls. Presumably for the companionship and lessons on how to survive in the bush.'

'Have you seen Ndlulamithi since then?'

'Once, about three years ago, I took a black and white photo of him standing at this very waterhole. Unfortunately, the picture's a bit fuzzy as my camera was crap and I knew nothing about taking photographs, as your mother often told me.'

'Do you think this elephant is still alive?'

'When I last saw him, I thought him to be somewhere around fifty years old. Ranger Krause at Punda Maria, who has seen him many times, told me my guess at his age was about right. You must remember elephants, providing they are healthy and not killed by poachers, can sometimes live into their eighties. Hell man, you could probably come back here in twenty years' time and still see him! And I hope one day you will do that.'

Theunis started the engine and drove back to the main road, turning south towards Letaba and the exit gate at Phalaborwa. 'I want you to know Andre, although I am sad you're going to England with your mother, I am also glad that she will not be alone there. After all, it's been nearly twenty years since she left her family behind, and a lot of things could have changed. At least I will have your sister to keep me on the straight and narrow!'

'Janet only wants to stay here because of her boyfriend.' Even as he said it, Andre realized how hurtful it must have sounded to his father. 'I don't mean it like that…'

'I know you don't; we often say things that don't sound too good when we think about them later.' A few moments went by before Theunis turned to his son again, 'Have you any idea what you would like to do once you finish school in England?'

'I've been thinking about joining the British army, or even becoming a policeman!'

His father laughed. 'Just so long as you don't join one of those regiments that fought against your great grandfather while he served in *Generaal* Ben Viljoen's commando during the Anglo-Boer War!'

'You have my word on that Dad; no regiment that fought against the Boers!' Andre said as he struggled to think of an English regiment that wasn't involved in that war.

CHAPTER 2

LONDON

A S THE DOORS SLID OPEN, Andre Meyer joined the rush of early morning commuters making their way up the escalators at Westminster Underground Station, and out onto the Victoria Embankment. He found the brisk morning air a welcome relief after the hot, crowded car on the Circle Line from Kings Cross. Crossing the road, he stood gazing at the lights of the London Eye and the passing riverboat traffic, muted by a light mist rolling in from the North Sea.

Glancing up at the newly renovated face of Big Ben, he realized he was fifteen minutes ahead of schedule for his eight o'clock appointment. Not wanting to arrive too early, he turned and walking slowly, followed the Embankment as far as the Royal Airforce Monument. Stopping under an ancient London plane tree, he looked out over the now mist-enshrouded river, all the while wishing he hadn't given up smoking. Checking his watch, he turned and retracing his steps, crossed over the road again and walked into the main entrance of New Scotland Yard.

Detective Inspector Andre Meyer was wearing his best charcoal two-button suit with an almost new, freshly ironed, white shirt and a conservative, dark blue tie. He was a tall man, probably about six foot with close-cropped, greying hair. His physique was lean and wiry as opposed to being muscular and when he smiled, which was often, the fine wrinkles around his eyes remained quite still.

'Good morning,' he said to one of the civilian receptionists behind the long counter, 'DI Andre Meyer, I'm attending a meeting with Detective Chief Superintendent Bryson and Detective Superintendent Webb.'

'Good morning, sir,' she replied, consulting her computer screen. 'DCS Bryson is expecting you. Please sign the visitor's book before reporting to the security desk.' The receptionist handed him a visitor's pass on a blue ribbon and directed him towards three uniformed officers standing around an airport style metal detector. 'Once you've cleared security,' she continued, 'follow the corridor to your left and take any of the lifts to the fifth floor. The duty security officer on that floor will let DCS Bryson know you have arrived.' Thanking her with a smile, he slipped the visitor pass around his neck and moved along the counter to the visitor's book. As he signed in, he was surprised to see that his boss, Detective Chief Inspector Guhrs, hadn't arrived yet.

Emerging from the lift on the fifth floor, he checked in with the duty officer. 'Please take a seat, sir. I'll let DCS Bryson know you've arrived.' Andre had scarcely taken a seat when his superior officer, DSU Webb, emerged from one of the lifts and joined him in the reception area.

'Good morning, sir,' Andre said rising to his feet. He had only met Webb once or twice since his transfer to serious organized crime at Caledonian Road and, like most of his colleagues, knew him to be a policeman's policeman. Webb, immaculately turned out in his uniform, wasn't much over five foot six, portly, with his thinning, dark hair brushed over in a failing attempt to conceal his bald spot.

'Ah! Meyer, good man, right on time I see,' Webb said by way of a greeting. 'Does Chief Superintendent Bryson know we're here?'

Andre was about to reply when the duty officer, taking a call on his intercom, invited them to go through to Bryson's office.

'Good morning, sir,' Webb said as they entered the office, 'this is DI Meyer from Caledonian Road.' An immaculately uniformed officer wearing the rank of Detective Chief Superintendent, rose from behind a large desk in the centre of the oak panelled office, its windows along one side overlooking the Thames River and Westminster Bridge.

Bryson was a tall man, about six foot two Andre thought, of slender build with an ascetic face topped by shock of white hair. Despite having been a member of the Metropolitan Police Service for close on twenty years,

Andre had never personally met more than two or three officers of DCS Bryson's rank.

'Good morning Meyer, I'm Chief Superintendent Bryson,' he said shaking Andre's hand. 'I'm sorry it's taken so long for us to finally meet. Would you like a coffee?'

'No, thank you, sir,' Andre replied taking the chair indicated while Webb, apparently unawed by his surroundings, poured himself a coffee and occupied the other. Andre couldn't help noticing the almost obsessive tidiness of the DCS's desk. All his files were colour coded, bound with thin red ribbons and neatly stacked in two trays separated from two telephones by a large, leather bound, green blotter.

'I don't suppose you have any idea why Superintendent Webb and I called this meeting?' Bryson asked breaking the silence.

'No idea, sir. Though I'm wondering why Chief Inspector Guhrs isn't here?'

The two ranking officers exchanged glances. 'We'll come to that later.' Bryson replied as he pushed his pair of rounded, metal rimmed glasses further up his nose. 'First off, I want to commend you and your team for your past successes in breaking up the various drug gang operations on your patch. But, and I'm sure you'll agree; your success rate has fallen off dramatically over the past few months.' Andre made ready to reply, but Bryson held up his hand stopping him. 'Based on reports I've received, you and your team carried out no less than three raids on various properties owned by this Clive Rylston but made no arrests or Class A drug seizures. Why do you think that is?' Bryson asked staring straight at Andre.

Andre stared right back. 'I've had to put it down to bad luck, sir. We've had no leaks that we are aware of. My Detective Sergeant and Detective Constables are the best officers I've ever worked with.'

'I don't doubt that for one moment Meyer; but take the raid on Rylston's furniture warehouse in Clement Street last Friday. Clearly you and your team were convinced there was a significant quantity of drugs on the premises. Is that not correct?'

Andre had been expecting this line of questioning from the moment he was ordered to attend this meeting with Bryson and Webb at New Scotland Yard. However, he had hoped his boss at Caledonian Road, DCI Guhrs, would have been there to back up his explanation.

'Sir, after more than a week of around the clock surveillance we identified and photographed a number of known drug couriers visiting the premises. Based on that, together with a tip from a usually reliable informant, we had good reason to believe Rylston and his lot were again cutting, weighing and packaging baggies of crystal meth, cocaine and heroin for sale by their street gangs throughout London. Unfortunately, when SCO19's Tactical Support Team effected entry to the building, all we found there were the three principle members of the gang sitting around a table in a back room playing cards.'

'So, the whole business was a complete waste of time and scarce police resources?' Webb chimed in.

Andre had not expected such an unfair and inaccurate criticism of his team's efforts to bring Rylston to justice so, for the moment, he was at a loss for words. Tamping down his anger, he smiled at Webb replying, 'Not really, sir. On the day before our raid, one of my alert Detective Constables noticed a member of Rylston's gang carry a large, black plastic garbage bag all the way to a dumpster behind a Tesco's supermarket, almost three city blocks away. Thinking this rather odd behaviour, he made the effort to retrieve the bag for closer examination back at the station.'

'And?' Bryson interjected, 'what did you find?'

'Along with the usual household rubbish, we discovered a thick batch of discarded, clear plastic wraps which subsequent tests confirmed, were used to wrap twenty, four pound bricks of cocaine. We estimated the street value of each brick to be somewhere in the region of £42,600; and this is before each brick is broken down into more saleable baggies. What we found especially interesting were the blue seahorse symbols stamped on each plastic wrap.'

'Ah!' Bryson snorted, '*Cavalo Marinho* – the Portuguese Blue Seahorse drug cartel! We've had several warnings from the National Crime Agency and Europol that this cartel is responsible for the majority of Class A drugs smuggled into this country. Most of it arriving in small craft masquerading as fishing boats, with London the preferred destination. As a result, the Home Secretary has been on my back demanding we break up this drug network before things get completely out of hand.'

'I can assure you, sir, we are doing the very best we can,' Andre replied. 'Were DCI Guhrs here, I'm sure he would confirm what I've just told you.'

'Unfortunately, Meyer, it pains Superintendent Webb and I to have to inform you that DCI Guhrs is currently suspended from duty, pending a criminal investigation by the Directorate of Professional Standards. The Directorate believes it has proof of his connections to the Seahorse cartel, which may explain why your recent efforts have come up empty handed.'

Andre sat in stunned silence trying to take it all in. The very mention of the DPS to any serving police officer was guaranteed to send chills running up and down their collective spines; and these are policemen who've never set a foot wrong. The effect on officers who may have something to hide could only be imagined. 'Perhaps, sir, I may have that coffee.'

'If you will excuse me, sir,' Webb said rising to his feet, 'I have to attend another meeting with the National Crime Agency in Tinworth Street. Meyer, I'll see you later at Caledonian Road.'

'No need to hurry away Meyer,' Bryson said as Webb closed the door behind him, 'let's take a few moments for an informal chat.' While Andre poured himself a coffee, Bryson paged through a report he picked up from a tray on his desk. 'Quite a resumé for a Metropolitan police detective,' he remarked. 'Born in South Africa; followed by six years in the Parachute Regiment, before joining us back in 1995. Forgive me, but I must ask, why on earth the Paras?'

'I promised my father I would never serve in an English regiment that had fought against the Boers during the Anglo-Boer War. The Parachute Regiment was the only one I could think of that never fought in South Africa!'

Bryson leaned back in his chair and laughed. 'I spent some time in Africa back in the 1980s. I was a member of a police contingent sent out to Rhodesia to oversee the so-called elections which Mugabe and his gang of incompetent thugs ended up winning. At the time, all of us believed something bad was in the offing for Rhodesia. Unfortunately, as it turned out, we were spot on.' Bryson sat staring out of the window for a few moments as though he were reliving his experiences in Rhodesia. Finally, he turned to Andre, 'How is it you ended up here in the first place?'

'My mother, who was born in England, met and married my father in South Africa, where my sister Janet and I were born. When my parents got divorced in 1985, I returned to England with my mother, while Janet stayed on in South Africa with my father. Although both of our parents have since passed away, my sister and I have stayed in touch over the years.'

'Quite a varied upbringing if you don't mind me saying,' Bryson commented. 'Have you been back to South Africa since you left?'

'Twice; once to attend my sister's wedding and again for my father's funeral.'

'So, I take it your sister still lives in South Africa?'

'She does. She and her female partner live in a place called Nelspruit; it's in Mpumalanga Province close to the Kruger Park game reserve. They run a bed and breakfast and arrange tours of the Kruger Park.'

I remember the Kruger Park!' Bryson said. 'After we finished our tour of duty in Rhodesia, a few of us took some time to travel around South Africa and spent a few days in the game reserve. I really enjoyed it and would like to return one day with my wife.'

'Sir,' Andre Meyer jumped in hoping to get the conversation back to the matter in hand, 'Sir, what will happen now DCI Guhrs is suspended from duty; will he be replaced by another officer from outside?'

'While it's always possible the Chief Constable may have other ideas, I, together with the full support of DSU Webb, have decided to appoint you acting DCI pending official confirmation in three months' time. I trust that answers your question.'

CHAPTER 3

POINT FREDERICK

'COME ON DANNY! IT'S TIME we got going. Tide will be coming in soon,' Mike Bewley said to his young son as he tied their fishing rods on the roof of his small car. 'I want to have our lines in the sea off Point Frederick before sunrise.'

'Why do we always have to go so bloody early?' Danny complained, 'we never catch anything anyway.'

'Watch your language son! For your information, we usually catch something, even if it's an eel or two,' Mike replied as they pulled out onto the Folkestone road.

'Dad, can I turn on our dashcam?'

'No harm in that – though it's not likely there'll be any other cars on the road at this time of the morning.'

'Oh yeah!' Danny replied as their headlights swept over the beach area illuminating a white van in the parking lot. 'Look at that, someone's already there before us!'

'Damn! I hope they aren't fishing in our favourite spot. I see there's a light on in old Mrs Davis's cottage,' Mike remarked as he parked alongside the van, 'hope they didn't wake her; you know how she feels about early morning fishermen.'

The first glimmer of dawn in the east made it easier for father and son to see where they were stepping as they followed the narrow footpath leading to the jumble of rocks and crashing waves on the Point. 'Where the hell do you think you're going!' a shadowy figure demanded stepping out onto the path and blocking their way. 'You'll fuck off back the way you came if you know what's good for you,' he said pointing what looked like a small submachine gun at Mike.

'Ok! Ok!' Mike replied holding up his free hand, 'no problem, we're going. Come on son, we'll go over the other side of the Point; if that's OK with you?' he said sarcastically to the gunman.

'As long as you stay away from this side of the Point, I don't give a flying fuck where you go!'

Mike steered his son away from the path and up over the headland that led to Point Frederick. 'Did you see his gun Dad? I thought he was going to shoot you.'

'Sorry you had to see that son; I just didn't fancy arguing with a man with a gun.'

'He sounded foreign Dad. Do you think they're smugglers?'

'Could be, I really don't know. But I'll tell you what we're going to do; we're going to take the long way back to the parking lot and get Mrs Davis to call the police. I'm not going to let some foreign bastard get away with pointing a gun at me. This is Britain; not some fucking third world country.'

'You should watch your language Dad,' Danny replied smiling.

———— ❦ ————

Father and son sat on the lounge in the enclosed porch of Mrs Davis's cottage facing Detective Sergeant Wilson from the Folkestone police. 'Sir, you said in your report that he sounded foreign?'

'At a guess I'd say possibly Spanish or Portuguese. You see, last year our family spent a week at a resort outside Lisbon; I know it sounds crazy but the man waving that submachine gun around sounded just like our waiter! Sergeant, do you have any idea why he didn't want us out on the Point?'

'According to Mrs Davis, a foreign sounding man came knocking on her door at around two this morning saying his small fishing boat had run aground on the rocks. He asked if he could use her phone to call a friend to help him retrieve some of his fishing gear. For her part Mrs Davis, not too happy at being woken so early in the morning, told him he should be calling the police or coastguard rescue for help. However, he insisted it wouldn't be necessary as his friend owed him a favour and would be only too happy to help. About an hour after he made the call, a white delivery van arrived in the parking lot. Mrs Davis told us that two men got out and walked along the path leading towards the Point. Then, fifteen minutes after you and your son left the parking lot carrying your fishing gear, four men appeared from the direction of the Point carrying several large bales which they loaded into the van. With her suspicions fully aroused, Mrs Davis tried to get the license number as the van drove off, but it was either too dark, or the license plate had been deliberately obscured.'

'Sergeant, we have a dashboard camera mounted in our car; when we checked it ten minutes ago, the van did not have a license plate.'

'Do you think they were smugglers?' Danny asked the Sergeant.

'Very likely son,' he replied. 'We've requested a dive team from Folkestone to search the wreck of the boat which, I'm told, is now lying in ten foot of water just off the Point.

———◆———

DSU Webb addressed the detectives gathered in the briefing room at Caledonian Road police station. 'Good morning everyone. As I'm sure most of you now know DCI Guhrs is currently suspended from duty pending an investigation by the DPS. Until further notice, DI Andre Meyer will assume responsibility for all investigations previously handled by DCI Guhrs. This matter is to be treated as highly confidential until the DPS releases its findings. That is all I have to say on the matter.' Waiting until the murmuring amongst the group died away, Webb continued, 'I will now hand you over to DI Meyer who will brief you on what could be an important breakthrough in our investigations into Rylston's drug distribution network.'

'Thank you, sir. In the early hours of this morning, a boat carrying a sizable quantity of drugs ran aground on a rocky headland just outside Folkestone on the Kent coast. The boat eventually sank, taking most of its cargo to the bottom. Police dive teams called in from Folkestone have recovered seventeen bales of cocaine and heroin from the boat to date. However, based on an eyewitness account, we have reason to believe a number of bales were retrieved from the boat before it sank and are quite possibly on their way to one of Rylston's packaging and distribution outlets in this area.'

'Sir, what evidence have we got that the drugs removed from the boat are on their way to one of Rylston's outfits around here; surely it could be going anywhere?' DS Adnan Banerjee asked.

'Good question. When the boat ran onto the rocks, one of the crew members hiked to a nearby cottage where he made a phone call to someone asking for help. The Folkestone police ran a trace on the number called and, to no one's surprise, it turned out to be registered to our friend Clive Rylston.'

Turning towards a photograph pinned on the whiteboard behind him, Meyer continued, 'This is a dashcam photograph of the white Mercedes Sprinter van that arrived to pick up the men and the bales from the sinking boat. Starting immediately, I want round-the-clock surveillance on all Rylston's known haunts, particularly his Clement Street warehouse operation. I want you all to treat this as a top priority for this department. Let's get to it everyone; let's put him out of business permanently.'

CHAPTER 4

CLEMENT STREET

WITHIN THE HOUR, A REPORT came in from one of the surveillance teams keeping watch on Rylston's Clement Street warehouse. 'A white van showed up a few minutes ago; definitely a Mercedes Sprinter. It circled the block a few times, apparently waiting for someone to crack the gates at the back. As soon as they were open, the van drove straight in and under a covered loading bay. What do you want us to do?'

DS Banerjee took the call. 'Have you got eyes on the van? What's it doing?'

'Nothing that we can see, Boss, though Bains managed to get up on the roof of a building a little way down the street. He confirms the van is parked in a closed loading bay and can't be seen from the street or any of the surrounding rooftops.'

'OK. Stay awake and let me know of any changes.'

'Sergeant, talking about changes, whenever someone entered or left the building through the street entrance, we saw that a new security grille has been installed just inside the door. You'll remember the last time we raided this place, we had to use a battering ram just to get in. It'll be a damn sight harder with that grille in place. We think this is something the DI will want to pass on to Tactical Support or SCO19.'

'Too bloody right it is! We always knew the bastards were up to no good in there! I'll see that DI Meyer gets to know about it.'

Andre Meyer knocked and entered DSU Webb's office, 'Sir, I think we've finally caught the break we've been looking for. One of our surveillance teams watching the Clement Street warehouse reported the arrival of a white Mercedes Sprinter van, which was hastily driven out of sight into the warehouse loading bay. What action can we take, sir?'

'It's your show Meyer; you're calling the shots. What do you suggest?'

'I think we should hit them right away, sir. Before they have a chance to move the drugs.'

'OK but do it by the book. Make damn sure you get all the necessary warrants and keep me in the loop.'

Meyer addressed the hastily gathered team of detectives in the briefing room at the Caledonian Road police station. 'Right, listen up. We've got the go ahead for a raid on Clement Street.' A collective groan went up from the detectives, many of whom had been down this road before. 'I understand how you feel, but this time I think we've got it right. Take the time to study the photos of Rylston and his known associates, as well as the layout of the double-storey building and the attached warehouse,' he said pointing to a number of photographs and building plans pinned to the whiteboard behind him.

'OK,' he continued, 'this is how we will do it. Two Tactical Support Teams, backed by SCO19 officers, will hit the warehouse entrance and the street entrance at the same time. We will be in close behind them, along with a dozen police constables drafted in to assist in the search and to control any crowds that may gather.'

Andre paused to take a drink of water from the glass on the table next to him. 'Given our previous experiences with Rylston and his lot, we can expect one or two of them to be armed. So, don't take any unnecessary chances; let Tactical and SCO19 lead the way. Also, be prepared for some fireworks! We've received information that a new steel, security grille has been installed behind the doors of the street entrance. Should this turn out to be the case, Tactical are planning to use an explosive breaching charge to effect entry. Any questions?'

He paused and looked around the room, 'None? Good; I take it we're all on the same page. Get kitted up; stab vests, everything. We go as soon as Tactical and SCO19 are ready to move. Good luck and be careful!'

Two Metropolitan Police Ford Transit vans, each carrying four Tactical Support Officers and closely followed by two Armed Response Vehicles, pulled out of the vehicle park behind the Caledonian Road police station. Meyer, along with two detectives, rode in a marked police car right behind the Tactical van tasked with entering Rylston's building through the street entrance. In another car, DS Banerjee and another three detectives followed the second Tactical van to the warehouse entrance at the rear.

Tactical Support and SCO19 officers took up positions on either side of the street entrance as Meyer pounded on the door, 'Open up!' he yelled, 'Armed police! We have a warrant to search these premises!' He gave the occupants one minute to respond before turning to the officer holding the red coloured battering ram known as 'The Big Red Key. 'Go ahead!' he ordered, 'take it down!' It took two swings of the battering ram before a number of deep cracks appeared in the door.

'Halligan bar!' the officer swinging the battering ram shouted, as he moved clear of the door. This enabled a second officer, carrying a pole-like device resembling a medieval halberd, to breakup what was left of the door, exposing a steel security grille.

Stepping forward, an explosives officer carefully taped two lengths of explosive detonating cord around the hinges and lock holding the grille in place. Ordering everyone to stand clear, he detonated the charge bringing the steel grille crashing down. With shouts of, 'Armed police! Get down!' SCO19 officers pounded over the collapsed grille and fanned out into the building. Meyer and his team of detectives, following hard on the heels of the SCO19s, searched frantically for Rylston and his gang, hoping to get to them before they started flushing drugs down the toilets.

'Good work,' Meyer said as DS Banerjee appeared from the direction of the warehouse with two suspects in tow, their hands tied securely behind their backs with plastic cuffs.

'Caught this pair in a shitter trying to dispose of bags of pills. All they managed to do was block the fucking toilet!' Banerjee laughed as he handed his prisoners over to one of the policemen guarding the entrance door.

'Still no sign of Rylston?' Meyer asked Banerjee, 'let's hope the bastard didn't scarper before we got here.' Turning to a SCO19 sergeant who appeared from the direction of the warehouse, he asked, 'Are you sure there's no one left hiding in the warehouse area?'

'We've been all over the place with a fine tooth comb, sir,' the sergeant replied, 'these two are the only ones we've found so far.'

'There's got to be more of them around than just these two. What about upstairs?' Meyer asked, glancing up the staircase as a pair of SCO19 officers shepherded two handcuffed men down to the ground floor. 'Are there any others left up there?' he asked one of the officers.

'None that we could find, sir,' they replied.

'I'm on my way up there now to make doubly sure, sir,' the SCO19 sergeant replied, 'you're welcome to come along, providing you agree to keep well behind me and do as I say.'

'You've got it,' Meyer replied.

"Give us a minute to get rid of this lot, sergeant,' one of the SCO19 officers who'd brought the two prisoners downstairs said, 'and we'll join you upstairs.'

Anxious to get the task over, the SCO19 sergeant turned to Meyer, 'If you're ready, sir, we can head on upstairs. It's been searched once already, so I don't believe we'll find anyone left up there.' Reaching a narrow landing at the top of the stairs, the sergeant ordered Andre to stay where he was while he checked the rooms leading off a long corridor. Waiting on the landing, Andre watched as the officer approached the closest room and pushed the door open. Checking inside, the sergeant turned to Andre, 'Empty,' he said with a quiet sigh of relief, 'clean as a whistle.'

The sergeant continued on and was about to open a second door, when an armed man suddenly appeared from a room at the far end of the corridor. The gunman fired a series of short bursts from an automatic weapon. The sergeant, hammered backwards by the violent impact of the bullets, collapsed to the floor. The gunman, apparently struggling to clear a stoppage on his weapon, dodged back inside the room.

'Officer down on the second floor! Medic, we need a medic!' Andre shouted, certain that the sound of gunfire would have alerted everyone to the danger. Ignoring instructions to stay where he was, he ran to the sergeant, grabbed the straps on his protective vest and began dragging him back towards the landing. Sensing further movement at the end of the corridor, Andre looked up as the gunman reappeared and fired the remainder of his magazine directly at him. The gunman's triumph was short-lived as an SCO19 officer racing up the stairs, returned fire, shooting and killing the gunman.

'Medics up here now! Two officers are down!' the SCO19 officer shouted stepping to one side as two paramedics rushed up the stairs to the fallen men. Acting separately, each medic quickly assessed his patient, 'We need more help up here, call it in,' one of them shouted to Banerjee watching anxiously from the staircase landing.

'Already done,' he replied, 'ambulances are on their way.'

'Better make that an air ambulance; both these men are in a bad way.' Less than fifteen minutes later, an air ambulance lifted off from the park across the road, transporting the two casualties to the Royal London Hospital in Whitechapel.

CHAPTER 5

CALEDONIAN ROAD

'How's DI Meyer doing?' DSU Webb asked Banerjee as he rushed into the Clement Street building.

'Fifteen minutes ago, the DI and the SCO19 sergeant were flown by air ambulance to the Royal London Hospital in Whitechapel,' Banerjee replied.

'How badly injured are they?'

'Well, sir, it took two teams of paramedics almost an hour to stabilize DI Meyer and the SCO19 sergeant to the point they could be safely transported to a hospital. I've just got off the phone to the Royal London's emergency department. The admitting doctor, a Dr Jane Krause, confirmed what the paramedics told me earlier; DI Meyer had been shot three times and is listed in critical condition.'

'What about the SCO19 sergeant?'

'He suffered a bullet wound to the head and, unfortunately, died shortly after arriving at the hospital. The gunman, who was shot dead by another SCO19 officer, closely matched the description we received of the supposed Portuguese drug smuggler who drove the white Mercedes Sprinter van at Point Frederick. This man was armed with a folding stock AKS-74 rifle firing a 7.62mm high velocity round which only the heaviest body armour can stop. DI Meyer and the SCO19 sergeant never stood a chance against such a weapon.'

'What the hell was DI Meyer doing inside that part of the building before it was declared safe?' DSU Webb asked angrily.

'We believed it to be safe, sir. All the rooms on the floor where they encountered the gunman had already been searched. Since we hadn't as yet apprehended Rylston, the DI wanted to make absolutely sure there was no one else hiding up there.'

'What about the drugs? Please tell me you've found them.'

'Not as yet, sir. We're still searching the building.'

'They must be in here somewhere. Tear this bloody place apart – no one goes home until we find them!'

<hr />

'Come in Webb,' DCS Bryson said, 'take a seat. Please tell me you have some good news.'

DSU Webb sat down, 'Yes, sir, I do have good news. My officers discovered a concealed space in one of the upstairs rooms at Clement Street and have seized a significant quantity of drugs marked with the blue seahorse symbol of the *Cavalo Marinho* cartel. They also recovered the seven bales of heroin and cocaine reportedly brought ashore at Point Frederick.'

'Why wasn't this so-called concealed place discovered on previous raids?'

'On the day prior to this raid, DI Meyer and his DS, a man by the name of Banerjee, brainstormed the idea of using a laser measuring device to compare room dimensions with the original building plans. This hiding space, complete with a secret entrance, can only be described as ingenious; in fact, it wasn't until later that day and only after we broke a hole in the wall, that we were able to confirm its existence.'

'Now what about this Rylston fellow; is he in custody?'

'Unfortunately, not as yet. However, as well as the drugs we also found two sleeping bags, a quantity of 7.62mm ammunition and food supplies in this concealed space. This led us to believe that at least one or two men had hidden themselves in the concealed space, just as Tactical Support forced entry to the building.'

'Well, I suppose that would explain how the gunman could suddenly appear even after the top floor had been searched,' Bryson mused, 'but it doesn't explain how Rylston could have got out of the building without being seen by your officers.'

'It pains me, sir, to tell you of our discovery of a number of yellow police high visibility vests stored in the concealed space. Anyone wearing one of these vests would have had no trouble mingling with police officers searching the building.'

Bryson seemed to accept this setback with surprising equanimity. 'Based on the fingerprints your department submitted to the National Crime Agency, it would appear Clive Rylston is wanted, not only by the Portuguese *Guarda Nacional Republicana*, but also by Europol. With so many regional and international agencies out looking for him, it shouldn't be too long before he's in custody!'

Clearing his throat, he turned to Webb, 'I want you to know I intend putting in a recommendation for DI Meyer to be awarded the Queens Police Medal for risking his life going to the aid of a fellow police officer under fire. Keep this under your hat though, at least until it's official.'

DSU Webb, flanked by DCS Bryson on his left and DS Banerjee and DI Sarah Paget, a Police liaison officer, on his right, sat at a table facing the dozen or so reporters attending the hastily convened press briefing. 'Thank you for coming,' Webb began, 'I will read a brief summary of the events leading up to the murder and attempted murder of two Metropolitan Police Officers in the pursuit of their duties. I will take questions afterwards.'

He cleared his throat nervously as he looked out at the faces staring expectantly at him. 'Yesterday morning, acting on information received, police officers raided a warehouse on Clement Street searching for a quantity of drugs believed to be concealed on the premises. A number of suspects were arrested during the raid. In the course of their duties, two police officers were shot. The suspected gunman was fatally shot by an armed officer.'

Webb paused, taking a sip from the glass of water on the table in front of him. 'The injured officers were air lifted to the Royal London Hospital where the SCO19 officer succumbed to his injuries. I can now confirm the other officer, Detective Inspector Andre Meyer, is listed in serious but stable condition. We are unable to identify the SCO19 officer until such time as his next of kin have been informed. I will take some questions,' he said pointing to a reporter waving his hand in the front row.

'What can you tell us about the gunman?'

'At this stage of our investigations, I can't tell you anything other than to confirm he is deceased.'

'What quantity of drugs did you find and what sort of drugs were they?'

Webb leaned over and conferred with Bryson. Straightening up, he continued, 'I can confirm a quantity of Class A drugs have been seized. I'm sorry, I cannot elaborate any further as it may hinder an ongoing investigation. From now on I would refer you to Detective Inspector Paget,' he said looking in her direction. 'DI Paget will keep you advised as further information comes to hand. Thank you all for coming.'

As the senior police officers left the room, Banerjee turned to Paget, 'Excuse me, ma'am, would you mind keeping our station up to date with DI Meyer's progress at the Royal London?'

'I'd be pleased to help in anyway, sergeant. I understand DI Meyer is very popular around the station?'

'Yes, ma'am. I've tried calling patient advice and liaison myself but, other than confirming the DI is in intensive care, I've not been able to find out anything further.'

'You have my word, sergeant, the moment I hear anything, I'll give you a call. In fact, here's my personal number; feel free to call me for an update.'

Banerjee's daily calls to DI Paget finally brought the news he had been hoping for. 'Your DI is between surgeries at the moment and I've arranged permission to visit him briefly this evening. If you like, you're welcome to come along.'

'Thank you very much, ma'am, I'd like that.'

'Before you ring off and providing you don't mind, I have a question for you regarding DI Meyer.'

'I'd be glad to help ma'am, if I can.'

'I have the DI's residential address as Russell Square, Bloomsbury. Is that correct?'

'Yes ma'am, that's quite correct.'

'My God, he must be one of the few policemen in London who can afford to live in a townhouse overlooking Russell Square!'

'It's a long story ma'am. As I heard it around the station, the DI, then a Detective Constable, was sent to investigate a break-in at a townhouse occupied by the widow of a leading London financier. Well, you can guess the rest.'

'Did they marry?'

'They did. A big society wedding, and by all accounts, were happily married for seven years, until she contracted cancer. She passed away three years ago; a blow he never fully recovered from.'

CHAPTER 6

ROYAL LONDON HOSPITAL

T OGETHER, DI PAGET AND DS Banerjee approached the reception desk at the Royal London, 'Good evening,' Paget said as they showed their warrant cards to one of the receptionists, 'We have permission to visit one of your patients in intensive care, a Detective Inspector Andre Meyer.'

'One moment please,' the receptionist replied, 'I'll call ICU reception for confirmation and to find out what ward your patient is in.'

'I never knew his first name was Andre; Andre Meyer, it sounds South African,' Banerjee mused out aloud while they waited.

'Oh yes,' Paget confirmed, 'DI Meyer was born in a town called Nelspruit; I'd say he's definitely South African. Does that bother you?'

'Heavens no! I'm also a South African, born and raised in Durban. I'll bet the DI didn't know that either.'

'Take the lift to the third floor,' the receptionist interrupted, 'ask at the desk for the ward sister on that floor, she will direct you to the SCP in charge of his unit.' Seeing the puzzled expressions on their faces, she hastened to explain, 'SCP's the acronym for surgical care practitioner; that's the nurse who is specifically looking after your patient,' she added with a smile.

Andre Meyer was sitting propped up in a chair in his private room watching television as they walked in. 'Good lord, Banerjee!' Meyer blurted out in surprise.

'No, sir,' Anand Banerjee responded with excellent timing, 'I'm still a lowly detective sergeant.'

'Not to me you're not! I can't tell you how good it is to see a friendly face and you've brought such an attractive lady to visit me as well.'

Stepping forward, Sarah Paget laid her hand on his, trying to ignore the intravenous cannula and other monitoring devices connecting him to a variety of machines making reassuring beeping sounds. 'It's a pleasure to meet you DI Meyer. I'm DI Sarah Paget, a press liaison officer with the Met.'

'Forgive me if I don't get up,' Andre smiled, 'I'm a little tied up at the moment, but please call me Andre and, with your permission, I'll call you Sarah and you Anand,' he said looking at Banerjee. 'How on earth did you manage to wangle a visit past my gatekeeper?'

'It's entirely due to Sarah's persuasive abilities that we managed to get permission to visit you.'

'And believe me I really do appreciate it. So, *howsit ou boet, hoe gaan dit in Durban*? How are things in Durban?' he said in Afrikaans enjoying Anand's surprised expression. 'You'll never believe the things you can learn in a hospital. Just in case you think I'm going mad; I should mention I had a visit earlier today from DCS Bryson; the man is a positive fountain of information on the goings on in the Met. So, Anand, what made you decide to leave South Africa?'

'A scholarship at the London School of Economics, where I fell in love with London and out of love with a higher education. Turns out the Met provided me with all the opportunities I ever wanted; also, it satisfied my father's hopes that I make something of myself.'

'A lot of fathers might have preferred a degree or two from an institution as highly regarded as the LSE,' Sarah observed.

'Not in my fathers' case,' Anand replied, 'he's a lieutenant colonel in the South African police service!'

At this opportune moment, their conversation was interrupted by the arrival of a matronly nurse who glanced disapprovingly at the two visitors. 'My patient is supposed to be resting, not exciting himself!' she chided.

'May I introduce Senior Staff Nurse Carter,' Andre said fondly, 'my surgical care practitioner, gatekeeper, temporary mother and best friend. It is only due to her courageous interventions that I am saved from the very worst excesses the surgeons would love to inflict on my poor, helpless body.'

'Oh! Get away with you, Andre. You know it's only the promise of your eventual discharge that keeps me coming into work every day,' Nurse Carter smilingly replied.

'If you don't mind me asking, Nurse Carter,' Sarah said, 'how is our colleague doing?'

Nurse Carter looked at Andre who nodded his permission. 'Your colleague is doing remarkably well, considering his arrival by helicopter suffering from three gunshot wounds; two of which could have easily proved fatal. And, as he well knows, he's not quite out of the woods yet.'

'Apparently,' Andre interjected, 'I still have a souvenir bullet lodged inside my pericardium, which some brilliant surgeon plans to retrieve sometime tomorrow. Then, if I'm still alive after that,' he said jokingly, 'I'll have to endure a bout of reconstructive surgery to repair damage to the inguinal canal, whatever the hell that is!'

'Perhaps now you can understand why I'm ushering the two of you out; your colleague needs all the rest he can get.'

The day before he was due to be discharged from hospital, Andre received a visit from one of the patient councillors. 'It's quite routine Mr Meyer,' the councillor replied in response to his query, 'may I call you Andre?' Andre smiled his approval, prompting his visitor to continue, 'You see Andre, we like to have a few words with any patient about to be discharged; particularly someone recovering from an event as traumatic as yours.'

Invited to speak freely and off the record, Andre revealed to the councillor his feelings of anxiety exacerbated by the thought of having to socialize with colleagues and friends who will want to congratulate him on his fortunate recovery. 'I must tell you; I have feelings of guilt over having survived this 'event' as you call it.'

'I can assure you, it's perfectly normal for anyone who has survived an incident in which others have suffered to a greater extent, to have feelings of guilt.' The councillor reached into briefcase, rummaged around and produced a business card. 'Let me give you the name and address of someone you can contact should you wish to talk over things later on.'

<hr>

'So, you're off now,' Senior Staff Nurse Carter remarked as Andre completed last minute preparations for his discharge. 'Come on, I'll wheel you out. Have you got someone meeting You?'

'I sincerely hope so.'

'It'll probably be that pretty little liaison officer, what's her name, Sarah?'

'That would be nice; but I expect it'll be Banerjee.'

'Considering how taken your liaison officer is with you, he'd have to fight her for the opportunity.'

'You exaggerate, Nurse Carter. Though, it would be nice wouldn't it?'

As Nurse Carter wheeled him out of the front entrance of the hospital, he looked around the patient loading zone and was somewhat disappointed to see DS Banerjee standing next to a police car, ready to drive him to his place in Russell Square.

<hr>

'Congratulations on your promotion to Detective Chief Inspector Boss,' Anand said opening the passenger side door, 'not to mention six weeks leave! What on earth do you plan to do with all that time on your hands?'

'I thought I may do a bit of travelling.'

'Good idea; they say it broadens the mind – any idea where you may want to go?'

'When I was admitted to the Royal London, our ever-efficient liaison officer DI Paget contacted my only living relative, my sister Janet in South Africa. Presumably, I believe, to forewarn her of my imminent demise. This news prompted my sister, whom I make a point of phoning at least once every five years, to get in touch. Anyway, my failure to shake off this mortal coil reinvigorated our brotherly and sisterly affections, resulting in an invitation to spend a few weeks with her and her partner in South Africa.'

'I envy you your opportunity to renew family ties,' Banerjee said thoughtfully, 'my parents, who are both getting on in years, badger me all the time to visit them. Maybe I will one day.' Brightening up, he added, 'If you get the chance, perhaps you may like to get in touch with my father. He's now a full colonel in the police service in Johannesburg; I know he would be delighted to meet you.'

'If I get the chance, I'll do that. Give me his phone number or his address and I'll do my best to get in touch with him.' Andre hated lying to Anand, because he knew, deep down, he had no intention of getting in touch with anyone; in fact, he was not even looking forward to meeting up with his sister.

'Not that it's my case anymore, but is there any news on Rylston?'

'I'm afraid not Boss; not so much as a sighting since the day before our raid. Rumours around the station would have us believe he was tipped off.'

'What do you think?'

'I think the bastard stayed in that hiding hole of his until he was able to slip out and mingle with the dozens of plods searching the building. You do know about the yellow hi-vis vests?'

'Yes, Bryson mentioned them. So, where do you think he went?'

'My money would be on somewhere out of this country. Probably Portugal, where most of his drugs came from.'

'You may just be right my friend; you may just be right.'

CHAPTER 7

KRUGER NATIONAL PARK

ABIO ANIMA WAS THE ELDEST son in a family of four boys and three girls, eking out a wretched existence in the slums of Port Harcourt on the banks of the Bonny River in the Niger Delta. His father deserted the family when Abio was eleven years old, placing the task of supporting his alcoholic mother and his younger siblings onto his young shoulders. Life was difficult for the Anima family but Abio was a good provider, even if he had to resort to burglary and violence to keep food on the table. Unluckily for the family, Abio's ability to support the family came to an end when one of his mugging victims, a well-known local businessman, died of his injuries forcing Abio to flee the country.

South Africa, as it turned out, was not the money-making paradise Abio Anima had hoped for. In fact, he never even recouped the airfare it cost him to get there in the first place. Then, to make matters worse, it cost him eighteen months of his freedom in Matatshe Prison for his botched robbery of a Musina taxi driver. However, his time in Matatshe enabled him to recruit two inept Zimbabwean criminals to his small gang of get-rich-quick hopefuls, the Masara brothers, Nyiko and Tiyani.

It was the younger of the two brothers, Nyiko, who came up with the idea of cashing in on the apparently successful outbreak of rural farm robberies. 'I worked for a white farmer not far from Musina. He's a rich man and has a nice motorcar we can take.'

'How do you know he's rich?' his older brother, Tiyani asked, sceptical at first, but ready to defer to the criminal wisdom of the man from Nigeria.

'When we were paid, this *mzungu* - white man - took big rolls of Rands out of his pockets. I never saw so much money in my life!'

Like most of Abio Anima's carefully laid plans, things went awry from the beginning. It started with the two large farm dogs which the trio, despite keeping a watch on the farmhouse over a two-day period, failed to take into account. The howls and yelps of pain from the dogs as the Masara brothers hacked and speared them to death, succeeded in rousing the farmer and his wife from their sleep. Armed with a handgun, the man rushed out of the backdoor only to have his skull split open by an axe wielded by Abio who had hidden in the bushes waiting for such an opportunity.

The sadistic excesses inflicted by Abio on the farmer's wife, before a merciful death ended her suffering, convinced Nyiko and Tiyani they were now doomed men in league with the devil himself. Driven by the urgent need to put as much distance as possible between themselves and the local authorities, the trio ransacked the farmhouse searching in vain for the money they believed to be hidden there. Despite their efforts, the murder of the farmer and his wife netted them the sum of two hundred Rand and loose change, a llama pistol with six rounds, an old Cogswell and Harrison rifle with three rounds and the keys to a beige Ford Escort.

Alarmed by increasing public pressure on the police to bring the murderers to justice, Abio decided to use this opportunity to put his newly-acquired rifle to more profitable use by killing a rhino for its horns or an elephant for its tusks. Convincing his two followers of the fortune that awaited those with the courage to take on such dangerous animals, they robbed a trading store for the supplies of food and blankets needed for their new enterprise.

It took them the best part of a day to arrive, undetected by police roadblocks, in the northern reaches of Limpopo Province. They spent half the following day hiding the Ford Escort in dense bush near Masisi, before crawling under the boundary fence of the Kruger Park in search of the Luvuvhu River and its herds of elephants.

***

It was cold as an early morning mist rose off the gently flowing Luvuvhu, covering its banks with a diaphanous silver cloak and softening the outline of the trunks of the sickly green, fever trees. Wrapping his two blankets around his shoulders, Abio Anima kicked the nearest of the two sleeping figures, 'You, get up! Make the fire and keep it small, there are too many *amaphoyisa* - policemen - all around here. I do not wish to go back to jail.'

With the coffee brewing and the effects of his *Tik* - crystal meth - pipe bolstering his courage, Abio unwrapped the Cogswell and Harrison rifle from its protective blanket. Pulling back the bolt, he carefully inserted the three brass .505 cartridges into the magazine. These three precious rounds were all he could find in the farmhouse, despite all his efforts to extract further information from the farmer's wife.

⸺◈⸺

Abio's plan to scout along the banks of the Luvuvhu River in search of an elephant with sizable tusks soon paid off. A glimpse in the distance of two bull elephants with large tusks, breathed new life into their poaching enter-prise. Convinced one of the elephants they were tracking was none other than the legendary Ndlulamithi, Abio assured Nyiko and Tiyani that its enormous tusks would guarantee them riches beyond their wildest dreams.

Tracks the size of dustbin lids left by the two bulls led them away from the river and its banks of lush vegetation and up into an area of small, rock strewn kopjes and dense stands of mopane trees. The mind-numbing heat of the midday sun, and too many *Tik* pipes, had dulled their bush senses to the point they failed to notice that the second of the two elephants had fallen back, and was now somewhere close behind them.

Shaking off the lethargy befuddling his drug-infused brain, Abio, at last, glimpsed the white gleam of a tusk and the sinuous movements of an elephant's trunk as it reached up into a marula tree searching for ripe fruit. Brusquely, he ordered Nyiko and Tiyani to get back as he crept cautiously into the dense tangle of mopane trees, straining to distinguish the head of the elephant from the mass of leaves and branches. Sweat poured down his face and flies crawled into his eyes as he struggled to find his aiming point for a fatal brain shot. Easing off the safety catch on the rifle and anxious to bring the hunt to an end, he raised the rifle to his shoulder and began to slowly squeeze the trigger. This slight movement prompted the second elephant, unseen but only yards away in the marula trees, to launch its deadly attack.

Panicked by the scream of rage from the attacking elephant, Abio jerked the trigger firing the copper-jacketed 400 grain bullet into the thick hide and bunched muscle behind Ndlulamithi's shoulder, inflicting a painful, but non-debilitating injury.

Abio Anima did not fare quite as well as his quarry. A powerful blow from the trunk of the charging elephant behind him, knocked him to the ground where the enraged animal trampled the life out of him before it turned and followed in the wake of the fleeing Ndlulamithi.

Despite their shock and dismay at this unexpected turn of events, Nyiko and Tiyani retained sufficient presence of mind to pick up the undamaged rifle before setting out on the long trek back to the boundary fence and the car hidden in the bush near Masisi.

CHAPTER 8

NELSPRUIT

THE BRITISH AIRWAYS AIRBUS A 380 was high over southern Zambia when the first officer announced the start of their descent into Johannesburg's O R Tambo International Airport. As the flight attendants bustled about the cabin clearing away the remnants of breakfast, Andre stared out his window watching the thin, silvery line of the Zambesi River slowly come into view then disappear beneath the aircraft. 'I used to work on the copper belt,' the elderly passenger seated on the aisle across from him remarked, 'six years at the Bwana Mkubwa mine. Made good money too; but that was before the Federation broke up and things changed.'

'Have you been back since?' Andre asked, not really wanting to start up a conversation.

'This is my first trip back since I left Rhodesia in 1980. Never thought I'd ever return, but here I am. Well, I suppose we'll be landing soon, so I'd better get in line for the loo.' Andre heaved a thankful sigh of relief as he turned back to his window. He watched as the green savannas of northern Botswana slowly gave way to the drier reaches of the region he once knew as the northern Transvaal, but now as Limpopo Province.

The landing was uneventful until some idiot pulling an excessively heavy, oversized suitcase out of the overhead locker, struck him on the back of the head. However, from then on everything went smoothly. Thirty minutes later, he was sitting in a comfortable lounge enjoying a coffee while keeping an eye on his luggage and the departures board for his afternoon flight to Kruger Mpumalanga airport.

The South African Airways Embraer short-haul jet banked steeply over the city of Nelspruit, levelled out and, touching down, rolled to a stop in front of the small airport terminal. With only twenty five passengers on board, they disembarked in a matter of minutes. As Andre and his fellow travellers walked into the cool of the terminal, they faced a half-dozen tour operators all waving placards displaying the names of those booked on local tours. 'Andre! Andre!' he heard his name being called out. Looking around, he caught sight of two women standing at the back of the placard-waving crowd gesturing in his direction. Waving an acknowledgement, he made his way through the crowd towards them.

Despite the ten-year gap since he last saw his sister Janet, he embraced her whispering, 'Hello Janet. My goodness you haven't changed a bit since I last saw you.'

'Oh,' she replied kissing him on his cheek, 'you probably say that to all the girls. Come on, let me introduce you to my wife, Elsie.'

Elsie, an attractive blonde was, by his estimate, a year or two younger than his sister and equally effusive in her greeting. 'Thank you both for coming to meet me,' Andre said, 'I wondered how I was going to get to your place in this Mbombela or Nelspruit, as I once remembered it.'

'Changing times little brother; but you'll get used to it,' Janet said holding him at arm's length. 'Let me look at you. You know we nearly died when we got that call from that policewoman telling us you'd been badly injured during a police raid. Bloody hell Andre! It was the sort of call we expected when you joined that bloody parachute regiment.'

'Sorry about that. Had I known the call would upset you, I wouldn't have got shot.'

'Come on you two,' Elsie jumped in, 'there's plenty of time for recriminations later. Let's get home before the afternoon rush; I'm dying for a sundowner or two.'

———◄━►———

Linking arms with Andre and Elsie, Janet led the way out of the terminal and across the parking lot, stopping beside an obviously new Toyota Corolla. 'Nice car,' Andre commented, 'I take it business is good?'

'Not really,' Janet smiled, 'just a little present to both of us for all our hard work. Would you like to drive?' she asked, handing him the keys. 'By the way, we still drive on the left; at least that hasn't changed.'

Andre followed the signs out of the airport parking lot and, within minutes, was on the road to Nelspruit. 'You know,' he said to no one in particular, 'I should have made enquiries at the airport about hiring a car.'

'I wouldn't worry about that right now,' Janet said, 'at least not until you decide what you'd like to do and where you may want to go. In the meantime, we have a second car, a small red Kia, which you're very welcome to use. At no cost of course,' she added.

'That's very kind of you both, I really appreciate it. But I must insist on being allowed to pay my way.'

'You won't get any arguments from us on that score,' Elsie said with a grin.

———◆———

Perched on the sunny side of a small hill, Meyer's View Bed and Breakfast overlooked the Crocodile River and the southern boundary of the Kruger National Park. 'Many of our guests tell us they've seen more big game from our garden lodges than on a typical day's drive through the Park itself,' Elsie told Andre as he drove in through the entrance gates.

Leaving the Toyota in the small parking lot, he followed the two women into the stone and thatch roof entrance to the main lodge. 'This is where we serve breakfast every morning and dinner in the evening,' Janet said waving towards an African-themed restaurant with an awe-inspiring view of the river and the Kruger Park beyond.

'Is that an elephant down there?' Andre asked, excitement evident in his voice as he pointed out a huge grey bulk pushing its way through a bed of reeds.

'It certainly is,' Janet confirmed, 'just wait until early evening, you'll see a lot more of them along the river when it's a little cooler.'

'Do they ever cross over onto this side?'

'On occasion they do; but we had a deep trench dug along the edge of our property facing the river, it tends to discourage their visits.'

'But it doesn't stop lions or leopards,' Elsie said with a straight face, 'which is why we offer a full refund to guests mauled by any of the big cats.'

Janet smiled indulgently at Elsie, 'At the moment, only two of our six lodges are occupied and, as their cars aren't in the parking lot, it's safe to assume they're out for the day. We've put you in the Nyala Lodge; it's a little further away from the other lodges so you won't be disturbed by guests coming and going.'

'I'd better go and get my suitcase out of the car,' he suggested.

'Don't worry about that. When you go down there later, you'll find everything unpacked and safely put away. But, a word of warning. Never leave the screen door on your lodge open when you're not there; if any of our Vervet monkeys were to get into your room, it will take days to clean up the mess! Now, what do you say we have those drinks we've been promising ourselves.'

Settling back in comfortable chairs, they watched, spellbound, as the dying rays of the setting sun turned the surface of the river to liquid gold. 'This is the life,' Andre remarked as he sipped his whisky.

'As someone who almost lost his life a short while back, you're in the best position to appreciate it,' Janet remarked. 'Are you able to talk about it or is it still too soon?'

'To be honest, there's nothing more I can tell you, other than it was a situation no one could have predicted. Unfortunately, the police officer I tried to pull to safety, died shortly afterwards. But I was lucky; mainly because the thug with the automatic weapon hadn't much of a clue on how to use it properly.'

'Did you shoot him?' Elsie asked.

'I certainly would've,' he admitted. 'However, as detectives, we're not usually armed; instead, we rely on specialist firearms officers for just that purpose.'

'The policewoman who called me, I think her name was Paget, told me it happened while you were trying to arrest a well-known drug dealer.'

'Did you get him?' Elsie asked, 'I mean before you were hurt,' she quickly added.

'Clive Rylston, that was his name; at least at the time that was the name he was using. No, we didn't get him, more's the pity. The last thing I heard before leaving England was that they had him living somewhere in Portugal. But that's someone else's problem now.'

'Refresh your drink?' Janet said taking his glass over to the bar. 'Now that we've got all of that out of the way, do you have any idea what you'd like to do now you're here?'

Andre sat back in his chair and took a sip from his whisky. 'When I was recovering from my operations in hospital, I found myself reminiscing about my childhood and the awfulness of our parents' divorce. Because you were a little older than I was, I'd always assumed you'd have a better understanding of what really happened between them?'

'Not really. I was away at boarding school in Pretoria at the time, so it came as much of a shock to me as it obviously did to you. Surely, when you went to England with mother, didn't the two of you ever talk about it?'

'No, never. It was a subject she adamantly refused to discuss with anyone, not even her own family in England. I asked her about it again just before I went into the army, but, as you know, she passed away suddenly while I was stationed in Northern Ireland. The closest I got to her was walking a few paces behind her coffin. I'm sorry, I should never have brought this up,' he said dabbing at his eyes with his handkerchief.

Janet came over to his chair and put her arms around him. 'Some reminiscences are good, while others are best forgotten. You know the old saying about sleeping dogs…'

'What a beautiful morning,' Elsie remarked placing a fresh pot of coffee on the table where Andre and Janet were sitting admiring the view over the river.

'You two are so lucky to be living in such a beautiful place,' Andre reflected, 'I envy you both.'

'Oh! It's not all beer and skittles you know. Sometimes its disgruntled guests, or guests who don't bother to cancel bookings ahead of time.'

'Not to mention our regular power failures, staff problems and hot water systems that fail at inopportune moments.'

'Or a bloody snake in a guest's bathroom,' Elsie added, 'but we wouldn't have it any other way would we my love,' Elsie said putting her arms around Janet's shoulders.

Andre smiled as he stirred his coffee. 'You asked last night what I would like to do while I'm here,' he said turning to Janet, 'after some thought I decided I would like to try and find out whatever became of that huge elephant that dad was so taken with.'

'Ndlulamithi! That was the name the local Tsonga people gave to that elephant; it means "taller than the trees." An apt name for an elephant believed to be close to twelve foot at the shoulder,' Janet remarked.

'Do you think this elephant may still be alive; given all the reports about ivory poaching in South Africa?'

'I remember reading something about him in a tourism brochure left behind by one of our guests,' Elsie added. 'You'd really have to speak to one of the Kruger Park game rangers.'

'Just before mom and I left for England, dad took me on a drive up to a place he called Panda, or something like that, to visit a waterhole where he once saw this elephant.'

'That sounds like Punda Maria; it's the furthest north rest camp in the Kruger Park,' Janet said, 'he often spoke about it and a game ranger he once knew up there. If I remember rightly, the man's name was Krause. But that was a long time ago and, you must remember, many of the old timers were laid off by the new Kruger Park administration.'

'Would it be OK with you both if I borrowed your little Kia and drove up that way to take a look around?'

'It would take you the best part of a day to get to Punda Maria,' Janet said looking at Elsie, 'what do you think?'

'Fine by me; especially if Andre came back through Phalaborwa. He'd save us the transport costs if he dropped off the bathroom supplies to Melanie at Leopards Rock.'

'Good idea! Would you be OK with that Andre?'

'Absolutely, I'd be glad to help in any way I can.'

CHAPTER 9

HOEDSPRUIT

'YES, I REMEMBER OLD JAPIE Krause,' Ranger Hanyani Maboko said taking Andre's phone call to the administration office at Punda Maria. 'Last thing I heard; he was living in an old-age home in Hoedspruit. I'm afraid that's about all I can tell you.'

'What I have to do now is phone all the old-age homes in Hoedspruit,' Andre said to Janet, 'there can't be all that many.'

'Why don't you give a friend of mine in Hoedspruit a call and ask her to make some inquiries on your behalf. That way, when you go up to drop off Melanie's supplies in Phalaborwa, you can stop off and see Japie Krause.'

'Providing he's still alive,' Andre replied.

———◆———

'Mr Krause, Japie Krause?' Andre said gently waking the old man dozing in an armchair on the *stoep* overlooking the garden.

'Ah! You must be Theunis Meyer's son, Andre. The nurse on the front desk said you wanted to talk to me about your father and Ndlulamithi.'

'Yes, I do. I appreciate you taking the time to see me.'

'Don't be silly young man; I have more time on my hands than you can shake a stick at. Sit down, take all the time you want. Now, what would you like to know?'

'Many years ago, my father took me to see the waterhole where he last saw that famous elephant, Ndlulamithi. All I can remember is that this waterhole was somewhere near Punda Maria.'

'Masiha. That's the name of the waterhole. If my memory serves me correctly, it's just west of the road from Punda Maria to Pafuri camp,' Japie Krause said pausing in thought. *Ja*, I often saw Ndlulamithi around that area. Unfortunately, the old boy died of natural causes around Shangoni back in the late 1980s. If you're interested, you can see his tusks in the Elephant Hall at Letaba.'

'I had no idea Ndlulamithi was dead. It's always been a dream of mine that one day I would see him in the bush, just as my father saw him back in the old days.'

'I spoke to Phuti Mabuza at Punda the other day,' Krause said, 'he's the section ranger in charge of that area now. He told me he recently saw a worthy successor to Ndlulamithi; an elephant they've named Nkovakulu. Phuti thinks it's possible that he's even bigger than Ndlulamithi! And, what's more, he says Nkovakulu is often seen around the Masiha waterhole.'

'According to Japie, if I head south on the R40 then east on the R531, I can enter the Park through Orpen Gate and be at Satara Camp within an hour or two,' Andre said calling Janet from the reception desk at the old-age home. 'From Satara, he says it's an easy day's drive to Punda Maria, where I hope to meet up with the section ranger, a Mr Phuti Mabuza. Apparently, he knows of an exceptionally large elephant they call Nkovakulu. Japie thinks this elephant may well be the one dad photographed all those years ago.' Taking a deep breath, he quickly continued, 'Afterwards, I plan to leave the Park through Punda Maria Gate and then drive down to Phalaborwa to drop off the supplies for Melanie.'

'Sounds like a good plan to me,' Janet replied. 'Now there's no need to rush, Melanie's supplies are not urgent. Take your time driving to Punda; it's a good time of the year to be in Kruger. But, please be careful on the road from Punda Maria Gate to Phalaborwa. It runs through a place called Giyani, which is not always safe because of unrest in some of the villages.

And for goodness sake, don't even think of driving it at night. Even if it takes longer, you should think seriously about coming back through the Park; it's a lot safer!'

CHAPTER 10

PUNDA MARIA

THE OCCUPANTS OF THE CAR stopped at the side of the road near the Nsemani Dam turnoff waved excitedly at him, pointing to something in the bush just off the road. *'Daar is ⊠ leeu!* There's a lion!' the driver of the lead car shouted as Andre slowed and stared into the bush, trying to see what all the fuss was about. 'Lion!' the driver shouted again, this time in English. As he pulled over, the head of a magnificent male lion rose above the grass and stared straight at him. Cursing, he remembered that the compact Nikon camera he had purchased in London was lying in his suitcase on the back seat of the car. Aware that it was against park regulations to get out of the car, Andre began the difficult job of climbing over the back of the front seat to reach his case. Struggling to undo the straps, he looked up just in time to see the lion walk slowly across the road, past his car and disappear into the long grass.

'Wasn't that fantastic?' the driver of the lead car shouted, 'he passed right in front of you. Did you get some good shots?'

'Yes, I did, thank you,' Andre lied, vowing never to go anywhere again without his camera on the seat beside him.

Forewarned by Japie that there could be problems with some of the restaurants in the Park, Andre had stocked up on a variety of canned foods, packs of frozen *boerewors*, coffee, boxes of rusks, and a couple of bottles of whisky. The truth be told, he was looking forward to the experience of grilling meat over a fire but was having a problem keeping the fire going in the grill outside his rondavel. A neighbour, noticing his struggle, appeared out of the darkness, 'Hannes Venter,' he said extending a huge hand, 'you can use my *braai* – barbecue, I've finished cooking.'

Andre introduced himself as Andy Meyer and expressed his appreciation for the neighbourly gesture. 'My wife and kids are out on a night drive,' the huge man began, 'are you visiting from overseas?' he said picking up on Andre's unmistakable English accent. 'We're leaving for Australia in a months' time so we thought we should take a look around the game reserve just in case we never come back.'

'Your decision to emigrate, is it because of not being able to get a job or worried about the political situation?' Andre asked.

'*Nee*, I had a good job with the police, but I don't like the way things are going. What, with all the drugs and violent crime, it's only a matter of time before something bad happens to one of us.'

Andre's ears pricked up. 'Where were you stationed?' he asked.

'Pietersburg or Polokwane as it's now called. It's a big town, north of Pretoria, do you know it?' Andre admitted he didn't. 'Lots of drugs,' Hannes continued, '*TIK*, you probably know it as methamphetamine, and *nyaope*, some crap they make out of heroin, dagga and, some say, anti-retroviral drugs. Sends them *blerrie* crazy.' He paused and stared out into the darkness, '*Ag* man, I'm sorry. Here I am keeping you from your dinner. Andy, I hope you have a good holiday. *Totsiens*! Goodbye!' he said as he disappeared in the direction of his rondavel. Although he would like to have questioned Hannes further about life in South Africa as a policeman, he was also looking forward to eating his dinner.

With the sun having set, Andre relaxed on the *stoep* of his rondavel sipping a whisky and staring out into the dark African bush just beyond the camp fence. It was for this reason he had asked the booking clerk for a rondavel close to the fence, resurrecting a vague memory of his father raising his hand saying, 'Listen Andre! Listen! That's what our ancestors heard as they trekked into the wilderness.' Somewhere, out in the darkness, he could hear the distant rumbling roar of a lion and the haunting sound of a Scops owl calling nearby.

Andre saw his first elephants a few miles from the entrance to Letaba rest camp. He'd turned off the tarred road onto a short, circular dirt road which led to a popular viewpoint overlooking the Letaba River. Almost right away, he spotted the grey backs of four elephants slowly making their way through the tall reeds lining the banks of the river. As other cars saw him parked and looking out over the river, they too turned off the road and joined him, anxious not to miss anything he may have seen. 'It's only a few elephants, and they're a long way away,' a woman in one of the cars remarked loudly to her companions as they drove off, disappointed at having wasted their time.

'Only a few elephants!' Andre muttered to himself, 'maybe, but they're my elephants, I saw them first.' Driving through the entrance gate he followed the signs to the Letaba Elephant Hall, parking close to the life-sized elephant statue looming over the entrance to the thatched building. Standing beside the statue, he was conscious of its enormous size and recognized, for the first time, the awful fear a fully-grown elephant must have exerted over early pioneers armed only with muzzle-loading, black powder guns. With a newfound appreciation of his father's fascination with elephants in general, and Ndlulamithi or Nkovakulu in particular, he walked into the cool confines of the Elephant Hall.

Looking at the enormous tusks of the 'Magnificent Seven' elephants arrayed around the Hall, he was drawn immediately to the tusks once carried by Ndlulamithi. Taking out the black and white photo his father had taken at the Masiha waterhole thirty years ago, he tried, unsuccessfully, to compare the tusks on the elephant in the photo to those mounted on the wall in front of him. 'It's likely only Phuti Mabuza will be able to decide which elephant my father actually saw,' he concluded, returning the photo to its folder as he walked back to his car.

The petrol station attendants agreed that, while it was a little over one hundred miles to Punda Maria, it could easily take up to six hours, factoring in game watching and elephant roadblocks. 'Elephant roadblocks! Does that sort of thing happen often?'

'Only when you're in a hurry,' one of them joked. 'Elephants have a sixth sense which tells them how late you are! So, don't forget, the camp at Punda Maria closes its gates at five thirty.' The drive proved to be uneventful. Elephant sightings were confined to hundreds of yards away from the road and, apart from a stop for a cup of tea and a sandwich at Shingwedzi, he made good time, driving into Punda Maria just before closing time.

'I'm staying in camp tonight,' he said to the receptionist, 'and I'm hoping to get in touch with Phuti Mabuza, the section ranger. How do you suggest I do that?'

'Not a problem, sir. Give me your mobile number, I'll call his office and leave a message for him to contact you.' Andre was about to sit down for his dinner in the restaurant when Phuti called.

'Mr Meyer, following your call the other day about Ndlulamithi; I've a suggestion that may interest you. One of my game scouts reported that a poacher may have wounded the elephant we call Nkovakulu. That's the elephant I suspect your father may have photographed. Anyway, I'm off early tomorrow morning to check on him; you're more than welcome to come along if you like.'

CHAPTER 11

NKOVAKULU

IT WAS STILL DARK AT six in the morning when Phuti Mabuza pulled up in his Land Rover *bakkie* - open back pickup - outside Andre's rondavel. 'This is very kind of you,' Andre said climbing in the passenger seat, 'while I'm looking forward to seeing this elephant, Nkovakulu, I hope we'll find he's not too badly wounded.'

'If my scouts' description is accurate, it's only a flesh wound in his left shoulder.'

'The area we're going to, is it a long way from here?'

'Not really. This elephant was last seen around the Masiha waterhole, it's about half an hour's drive from here. We should get there around sunrise.' The headlights of the Land Rover cut through the darkness, picking out scattered groups of startled impalas as they leaped away from the roadside. 'Would you rather we spoke in Afrikaans?' Phuti asked.

Andre laughed, 'Chances are I wouldn't understand a word you were saying.'

'An Afrikaner who can't speak Afrikaans?' Phuti said glancing sideways at Andre.

'*Ja*,' he replied, 'I was born an Afrikaner, but from the age of fourteen onwards, I lived in England.'

'Are you planning on returning to live here?' Phuti asked.

'No. I'm only here for a bit of rest and recuperation and to follow up on the story behind a photo my father took of an elephant he believed to be the legendary Ndlulamithi.'

'Do you have the photo with you?'

'Not with me; it's back in my rondavel at the rest camp.'

'Good; when we get back, I'll take a look at it for you. Here we are,' Phuti said pulling the Land Rover over in front of a small thatched hut as an African game scout emerged from the darkness carrying a rifle. 'This is Vukosi,' Phuti said as Andre moved to the centre seat allowing the scout to sit next to him, his rifle gripped between his knees. 'Vukosi's been out here for the last few days keeping an eye on Nkovakulu. That way, we won't have to spend all day looking for him. *Het jy jou geweer ontlaai*? Did you unload your rifle?'

'*E-ee*,' the scout replied sheepishly.

'Get out and do it now. *Blerrie mampara*! Bloody fool!' Phuti said sharply, stopping the Land Rover. Vukosi got out, unloaded the rifle and dropped the rounds into his jacket pocket. 'Despite our best training, some of these guys occasionally forget the most basic rules,' Phuti observed. 'Being shot is an experience I would like to avoid at all costs.'

'And it hurts like hell; I can tell you,' Andre replied, immediately regretting he said that.

Phuti looked at him. 'Were you wounded while you were in the army or something?'

'No; I was in the Metropolitan Police Service in London when it happened to me.'

'I thought most English criminals only carried knives?'

'And you'd be quite right; only my experience was at the hands of a thug carrying a submachine gun. Fortunately, he was a poor shot and only hit me a few times.'

'Fucking hell!' Phuti swore, 'and I thought my job was dangerous.'

<hr />

Phuti parked the Land Rover *bakkie* on the top of a steep rise and handed around a flask of coffee, 'I'm sorry, we'll have to share, I've only got one cup,' he apologised. Once all three had had coffee, they sat looking out over the Luvuvhu floodplain as the rising sun brushed the tops of the of mopane and corkwood trees with fingers of red and gold.

'*Languta*! Look!' Vukosi said triumphantly pointing to a large elephant as it walked out of the mopane trees and into the open. 'Nkovakulu.'

Phuti reached into the glovebox and took out a pair of compact binoculars. After a few moments he gave up, 'He's too far away and the light isn't good enough yet. We'll have to get a lot nearer. You stay here Andre, Vukosi and I will go and take a closer look.'

'Now that's not fair. I flew all the way from England just to see this elephant; if you don't mind, I'd like to come with you.'

'As you wish,' Phuti said shrugging his shoulders and smiling. He unclipped a rifle from the top of the dashboard and, climbing out of the vehicle, took a handful of cartridges from an open container in the glovebox. 'Brno .458, a game rangers' friend in any bad situation,' he said to Andre's unspoken question. Pulling back the bolt on the rifle, he inserted three rounds in the spring-loaded magazine and pushed another round into the breech. 'OK. Let's go,' he said leading the way down the hill.

<hr/>

It took them a little over half an hour to get within two hundred yards of Nkovakulu who was peacefully destroying a molala palm tree to get to the fruit in the upper branches. 'Close enough,' Phuti whispered, focussing his binoculars on the wound in the animals left shoulder. A hiss from Vukosi drew their attention to another elephant as it emerged from a stand of mopane trees and strode purposefully towards them. 'Hey! Stop it! Hey!' Phuti shouted out waving his arms and his rifle above his head. Taking no notice of his shouts, the approaching elephant, tucked its trunk between its front legs and broke into a shambling run towards them. 'Don't run!' Phuti shouted to Andre as he fired a shot into the ground in front of the animal, causing it to swerve away. Another shot into the air sent the elephant back in the direction it came from. 'Let's get out of here,' Phuti whispered as he led the way back to the relative safety of their Land Rover.

'I couldn't have run even if I wanted to,' Andre said as he struggled to get a grip on his trembling legs. 'Was that a serious charge?'

'About as serious as I've ever experienced,' Phuti replied with a grin. 'Clearly he saw us as a threat; but whether to him or to his friend Nkovakulu, I've no idea.'

'You mentioned in your phone message yesterday that you planned to drive to Phalaborwa later today,' Phuti remarked glancing towards Andre.

'Yes, I've got some things to deliver to a friend of my sister, who lives there. As long as I'm on the road by noon, I should be able to make it.'

'It's only gone nine thirty, so we should be back in Punda in plenty of time. I don't think I mentioned this yesterday, but one of our patrols found the body of an African male apparently trampled to death by an elephant. We think this may have been the poacher who wounded Nkovakulu.'

'Good Lord,' Andre said, 'did they find the weapon he used?'

'Spoken like a true policeman!' Phuti laughed. 'No, we didn't; but we did find an empty .404 cartridge case near the body.'

'So, what does this all have to do with me driving to Phalaborwa?'

'You see Andre, any time someone dies or is killed in Kruger Park, it falls under the jurisdiction of the South African Police Service. This means that in less than thirty minutes time, I'm due to meet some policemen at the Mashikiri waterhole and escort them to where this man was killed.'

'If you have no objections, I'd like to go along with you. I must admit I'd be interested to see how they go about investigating this type of incident.'

'Of course, I have no objections; besides, you'd be saving me from a hurried drive taking you back to camp. And don't worry, I'll be sure to get you back to Punda in good time.'

'They're already here,' Phuti remarked as he turned down a short, bumpy track that led to the Mashikiri waterhole.

'I take it the white van with the blue and yellow stripes along its sides is the police vehicle,' Andre said, 'but who'd be driving the little white SUV?'

'That's Captain Annette Fourie's little Mahindra four-wheel drive. To be quite honest, I was hoping someone else would be handling this case today.'

'A little difficult, is she?' Andre asked.

'A little difficult would be the understatement of the year. She's a good detective, but not very easy to get along with and her public relations skills leave a lot to be desired,' he said parking next to the police van. 'Come and meet her, you'll soon see what I mean.'

'Good morning Annette, it's so nice to see you again.' Annette Fourie was dressed in the South African police uniform of dark blue trousers, lighter blue shirt and heavy boots. Looking at her, Andre saw an attractive woman of medium height with a nice figure and curly blonde hair which she kept tucked under her peaked police cap.

'Cut the bullshit flattery, Phuti,' she said abruptly, 'how far is it to where this unfortunate wretch was trampled to death by one of your elephants?'

'One of our elephants Annette, owned and protected by the people of this great country. Now, to answer your question, it's about a fifteen-minute drive in a Land Rover, but quite possibly too far for that quaint little piece of crap you're driving,' he answered with a smile.

'Before I tell you to fuck off, Phuti, you'd better tell we who this guy is,' she said nodding towards Andre.

'A real Scotland Yard Detective, Annette. He's out here hoping to find out to what extent public relations skills have improved in the SAPS.'

She glanced in Andre's direction, 'I don't care who he is, just make sure he stays out of my way. Right,' she said walking over to her SUV, 'let's get this show on the road.' Andre watched as she climbed in, started the motor and, accelerating hard, drove off in a cloud of dust.

⟨✦⟩

'Well my friend,' Phuti said as they drove past the Mashikiri waterhole on the road back to Punda Maria, 'now that you've met her, what did you think of our Captain Annette Fourie?'

'You were absolutely right when you said she could be difficult,' Andre said laughing, 'however, you forgot to add rude and abrasive to her résumé. Otherwise, she struck me as a competent and meticulous detective and not at all bad looking either! Though I imagine being around her all the time would be a bit trying.'

'That's probably how her husband must have felt.'

'She was married?'

'Yes, she was once. I met her husband, Japie Fourie, a few times. He was a big shot lawyer in Phalaborwa who defended one of our rangers in a court case. He died about three years ago in a traffic accident. Drunk driver I believe.'

'Did they have any children?'

'Yes, a daughter. Unfortunately, they lost her to SIDS shortly after they were married. Then, three months later, Japie was killed.'

'God almighty! What an awful turn of events. The poor woman.'

———◆———

Phuti parked his Land Rover outside the restaurant in Punda Maria camp. 'Let's have something to eat while I take a quick look at that photograph your father took all those years ago.'

'Thirty seven years ago to be exact,' Andre said handing the grainy black and white photo across the table to Phuti.

'Now, I've never seen Ndlulamithi in the flesh; he was well before my time. However, I've seen enough photographs and 16mm film to confirm that this is definitely a photo of the famous elephant himself. Although you may now be thinking your journey a waste of time, I honestly believe you have seen the next elephant in line for that title, Nkovakulu. Not to mention the added bonus of having had a close encounter with one of his friends. What more could you ask for?'

CHAPTER 12

GIYANI

BEFORE LEAVING TO RETURN BACK through the Park to the Phalaborwa Gate, Andre called Janet on his mobile to let her know how things were going. 'You're leaving it a little late if you want to get through Phalaborwa Gate before closing time,' Janet chided him.

'I don't think I'll have a problem. I'll be on my way as soon as we end this call, though I'd appreciate you giving Melanie a call to keep her in the loop.' Ending the call, Andre drove over to the camp store and bought a few cold drinks and a meat pie for later on the road. As he walked out of the store, a customer on his way in pointed to his left front tire, '*Ag* sorry my friend, but it looks like you've got a flat tire.'

Cursing, Andre opened the boot removing, amongst other things, a first aid kit and the half dozen boxes of supplies he had promised to deliver to Melanie at Leopard's Rock. When he lifted the floor cover to get to the spare tire, he was disappointed to find it missing. Fortunately, both the jack and the tire wrench were there, so he was able to take off the tire, all the while blaming himself for not having checked on the spare before leaving Meyer's View. To make matters worse, the camp service station was busy, and it took over an hour to get the puncture repaired. 'How long will it take me to drive to Phalaborwa if I go out of the Park and take the road through Giyani?'

'Much quicker, Baas,' the service station attendant assured him, 'good road through Giyani all the way.' Andre thanked him for his help and gave him a good *bonsela* - tip. Hoping to make up lost time, he decided to ignore

Janet's warning about taking back roads and checked out of the Park, taking the R524 road to the Giyani turnoff.

Once on his way, he began feeling a lot better about his decision. The R524 was in fair condition and he made good time to the junction with the R81, which branched off turning south to Giyani, a sprawling town that seemed to stretch for miles. It was a little past mid-afternoon when, passing a service station, he thought it a good idea to fill up with petrol. 'Is it much further to Phalaborwa?' he asked the clerk in the office as he paid for the petrol.

'There's a good shortcut if you take the secondary road through Mbaula; it'll save you a good half hour.' However, like most shortcuts, it didn't save him any time at all. As Andre soon discovered, the road was poorly maintained and crowded with foot traffic, donkey carts and stray cattle around almost every bend. Concerned the sun was about to set, he was regretting his decision to take the shortcut, when a car travelling at high speed, swerved out and overtaking him, narrowly missing a dilapidated lorry travelling in the opposite direction.

'He's going to kill himself, the crazy bastard! He must be drunk or out of his mind,' he swore as he watched the car, now a half mile down the road, weave from side to side as it rapidly approached a sharp bend. There was a brief flicker of red brake lights as the driver, losing control of the car, swerved off the road and down a steep embankment, raising a cloud of dust as it ploughed its way into a bush-choked ravine..

Andre began slowing down almost at once and was about to go to the aid of the driver, when another vehicle, a large black SUV with tinted windows, flashed past at high speed, hooting for him to get out of its way. 'I hope you crash as well,' he muttered, watching as the SUV successfully negotiated the bend and continued on its way never slowing for even a second.

———◆———

The sun had just dipped below the western horizon as he searched for skid marks or other signs to indicate where the car had left the road. Noticing some shallow gouges in the gravel at the side of the road, he pulled his car over and, taking a small torch from the glovebox, began the steep climb down the embankment.

The beige Ford Escort lay pitched forward at a steep angle, its right front bumper crumpled up against a large rock. Shining his torch through the driver's side window, Andre saw the driver, a black man, lying sprawled across the front seat. Unable to pull open the jammed and buckled driver's door, he went around to the passenger side and managed to pull the door open. The light of his torch revealed a huge amount of blood covering the front seat and most of the driver's clothing.

Appalled at the sight and growing more concerned by the minute over the strong smell of leaking petrol, Andre leaned into the car to see if the driver was still alive. The injured man groaned in pain as he placed his hand on the man's neck feeling for a pulse. While his pulse was strong, the man seemed to be in a daze, possibly the result of the deep gash to the right side of his head and an ugly looking wound in his left shoulder. 'Can you hear me?' Andre asked. There was a garbled, almost inaudible reply. 'Well, you're not dead yet, but you soon will be if I can't get you out before the petrol tank catches fire.' Opening the door, Andre reached in under the driver's shoulders and, ignoring his cries of pain, pulled him out and dragged him a safe distance away from the car.

'Help us please,' the injured man cried out, clutching at Andre's jacket with his good arm, 'they want to kill us.'

'Who wants to kill you? Who are they? Do you mean the men driving a black SUV?'

'Yes! They will kill you too if they find you here with us. Please help us, sir, we must get away from here. Where is Tiyani? Look in the back of the car; please you must help him. We must go quickly, they will come back if they cannot find us,' the man said as he struggled to get up.

'You've been injured; you must lie still until help arrives. I'll go and see how your friend is doing, but for now you must stay here,' Andre said easing the man back down on the ground. Returning to the car, he opened the rear door and shone the torch around. 'Oh My God!' he said as the now failing light from the torch revealed six or seven bullet holes in the rear window and black, ugly-looking tears in the upholstery on the seat back. 'Christ Almighty!' he exclaimed as he found the second man lying on the floor, wedged between the front and back seats.

There was no need to check for a pulse. The top half of the man's head was missing, proving that at least one or two of the bullets that came through the rear window had found their mark. With the light from his torch dimming, he reached into the car and feeling around the back seat, brushed against a canvas bag wedged against the far door. Pulling the bag towards him, he dislodged an automatic pistol lying on the top of the bag. Picking up the pistol, he used what little day light was left to make sure the weapon was safe. While ejecting the empty magazine, the strong smell of cordite from the breech, proved it had only recently been fired.

He tried to open the canvas bag, but found it securely closed by two, heavy-duty plastic cable ties. Slipping the pistol into an open side pocket on the bag, Andre moved around to the back of the car and tried the boot. To his surprise, it opened easily. Feeling around, he found it empty, but for a rolled-up blanket lying sideways across the back of the boot. Thinking to use the blanket to cover the injured man, he reached in and pulled it towards him, uncovering a rifle. Making sure the weapon was safe and its magazine empty, he was using what little battery power remained in his torch to search the rest of the boot, when he heard a vehicle skid to a stop on the road above.

'Oh Shit!' Andre cursed. Fearful that the black SUV had returned in its search for the Ford Escort, he pushed the canvas bag and rifle under a clump of bushes, before running over to the injured man and covering him with the blanket. 'You must keep very quiet,' he whispered, 'a car has stopped on the road above and, until I find out who it is, we must assume the people who are trying to kill you have come back.' Carrying his almost dead torch in his hand, Andre started up the slope of the embankment to his car.

'*Hier is hy!* - Here he is!' a voice above warned someone in Afrikaans. '*Wat die fok doen jy daaronder?* - What the fuck are you doing down there?' the voice asked. While Andre recognized the language as Afrikaans, he had no idea what was being said and replied to that effect in his best plummy English accent.

'OK, white Englishman, what the fuck are you doing down there?' a black man growled emerging from the darkness and poking Andre in the chest with what Andre recognized as a Skorpion machine pistol.

'Trying to have a shit, if it's anything to you. Then my torch gave out on me and I think I stepped in my own crap,' Andre replied, scraping his shoe around in the dirt and trying to ignore the weapon pointed at his chest.

The gun toting man laughed at this, 'White Englishman, have you seen a car around here, a small Ford with two men in it?'

'A while back on the road a small car passed me going like hell then, a short while later, this car here passed me going almost as fast,' Andre said pointing to the large black SUV parked nose on to his car. 'What's this all about? Are you guys from the police?'

The two men laughed at this suggestion. Their mirth was short-lived as a third man, emerging from the dark shape of the SUV, shouted something at them in what again sounded like Afrikaans. 'OK *meneer - mister*,' one of the black men said to Andre, 'my boss wants you to fuck off out of here before something really bad happens to you.'

'No need for that, I'm on my way,' Andre replied, as he got into his car and started the engine. As he pulled off, his headlights lit up the front of the SUV which he recognized as a Cadillac Escalade. His lights also exposed a number of bullet holes in its windscreen and around the bonnet area, clearly the work of the dead man in the Ford Escort. He was hoping to get a glimpse of the SUV's license plate, but it appeared to be missing. He did, however, get a brief look at the face of the third man who apparently gave the orders; he was a white man.

Andre knew he had to get back as quickly as he could to get the injured driver to a hospital and the canvas bag, pistol and rifle to the police, who'd be in a much better position to sort out what was actually going on.. Assuming the men in the SUV were watching to make sure he left, he followed the road around the bend, over a small bridge and up a gentle rise. As he crested the top of the rise, he switched off his lights and coasted to a stop, careful to use only his handbrake to avoid showing tell-tale red brake lights.

Now out of sight, he turned the car around and, without turning on his lights, drove back over the rise and coasted down towards the bridge and a rough dirt track he had spotted just before the bridge. He was almost at the bridge, when a bright yellow and red fireball erupted into the sky from the direction of the little Ford Escort. 'Bloody hell! Either the bastards set it alight or the leaking petrol finally reached the hot engine.' Coasting over the bridge, he turned off down the dirt track and stopped the car. Switching off the engine, Andre got out and quietly closing his door, made his way back up onto the road.

It was dark as he walked along the edge of the road to where he had parked earlier. Occasional flickers of flame coming from the wreck, made it easier for him to see as he climbed down the steep embankment to where he had left the driver. His heart sank, when the only sign of the man he could find was the discarded blanket he had covered him with just before the black SUV arrived.

He made his way over to the clump of bush where he had hidden the canvas bag and the rifle. Getting down on his hands and knees, he crawled into the bush feeling around for the bag or the rifle. 'Shit! It must be here somewhere,' he muttered aloud, 'I hope to hell they didn't find it.'

'Baas! It is I, Nyiko,' a voice called to him from the darkness. 'I hear them coming, so I hide. They light fire and call for me, but I know they will kill me if I go to them.'

'You did well to hide from them. Are you able to walk? We must get away from here; those men may come back. Did you find the rifle and bag I hid in this bush?'

'Yes Baas. Take rifle, but leave bag, too much bad things in bag. Make peoples crazy. Much better we leave bag here.'

'What's in the bag Nyiko? Why do these men want to find it?'

'Things we find in *ndege*. Tiyani says we can sell things we find in bag to these men, but they do not pay and want to kill us.'

Probably drugs or diamonds Andre thought to himself, even more reason to get away from here. 'If I help you, can you walk?'

'I can try.'

'Good. I've left my car near the bridge. There's a first aid kit in the boot – perhaps I can find a dressing for your shoulder and maybe some painkillers. But we'd better keep to the bush and not walk along the road, just in case they come back.'

CHAPTER 13

CAVALO MARINHO

WORKING IN THE DIM GLOW of his Kia's dome light, Andre taped a dressing over the deep gash running along the side of Nyiko's head. 'Given the huge number of shots fired into your car, it's a wonder you survived at all,' he remarked, tying a compression bandage over the bullet wound in Nyiko's shoulder. 'That's the best I can do for now; its straight to the hospital for you as soon as we get to Phalaborwa.'

'Please Baas, better I go to friend's house, I have much troubles with police.'

'I'm sure you do Nyiko,' Andre replied as he helped him stretch out on the cramped back seat of the little car, 'but it would be better for you if you told me, truthfully, where you got the rifle and pistol and the story behind this canvas bag.' Andre paused as he examined both firearms more closely under the car's dome light. The rifle was an old, bolt-action .505 Cogswell and Harrison and the handgun, a cheap Llama pistol of Spanish origin. 'It's important Nyiko, you must tell me where you got these guns.'

'Abio buy rifle, small gun and car from friend in Musina to shoot animals to eat.'

'And not to shoot elephants?'

'*Aau* Baas! We no shoot elephants.'

'OK. Now about this bag, what will I find when I open it?'

'Bad things Baas! We try sell these things, but bad peoples don't pay and want to kill us.'

Andre reached into the glovebox, took out a pair of pliers and cut the two plastic cable ties. Unzipping the bag, he pulled aside a cloth towel exposing a number of white, plastic wrapped, four by eight inch bricks, all prominently marked with the blue seahorse symbol of the Portuguese *Cavalo Marinho* drug cartel. 'Fucking hell!' Andre yelled, pulling out block after block, 'Nyiko, this is heroin! No wonder those bloody people want to kill you; this stuff must be worth hundreds of thousands of Rands. Where the hell did you get it from?'

'We find in Kruger Park Baas. Broken *Ndege.*'

'What the fuck is that?' Andre shouted looking back over the seat at Nyiko. The man made a flapping motion with his hands. 'A bird?' he asked puzzled, before it finally dawned on him what Nyiko was trying to tell him. 'Ah! An aeroplane. Did it land in the Kruger Park?'

'No Baas, fall down, one dead people in *ndege.*'

'OK. So, you and Tiyani took this bag out of the crashed aeroplane to sell. Did you take it all?'

'No Baas, too much bags to carry. We take one bag.'

'Bloody hell! I'll bet Phuti and that Detective Fourie will be surprised to hear there's a crashed aircraft full of heroin right in their backyard! I'm sorry my friend, but this is now a matter for the police.'

Nyiko did not reply, instead lapsing into a sulky silence.

Andre placed the canvas bag on the floor in front of the passenger seat and propped the rifle up against the side door. Starting the car, he drove back up the track and onto the road continuing in the direction of Phalaborwa, thirty miles away by his calculation. A few miles down the road, he decided it was safe enough to turn on his headlights as the chances of running into stray cattle grew with every small community they passed. Fifteen minutes into their journey, he saw the lights of a roadside store that appeared to be open. Thirsty after the stress of the past hour, he pulled the car over and stopped. Turning to Nyiko he asked, 'Would you like a cold drink?'

'*Aau*, please Baas,' he replied.

Andre went into the store and a few minutes later, emerged with two cans of beer, 'I'm sorry, this is all they have; this place is more of a *shebeen* - bar than a store.'

Sitting up, Nyiko took one of the beers from Andre and looked out of the car window towards the store. '*Aieee!*' he shouted in alarm pointing to a black Cadillac Escalade driving out from behind the store.

'Sit still,' Andre ordered Nyiko, 'they may not have seen us.' But it was only wishful thinking. Two incredibly bright spotlights and a brace of headlights lit up the sandy parking lot as Andre threw his beer out of the window, started the Kia and drove off, spinning sand and dust into the air. 'Let's hope they've had a lot to drink or smoke in that den of iniquity. Anyway, this will be my chance to find out whether the Metropolitan Police advanced driving course was worth a month of my time.'

To their good fortune, the road was reasonably free of traffic, with most locals now gathered around cooking fires preparing their evening meals. A quick look in the rear-view mirror left Andre in no doubt that the powerful V8 engine in the Cadillac was more than a match for the little Kia. Hoping to exploit the tight turning circle of the Kia, Andre turned off onto the network of dirt roads winding through the "informal" settlements, which increased in number as they neared the R71 turnoff into Phalaborwa.

Skidding back onto the road after one of his off-road excursions had left the lumbering SUV half a mile behind, he began congratulating himself on getting the better of their opponents. Of course, this was before the shooting started. At first, he thought it was just a stone thrown up from the road, but the spiderweb shaped pattern that appeared with a sharp crack in the windscreen, proved something a lot more serious was about to happen.

'Baas!' Nyiko shouted, 'they shoot now!'

'Thanks, Nyiko, I worked that out myself. If only we had ammunition for that bloody pistol, we could have at least defended ourselves!'

'I have two bullets for rifle, Baas.'

'Bloody hell! You could have told me earlier; have you got them now?' Nyiko stretched a hand over the front seat holding two brass cartridges, each three inches long and as thick as a man's index finger. 'Right you bastards, let's see how you like this,' Andre shouted bringing the Kia to a skidding stop at the side of the road. Grabbing the rifle, he jumped out, opened the bolt and inserted both cartridges into the magazine, praying there was no dirt blocking the barrel. Cycling the bolt, he pushed the safety catch off and raised the rifle to his shoulder. 'I hope this is where you shoot a charging Cadillac Escalade,' he muttered as he aimed between the rapidly approaching headlights and pulled the trigger.

Despite having fired Energa anti-tank rifle grenades while with the Paras, a weapon renowned for its punishing recoil, the blast and the punch to his shoulder surprised him. Almost as much as the impact from the solid round surprised the driver of the SUV as it punched a hole through the radiator, ricocheted into the cab and wounded him in the leg. Working the bolt again, Andre fired his second shot into the side of the SUV as it slewed off the road and crashed into a ditch. Whooping with uncharacteristic joy and exuberance, he jumped back into the Kia and raced off in the direction of Phalaborwa before the occupants of the SUV could get over their shock.

CHAPTER 14

CAPTAIN FOURIE

ENTERING PHALABORWA FROM THE WEST, Andre followed the Police Service signs into the parking lot behind the police station. 'Please watch this vehicle and don't allow the man sleeping on the back seat to leave without talking to me or Captain Fourie,' he said to the constable on the gate. Locking the car, he walked into the charge office and asked the desk sergeant on duty to contact Captain Fourie as a matter of urgency.

'Captain Fourie has gone home, *meneer*; she's off duty now,' the sergeant replied.

'A police officer is never off duty. Please call her at once and tell her I have a man in custody who is wanted in connection with a crime she is currently investigating. And, if that's not enough, tell her I also have a major crime to report.'

'Who should I say you are, *meneer*?'

'Detective Chief Inspector Andre Meyer from the Metropolitan Police Service in London. I'm here to assist her with her investigations. Kindly tell the Captain I will be waiting for her in the little red Kia parked behind the station.' That should get her attention, or get her goat or both, he mused as he returned to his car to await developments. They were not long in coming.

'Just who the fuck do you think you are, *jou donnerse Engelsman*! - you damned Englishman! You've got no jurisdiction coming here ordering me to come to my station when I'm off duty. And what the hell do you mean by telling my sergeant that a police officer is never off duty! I only came all the way over here to tell you to …'

'Fuck off. I know that's exactly what I would have said were I in your position. But, if that's the way you feel about it, I will leave you in peace and let my prisoner go. I'm sure he, of all people, will appreciate the gesture.'

'Don't threaten me, you damned Englishman with an Afrikaner name! I could have you arrested and thrown in jail!'

'On what charge?' Andre asked with a smile.

'Oh, I'd soon think of something.'

'Look Captain Fourie, I didn't come here to fight with you. I honestly believe I can help you deal with a growing drug problem which, you may or may not realize, is about to hit this part of the country. Also, as long as we're not arguing with one another, I've information that will help you solve the poaching case you were investigating the other day.'

'Alright Mr English Detective Inspector, I'll give you five minutes. Come inside to my office and let me see if you are on the level, or just full of shit!'

'Fair enough! In the back of my car there's a man, Nyiko Masara, who has two minor gunshot wounds, which require medical attention. After he's received treatment, I suggest he spends the night in a cell, as we will have need of him tomorrow.' While Annette Fourie gave her orders, Andre took the rifle and the canvas bag from the front seat of the car and followed her into the station.

⚬

'*Jislaaik*, that's quite a story!' Annette Fourie said pushing her chair away from the desk and staring at him. 'I hardly know where to start!'

'If I may respectfully suggest,' Andre began getting a smile from her, 'the Cadillac will likely still be at the side of the Giyani road, which will also take us to where we can properly examine the burnt-out car and retrieve Tiyani Masara's body.'

'What do you mean 'us' Detective Inspector?' she asked with a straight face, 'this is a matter for the South African Police Service only.' Seeing the look of disappointment on Andre's face, she relented and smiled, 'I'm only joking, my station commander, Major Baloyi, insists I take you along. Providing you can report here at seven tomorrow morning, you're welcome to join us. Of course, I'll have to keep the rifle, pistol and the drugs as evidence. I take it you have a place to stay tonight?'

'I expect my sister's friend, Melanie, who operates the Leopards Rock Bed and Breakfast will rent me a room for the night, and thank you Captain Fourie, I'll be here at seven sharp tomorrow morning.'

------◆◇◆------

They drove out of the parking lot at the rear of the Phalaborwa police station in three vehicles. Captain Annette Fourie and Andre led the way in her little Mahindra SUV while Nyiko, handcuffed and clearly unhappy, travelled in the first of the two police double-cab bakkies, each carrying three uniformed constables and a corporal. 'I've brought along a few more officers than I would normally,' she said to Andre, 'just in case we have to leave some behind to secure any vehicles we may come across.'

It didn't take them long to arrive at the shuttered and locked roadside store, which Andre thought was more of a *shebeen* than a store. As he expected, there was no sign of the Cadillac Escalade or the owners of the store. 'It would have been driven or towed away as soon as they realized we'd got away. Not to worry, they sure as hell won't be able to drive or tow away the next car I'll be showing you.'

He was right about that. The burnt out wreck of the little Ford Escort lay at the bottom of the embankment where Andre last saw it. It did not appear that anyone had been near the car since the fire, and the charred body of Tiyani Masara was undisturbed. 'OK,' Annette ordered one of her officers, 'Corporal Mbata get two of your men to place these remains in a body bag while you and the other constable check over the car. I'm looking for serial numbers and, if you can find it, a legible license plate.'

'*Here God!*' she said to Andre as they stood looking at the car, 'I can count at least eleven bullet holes in and around the boot alone.'

'You could have added another five or six in the back window, if that hadn't been destroyed in the fire!' he added.

Annette ordered Corporal Mbata and his men to return to Phalaborwa once they'd completed their investigation. 'Put your prisoner, Nyiko, into Corporal Ngwazi's bakkie and, when you get back to the station, pass on any serial numbers and license plate information you've found to the desk sergeant. Tell him to get onto motor vehicle registrations. We need to find out who really owns this car.'

Back on the road, the little Mahindra, followed by Corporal Ngwazi in the remaining police double-cab bakkie, passed through Giyani and joined the R81. 'We're about an hour from Punda Maria Gate,' Andre said breaking a long silence, 'what are your plans when we get there?'

'I was wondering when you'd finally ask,' she laughed. 'OK. I spoke to Phuti early this morning before we left Phalaborwa. He will arrange for us to enter the Park and drive through to his section station outside Punda Maria where we will discuss plans to search for this aircraft. Not surprisingly, Phuti insists he must accompany us to the area where this Nyiko claims he and his brother supposedly found this drug smuggling aircraft.'

'I get the impression you don't really believe Nyiko's story about this aircraft and its cargo of drugs,' Andre commented.

'Come on, even you must agree it sounds a little farfetched. I think it more likely these two came across a stash of drugs left behind by smugglers passing through the Park, probably intending to pick up their merchandise at some future date.'

Always the evidence-conscious policeman, Corporal Mbata got his three constables to search the area surrounding the burnt-out Ford Escort for anything that may be relevant to the investigation. 'Pick up any cigarette *stompies - butts*, bits of paper, anything that could be important. If it's just rubbish, we can throw it away later. Jonte,' he ordered one of his constables, 'take Akani with you, go to the top of the embankment and search along the roadside where our van is parked.'

Minutes after Constables Jonte and Akani left to carry out this order, the sound of a gunshot, followed by a scream and a second gunshot, shattered the silence. Mbata drew his Z88 service pistol and, signalling to the remaining constable to follow him, began the climb up the embankment to where the shots appeared to come from. A hail of bullets from two automatic rifles fired from the top of the embankment, killed Mbata and the accompanying constable before they got even halfway up.

The two gunmen stood at the top of the embankment looking down at their handiwork. 'I knew it! We're too fucking late!' the white gunman complained to his black counterpart as they reloaded their weapons.

'The kid must have gone with them in the bakkie or in the white jeep,' the black gunmen replied as he followed the limping white gunman back to the black SUV parked behind the police bakkie. 'You realize this leaves us no choice but to go into the Kruger Park after them,' he added.

'*Ja*; thank fuck we've got their *blerrie* map. OK, you lot, get your black arses in gear and get all these dead *amaphoyisa* into the back of the police bakkie,' the white man shouted to the three men standing around the SUV. 'And you,' he shouted singling one of them out, 'once that's done, get that fucking bakkie out of here and hide it where it won't be found in a hurry. And pick up all their guns,' he added, 'I've a feeling we're going to need all the firepower we can get.'

CHAPTER 15

CHIPANGA HILLS

SECTION RANGER PHUTI MABUZA CAME out of his office to greet them as they parked their vehicles in the yard. 'Come on inside,' he said shaking hands all round before ushering them into a spacious room with a number of large scale topographical and physical maps spread out on a table. 'There's coffee brewing on the counter over there, so please help yourselves.' Taking Andre aside as everyone helped themselves to coffee, he said, 'Don't tell me you rode all the way here from Phalaborwa in the Mahindra with Annette Fourie driving?'

'I survived unscathed,' Andre replied with a smile.

'Then you're a better man than I, Andre Meyer!'

'OK! If everyone would gather around,' Annette said standing in front of one of the maps on the table. 'I'm Captain Fourie with the police service in Phalaborwa. I'd like to begin by bringing you all up to date on what we know so far, and what we are hoping to accomplish today,' she said looking around at the faces hanging on her every word. 'A few days ago, three men driving a stolen Ford Escort arrived in Masisi on the western boundary of the Kruger Park. They concealed the vehicle in the bush and entered the Park on foot with the intention of illegally shooting an elephant.'

Annette paused as she consulted her notes. 'One of these men,' she continued, 'Abio Anima, an illegal immigrant from Nigeria, succeeded in wounding one of our emerging tusker elephants, only to be trampled to death by a second elephant he had failed to see. His fellow poachers, the brothers Tiyani and Nyiko Masara, illegal immigrants from Zimbabwe, picked up his rifle with the intention of selling the weapon to a criminal contact they had met in Masisi,' she said pointing to a small community west of the Pafuri Gate.

'Now this man, Abio Anima, was killed a few miles east of the Mashikiri waterhole; somewhere about here,' Annette said pointing to a location on the map. 'This is important because it was during the Masara brother's trek back to their vehicle hidden in the bush near Masisi Village, that they claim to have come across the wreck of an aircraft carrying a quantity of Class A drugs.'

'What proof do you have that this aircraft was actually carrying these drugs?' Phuti asked.

'The Masara brothers removed a canvas bag containing twelve bricks of heroin from the aircraft, all marked with the blue seahorse symbol of the Portuguese *Cavalo Marinho* drug cartel. We now have this bag in our possession. Unfortunately for the brothers, their efforts to sell the heroin to their contact in Masisi drew them to the attention of a criminal gang. In their efforts to get away from the gang, the one brother, Tiyani, was killed and the other brother, Nyiko, was wounded. Fortunately for Nyiko, Andre Meyer happened on the scene and, after helping him escape from the gang, he delivered him, the rifle and the bricks of heroin to us at the Phalaborwa police station.'

'So, I take it this Nyiko will guide us to the aircraft wreck and its cargo of drugs?' Phuti asked.

'That's the general idea,' Annette replied, 'though I should warn you all, it's likely this criminal gang has the same idea. I had Nyiko questioned at length by one of my constables who is fluent in Shona. This constable told me that Nyiko believes his brother may have provided the gang with a map of the location of this aircraft in an effort to prove his good faith.'

'Has this man, Nyiko, given you any idea where we should start looking for this aircraft crash site?'

'All we've been able to get out of him so far, is that the wreck lies in an area of large granite boulders and deep, bush choked ravines. All of which probably explains why the crash site was not discovered during routine patrols.' Annette paused and took a sip from her coffee. 'Well, the ball is in your court now Phuti. How would you suggest we go about this?'

Phuti Mabuza stood facing the topographical map. 'OK. If we start moving west from the Mashikiri waterhole,' he said pointing to its location on the map, 'the first place that fits the description is the Chipanga Hills. This is an area known for its granite outcrops, rocky gorges and stretches of deep sand; in short, difficult terrain for motor vehicles. From what I remember, we should be able to drive as far as the Shinkuwa River but, depending on sand conditions, we may have to cover the last few miles to the Hills on foot.'

'Thank you, Phuti,' Annette said taking the floor again. 'Considering the possibility that we might encounter this gang of criminals out for the same reason we are, I've authorised my policemen to carry assault rifles in addition to their Z88 service pistols. I suggest your patrol rangers do the same.'

'I will be accompanying your group together with patrol ranger Hanyani who is familiar with the area. Rest assured, we will both be armed.'

Anxious not to alert anyone keeping watch as they approached the Chipanga Hills, they left the three vehicles in the shade of a large sycamore tree and waded across a shallow stretch of the Shinkuwa River. Hanyani set off at a steady pace towards the hills whose dark, reddish coloured shape dominated the western horizon. Aware of the need for a stealthy approach, Hanyani kept the group in the shadows cast by mopane trees and the stands of red bushwillows that dotted the area.

As they neared a jumble of red granite boulders, Nyiko, handcuffed to one of the police constables, called softly to Andre, 'Baas! Baas! I know this place. Not far, we go up there,' he said pointing to a narrow cleft between two huge boulders, each the height of a two-story building.

Hanyani called a halt while he went forward to make sure it was safe to go any further. After what seemed like ages, he appeared on the top of one of the boulders and signalled the group forward. After a short distance, the cleft opened up into a flat, sandy area half the size of a football field, and surrounded on all sides by a series of low, bush covered ridges. Almost completely invisible behind a pile of rocks, lay the wreckage of a small aircraft. Shouting with joy, Nyiko dragged the police constable up to Andre, 'Hau Baas! You see Nyiko is right. Here is *ndege*! - aeroplane!'

'Looks like a single engine Cessna,' Phuti commented, 'though judging by the way bushwillows have grown into the fuselage, the wreck's probably been lying here for at least a few months.'

'This is where Nyiko and his brother found their canvas bag of heroin,' Annette said pulling open the cabin door behind the pilot's seats, exposing three more dust covered, black canvas bags. 'I can also see what appears to be a mummified body seated at the controls, but there's no sign of any other passengers. I'm treating this crash site as a crime scene,' she said as everyone gathered around anxious to look inside the aircraft. 'No one is to remove anything from the aircraft without my permission.' Turning to Corporal Ngwazi, she said 'Get your men looking for any paperwork, maps, identifying numbers or registration lettering; in short, anything that will help us identify the owners or the origins of this aircraft.'

'Annette,' Andre began, 'may I suggest you post one of your men on some high ground to keep a lookout for anyone approaching this place. As you mentioned earlier, we're not the only people interested in this aircraft.'

'Good idea! Corporal Ngwazi, you heard the English Detective Chief Inspector, please get one of your constables up on top.'

Phuti caught Andre's eye, giving him a smile and a wink.

CHAPTER 16

NYIKO

'WHY DO YOU THINK THE pilot ended up crashing into these hills?' Phuti asked Andre, 'they're probably not much higher than five hundred feet at most.'

'At a guess, I'd say he was flying on instruments at night, and at an altitude he thought low enough to avoid detection on radar. If you look up there,' Andre said pointing to a gouge high up on the face of the cliff, 'I think that's where he came a cropper and ended up down here. Poor bastard! He probably never knew what hit him.'

As Annette removed the three canvas bags from the crumpled, dust filled interior of the Cessna, Phuti walked over and cautioned her to be careful of snakes, 'Just the sort of hiding place that would appeal to a Mozambique cobra, or something even worse.'

'I can't imagine what could possibly be worse,' she quipped at the same instant a scream of fear drew everyone's attention to where Nyiko and the constable were lifting up a section of the aircraft's wing. A long, black snake rearing up from beneath the wing, struck repeatedly at Nyiko and the constable.

'Black mamba! Give it room; don't crowd it!' Phuti yelled as others rushed to the aid of the two men, 'let it escape – we don't want anyone else bitten. Hanyani, how fast can you get to my Land Rover and back with my first aid and snake bite kits?'

'Very fast, Nkosi,' Hanyani shouted as he took off at a dead run, disappearing out of sight into the rock cleft.

'Damn! I meant to tell him to come back in the Land Rover,' Phuti said, 'we may need it to get these men to a hospital. I'd better go after him,' Phuti said as he started off towards the cleft, 'I'll catch him on his way back, he'll be exhausted!'

'No, Phuti, I'll go,' Andre said trotting towards the cleft, 'you stay here and keep these people safe.'

'Andre!' Annette shouted as she tossed him her vehicle keys, 'do me a favour, bring my Mahindra on your way back.'

<hr />

Emerging from the cleft into bright sunshine, Andre settled into a steady trot making good time through the occasional stretch of soft sand all the while hoping to catch sight of Hanyani. 'Bloody hell! He's running like the wind,' he muttered, wishing he'd left his rifle behind with Annette. Getting his second wind, his thoughts drifted back to the days he spent running up and down Pen-y-Fan in the Brecon Beacons with his mates in the Parachute Regiment lugging their forty-pound Bergens.

As he breasted a rise, he slowed to get his breath back while making sure he was still following the deep footprints left behind by Hanyani. Above the sound of his laboured breathing, a distant crackling sound got his attention. He listened intently trying to decide what could be making those sounds. 'Bloody hell! That sounds like gunfire! What could they possibly be shooting at; not that bloody snake, I hope!' As he struggled to make sense of what he was hearing, a growing unease swept over him, prompting him to turn around and start running back as fast as he could.

As he got closer to the reddish-brown bulk of the hills, he heard the unmistakable growl of a Land Rover in four-wheel drive, as it made steady progress through patches of deep sand. Slowing to a fast walk, Andre waited for Hanyani to come up to him. 'I'm fairly sure I heard shots fired back at the crash site,' he said as he quickly climbed into the passenger seat, 'did you take your rifle with you?'

'*Yebo*,' Hanyani confirmed, 'perhaps they were shooting at the mamba,' he said hopefully as he stopped the Land Rover a few hundred yards from the entrance of the cleft in the rock. 'Just in case,' he added as he slipped his arm through the shoulder straps of the first aid and snake bite kits and cocked his rifle, 'just in case, we should tread carefully.'

The acrid smell of cordite hung in the air as they emerged from the cleft into the open area where the crashed aircraft lay. 'Oh My God! What the hell happened here?' Andre said reacting with shock and horror at the scene of bloodshed and death that greeted their eyes.

'Andre, Hanyani! Over here,' Phuti yelled, waving his arm to attract their attention. 'I've been shot!'

'Where have you been shot?' Andre asked running to his side.

'My leg, but it's only a flesh wound. A white man, who seemed to be in charge, swore he'd kill anyone who tried to stop them taking the bags of heroin from the aeroplane. To make sure no one followed them, they took Annette along as a hostage, promising they'd rape and kill her if he so much as caught sight of anyone on their trail.'

'The bastard! You're lucky he didn't kill you like he did the others!'

'He said the only reason he left me alive was because I wasn't a policeman; otherwise he'd have shot me along with the rest,' Phuti said wiping tears from his eyes. 'God help us Andre! What sort of monsters are they to shoot and kill these young men?'

'Hanyani, bring the first aid kit and help me bandage up his leg. I don't understand how the hell this could have happened. I heard Corporal Ngwazi send one of his constables up there to keep a lookout,' he said gesturing to a high rocky outcrop.

'While we were all running around worrying about Nyiko and the constable and looking out for that mamba, this bloody lot probably took him by surprise. Then, before we knew it, these murdering swine were amongst us.'

'Oh My God! Annette! Where do you think they're headed?'

'Most likely towards the border.'

'We've got to get after them.'

'He promised to kill her if anyone tried to follow them. They also took the three bags of heroin we had removed from the aircraft. When I asked the white guy if this was their aircraft, he threatened to shoot me in the other leg if I asked any more questions.'

'This white man, was he South African?'

'No. I'd say he was Portuguese. I got the impression he'd met Nyiko before because, after questioning him for a few minutes and apparently unhappy with his answers, he shot Nyiko and the constable to death.' Phuti's body trembled as he struggled to get a grip on his emotions. 'Thank God,' he said taking hold of Andre's hand, 'they had no idea you and Hanyani had gone to get the vehicles. Please help me up; I've got to get to the radio in the Land Rover. The sooner I call this in, the quicker we'll get some help out here.'

'I've got to go after these murdering swine before they get too far,' Andre said getting to his feet.

'Bad idea. There are at least five of them, including the white man, and they're all armed to the teeth with automatic weapons and pistols. You'd only get yourself killed and endanger Annette's life.'

'At least I can get some idea where they may be taking her. I've no doubt Major Baloyi, he's her boss in Phalaborwa, will want to bring in the heavies. The police will never let them get away with killing three policemen in cold blood and kidnapping a police captain.'

'That would almost certainly get Annette killed,' Phuti replied. 'Surely with your military and police experience, you'd know that blundering efforts to rescue hostages seldom work in favour of the hostage. Believe me, despite all the jokes we make about Annette, we all want to see her back safe and sound. Come on! Get me to the radio in my Land Rover. If we're in luck, I may be able to get one of our elite anti-poaching teams here within the hour. These guys are our best chance at stopping these thugs before they slip over the border. Once they get into the general population, it'll be a lot harder, if not impossible, to track them down.'

'Fair enough. I still think I should get onto their trail, if only to keep tabs on them. Give me one of your patrol radios and a GPS and I'll keep you posted on their location until one of your anti-poaching teams arrive. Come on Phuti! You know that makes good sense.'

'OK, but only if Hanyani goes with you.'

'No way! He's better off staying here with you.'

'Andre, I'm section ranger in this part of the Kruger Park. What I say goes! Now the two of you bugger off before I change my mind.'

CHAPTER 17

HOSTAGE

'Even I can see their *spoor*,' Andre said as he and Hanyani took off following the deep tracks left by the five men and their hostage. 'These people are *tsotsi's* from *Jozi* - Jo'burg and one of them is injured; look how he limps. They do not know the bush or how to walk softly, soon we will catch up to them and kill them.'

'As much as I would like to do that Hanyani, it is against the law. Unless, of course, they shoot at us first, then all bets are off.' They were making good progress until the tracks stopped at the side of a shallow stream. 'Now what?' Andre asked as Hanyani cast about looking for signs in the soft sand along the riverbank. 'What do you think they're up to now?'

'If you'd asked me ten minutes ago, I would have said they're on their way to the Luvuvhu River and Masisi Village; much the same route Nyiko and his brother took after finding the aeroplane. But now I'm not so sure. Andre, check up and down this side for any tracks while I wade across to see if they've continued straight on or are just trying to confuse us.'

Walking a short distance along the bank of the stream, Andre stopped in the sparse shade of a mopane tree recently shredded by an elephant looking for food. Looking around at the confusing pattern of tracks, he noticed a white object lying half buried in the sand. Walking over, he picked it up. It was a button off a shirt. 'Annette was wearing a white blouse,' he thought to himself, 'it's possible she tore the button off and dropped it so anyone following them would know she was still with her kidnappers.'

Retracing his steps, he met Hanyani wading back across the stream. 'I think they've realized someone's following them, so they've split into two groups,' Hanyani told him. 'I expect each will now go in a different direction hoping to confuse us as to which group is holding Annette. Judging from their *spoor*, I'd say one lot is headed towards the Luvuvhu Gorge, but I'm not sure in what direction the others are going.'

'I may have found something that will help us,' Andre said showing Hanyani the button he had found.

Retracing Andre's steps back to the mopane tree, Hanyani soon found the tracks he was looking for. 'Clever of her,' he complimented Annette, 'it looks as though her kidnappers are now heading in the general direction of the Punda Maria rest camp.'

'Why on earth would they go in that direction?' Andre asked. 'Surely they must realize that with the amount of visitor and game ranger activity in the area, they'd be easily seen by anyone looking for them.'

'Well, I may have an answer to your question. Back across the stream, I found a roll of blood-soaked bandages hidden under a bush. It's my guess that one of them is injured, and they're hoping to find medical attention for him.'

'Or they've made arrangements to meet up with someone on the road driving a car,' Andre suggested.

'Good point! Just in case that's what they're up to, I'd better bring Phuti up to date,' Hanyani said switching on his patrol radio.

Andre kept careful watch on the surrounding bush as he knew from his time with the Paras that the sound of radio conversations, no matter how quietly they're conducted, can travel long distances in open areas.

'Well, what did Phuti have to say?' Andre asked.

'He agrees with your idea that they may have arranged to meet up with someone with a car on the road near the camp. He said he would look into it and get back to us.'

'Well, let him worry about that while we try to get closer to them,' Andre suggested as Hanyani picked up the trail again.

Five minutes later, their patrol radio vibrated with an incoming call. 'I've just spoken with the camp supervisor at Punda,' Phuti told Hanyani, 'when I mentioned our interest in visitor traffic on the road, he told me the road is closed to all traffic while a road maintenance crew conducts a controlled burn along its northern edge.'

'I'll bet our friends never thought of that,' Andre chuckled, 'I can already smell the smoke and once they encounter the flames, they'll be forced to retreat back this way. This could be the chance we've been waiting for,' he said clapping Hanyani on his shoulder, 'let's keep heading towards the smoke until we find a good place to set up our ambush.'

The vibrating patrol radio heralded another problem. 'The road crew originally planned to let it burn as far as the Mahembane River, hoping it would burn itself out there,' Phuti reported, 'but with the unexpected arrival of a strong southerly wind, it's looking more and more like a major problem for the local fire crews. Both of you urgently need to get to the river before the fire reaches you.'

<hr>

Dense clouds of reddish-brown smoke, interspersed with burning embers and heralded by a roaring sound, drove small herds of impala, flocks of birds and clouds of insects from the path of the rapidly-approaching wall of flames. As the fire drew closer, a male Greater Kudu, his magnificent horns swept low over his back raced by, closely followed by three female kudus. 'We've got to keep watch in case Annette and her captors didn't make it through to the road,' Andre shouted to Hanyani. With their jackets pulled up over their noses to help them breathe in the dense smoke, it was Hanyani who first saw them.

'Over there!' he shouted, 'Two people, it looks like a man and a woman! They've wrapped cloths around their heads, but they're running the wrong way! No Andre, leave them, the fire is too close!' But Andre was already up and running, dodging and jumping over burning branches as tongues of flame reached out to stop him getting to the desperate couple. Throwing his jacket over the woman's head to smother her already smouldering hair, he grabbed her by her waist and tried to pull her away from the fire now burning all around them. Feeling a resistance, he looked down and was horrified to see she was handcuffed to the man's wrist.

'Hanyani! Help me!' He needn't have yelled, Hanyani was right there, half lifting half dragging the man towards the safety of the river. Picking up the woman in his arms, Andre followed Hanyani as they all jumped or fell into the cooling depths of the Mahembane River.

CHAPTER 18

PHALABORWA

'MY FIRST THOUGHT WAS WHAT about crocodiles! My second thought was there can't be any, otherwise Hanyani wouldn't have jumped in either!'

Phuti, lying in his hospital bed with his wounded leg in a sling, looked up at Andre and laughed. 'Take it from me, there are crocs in the Mahembane! In fact, some of the largest crocs I've ever seen are in that river. But, with that raging inferno all around you, what choice did you have? Now Andre, how are they treating your burns?'

'Painfully!' he joked. 'To tell you the truth Hanyani and I got off lightly. Apart from singed hair and a few minor burns on our hands and backs, we came out of it relatively unscathed. Other than all of us jumping into the river to escape the fire, my recollection as to what happened next are a little hazy.'

'Let me enlighten you,' Phuti said. 'The four of you were pulled from the river by one of our anti-poaching teams which had arrived in the nick of time on their ATV's. You and Hanyani were transported here to Phalaborwa by ambulance, while Annette and her captor were airlifted to a hospital in Nelspruit that specializes in the treatment of burn victims. In case you're wondering, everything was arranged by Major Baloyi, who commands the local police detachment. Incidentally, he's now taken over this investigation from Annette.'

'She won't be too happy about that; this drug smuggling business was very much her baby,' Andre said. 'There was another man with Annette and her captor, did he...'

'Burnt to death in the fire along with his canvas bag of heroin, which he stupidly refused to drop, even to save his own life. The other three who were headed towards the Luvuvhu Gorge, were picked by another anti-poaching team and have been handed over to the police, together with two bags of heroin.'

'And how are you doing Phuti? What's the doctor got to say about your leg?'

'All good news I'm glad to say; with any luck I should be discharged by the end of the week. Now my friend, what are your plans?'

'Well, as you probably know, Hanyani returns to work in two days' time and I'm driving my sister's little red Kia back to Nelspruit first thing tomorrow morning; now that all the bullet holes have been patched up of course,'

'Do you think she'd ever let you use her car again?' Phuti laughed.

'Well, when I arrive at her bed and breakfast and the gates are open, only then will I know if I've been forgiven.'

They shook hands. '*Hamba kahle* Andre - Go well Andre. Keep in touch my friend and say hello to Annette for me.'

***

Nearly four hours after leaving Phalaborwa, Andre arrived at the gates to Meyer's View Bed and Breakfast in Nelspruit. He chuckled to himself, the gates to the B&B were wide open, giving him reason to believe he would not be entirely blamed for the damage to Janet's little red Kia. The effusive greeting from Janet and her partner Elsie confirmed that all was forgiven.

'But don't think you're going to get off that lightly!' Janet said enveloping him in a warm embrace, 'you've brought nothing but disgrace to our vaunted notion of South African hospitality by being nearly killed by an elephant, shot at by drug dealers and almost burnt to death in a bush fire. And all within a few days of arriving at our bed and breakfast!'

'You make it sound a lot worse than it actually was,' he protested.

'Well that's not how Annette Fourie describes it.'

'Captain Fourie? How on earth do you know about her?'

'Oh! She's a captain, is she? I see you don't believe in starting at the bottom. Actually, Elsie and I spent an interesting hour this morning visiting your captain at the burn treatment centre in the hospital. For reasons that are beyond both of us, she speaks rather highly of you.'

'How is she doing?'

'Annette asked us to make sure you visited her as soon as you got here, so my big brother, off you go.'

'I'll need to borrow your Kia again, is that OK?'

'Of course, but please try to bring it back without any more bullet holes!'

Annette was asleep when the charge nurse led Andre to her private ward. 'Captain Fourie said I was to wake her when you arrived,' the nurse told him.

'Please don't do that right now; I'd like to sit here with her for a few moments. Though, before you go, can you tell me how she's doing?'

'Actually, she's doing surprisingly well for someone caught in a bush fire. The same can't be said for the prisoner she brought in; he was more badly burned. The story we're hearing is that she managed to pull her jacket up over her head which protected her from the worst of the fire.'

Thanking the nurse, Andre pulled a chair up to her bedside and looked at her face as she slept. He winced at the hydrogel burn dressings that covered part of her arms and hands but was grateful he'd managed to save her hair and face from the worst of the flames. 'And the fact that the crocodiles of the Mahembane were distracted by the hundreds of animals jumping into their river to escape the fire,' he thought smiling to himself.

'I don't know what you're smiling about, English policemen! I'm burned all over and it hurts like hell!' Annette said looking accusingly at him.

'Ah! You're awake. I've been told you're doing rather well.'

'Not from my side I'm not! But I don't want to fight with you, so if you say I'm doing rather well it's only because you put your jacket over my head and threw me in that river. Just as well there were no crocs, hey!'

He laughed. 'Phuti tells me that river has some of the largest crocs he's ever seen!'

'Well, we should all be grateful they were busy elsewhere. Talking about threats lurking beneath the surface, you've no doubt heard I've been relegated to a desk job by Baloyi who's taken over my drug smuggling case. The bastard, after all I've been through.'

'Based on my experiences in England, a clever and determined detective can do a hell of a lot from behind a desk,' he said hoping to put a positive spin on the way things were shaping up. 'Your nurse tells me your prisoner, who was badly burned, is currently being treated under guard in this hospital.'

Annette chuckled, 'My prisoner indeed! Well, you and I know differently.'

'Point is, as your prisoner, it would be quite OK if you urgently needed to question him as soon as possible with your overseas liaison officer in attendance.'

'With you being the overseas liaison officer, I assume?'

'And why not? I probably know more about the *Cavalo Marinho* or blue seahorse drug cartel than most people and, what's more, I have the wounds to prove it.'

A request from Annette to the doctor in charge of the burns unit, gave Andre access to the handful of personal effects taken off the "prisoner" currently suffering from second and third degree burns. His possessions didn't amount to much. A plastic wallet containing a Mozambique driver's license, a few five-hundred Metical bank notes and two business cards. One representing a shipping agency in Maputo and the second a customs agent in Moamba on the main road from Maputo to Komatipoort. 'His name is Octavio Gobuzo and he lives in Zangeni, Mozambique,' Andre briefed Annette. 'Not much to go on, but the card from the Escudos Shipping Agency in Maputo could provide a lead of some sort.'

'Not much use to us unfortunately. South African police officers have no jurisdiction in Mozambique and any efforts we've made in the past to secure co-operation from *Policia da Republica da Mocambique* or PRM, are usually rebuffed and, need I remind you, I'm officially off the case.'

'How much off duty time do you think you'll be allowed to make a full recovery?'

'Andre Meyer, are you suggesting we take a holiday in Mozambique to aid in my rehabilitation?'

'Sea air, sunshine and saltwater is renowned for its restorative qualities,' he added, 'however, according to your doctor he wouldn't agree to your discharge for at least a week. Which leaves me with a little time to explore another avenue of inquiry.'

'Sounds interesting! Tell me more.'

'I'd rather not, just in case my idea proves to be a dead-end,' he said kissing her on her cheek. 'If I don't leave now, I might not be allowed to visit you tomorrow,' he said as the ward matron entered looking pointedly at her watch.

CHAPTER 19

COLONEL BANERJEE

Sitting in Janet's little red Kia in the hospital parking lot, Andre used his new mobile to call London. 'Caledonian Police Station,' said a pleasant-sounding female voice, 'how can I help you?'

'Please put me through to Detective Inspector Banerjee,'

'May I say who's calling?'

'Detective Chief Inspector Meyer.'

'DCI Andre Meyer?' the female voice asked excitedly.

'The same.'

'It's so good to hear your voice again, sir. I'll put you through right away.' He heard the click as his call was transferred.

'Good morning, sir. How are you?'

'I'm very well, thank you. And Anand, for God's sake please call me Andre!'

'Of course, Andre, thank you. You've been gone for less than two weeks; are you planning on coming back earlier?'

Andre laughed, 'No, no, nothing like that. Actually, I'm calling to ask you to email me a photo of Clive Rylston. I think we have a few good ones taken during our surveillance of his warehouse in Clement Street.'

'Not a problem. I'll send them off within the hour. Have you had a chance to get in touch with my father yet? When I called him yesterday, he had a lot of questions about the *Cavalo Marinho* or blue seahorse cartel. Any idea why he'd even heard of them?'

'Nothing I can discuss at the moment, but thanks for the heads-up. I'll be phoning the Colonel as soon as we end this call. But, before I let you go, have your inquiries come up with any idea where Rylston may have gone into hiding?'

Anand laughed. 'We've looked into rumours that range from a crofter's cottage in the Scottish Highlands, to a flat in Beirut and even a castle in Portugal! You're welcome to take your pick.'

'Seeing as the *Cavalo Marinho* cartel is based in Portugal, I'd opt for the latter.'

'Banerjee,' the Colonel said answering his personal line right away. Identifying himself, Andre explained the reason behind his call. 'Detective Chief Inspector Meyer, I was about to call you. I take it you've heard from my son Anand?'

'Yes Colonel, I just got off the phone with him. He mentioned your interest in the *Cavalo Marinho* or blue seahorse cartel which, as you are aware, has raised its ugly head here in Limpopo province.'

'I have in front of me a report from a Major Baloyi stationed in Phalaborwa, outlining the discovery of a substantial amount of Class A drugs in a crashed aircraft in the Kruger Park. Apparently, you played a not insignificant role in this affair.'

'Along with a Captain Fourie, who is also stationed in Phalaborwa,' Andre added.

'Yes, Baloyi mentions in his report that this officer recently arrested a man by the name of Octavio Gobuzo. This man is believed to be responsible for the murder of four police officers at the site of a road accident near Giyani, as well as another four officers at the site of the aircraft crash in the Kruger Park.'

'It may surprise you Colonel, as much as it surprised me, to hear Captain Fourie has been taken off the Gobuzo case. This is despite her having made such a high profile arrest under extremely difficult circumstances.'

'I am surprised to hear that too! Which reminds me why I was about to call you. I'm flying out your way tomorrow afternoon and would be grateful if you would meet with me at the Kruger Mpumalanga Airport prior to any meetings I may have with Captain Fourie or Major Baloyi.'

'Not a problem Colonel. I look forward to meeting you.'

'Thank you, DCI Meyer. My son speaks very highly of you. I too look forward to meeting you.'

———— ◆ ————

Arriving back at Meyer's View Bed and Breakfast, Andre joined Janet and Elsie on the terrace overlooking the Crocodile River. 'Gin or whisky?' Janet asked as he sat down.

'Whisky please; and not too much water.'

'Been that kind of day?' she asked going over to the liquor cabinet and pouring him a double tot of Laphroaig. With a tired sigh, Elsie got up off the couch to answer a phone ringing in the background.

'It's the hospital Andre!' Elsie shouted. 'Annette is asking for you to get up there as fast as you can.'

'Tell them I'm on my way!' he replied grabbing his jacket and racing out the front door. Jumping in the little Kia, he broke every speed limit and the rules of the road as he drove through the deserted streets and into the hospital parking lot, which he had left only an hour ago. The sight of two police cars parked near the entrance way did nothing to relieve the fear he felt believing that something bad may have happened to Annette.

Identifying himself to the policeman on duty in the reception area, he was directed to floor three, secure wing. 'Shit!' he swore under his breath, 'that's where they're treating Gobuzo.' Fearing the worst, he took the stairs two at a time and ran down the corridor leading towards the secure wing, almost bowling over Annette. 'What an earth are you doing out of bed!' he shouted taking her by her arm.

'He's dead. The bastards, they've cut his fucking throat!'

'Who's dead?' he asked, 'Oh God! Not Gobuzo.' The look on her face confirmed his worst fear. 'I was planning on questioning him tomorrow morning to see if there's any connection between his lot and the Rylston gang in London.'

'Bit of a long shot wouldn't you say?'

'Wouldn't surprise me though. The *Cavalo Marinho* cartel is based in Portugal and Octavio Gobuzo was of Mozambican-Portuguese parentage. I don't suppose anyone has any idea who may have carried out this murder?'

'No idea. It seems the police constable guarding Gobuzo was called away to deal with a fictitious assault taking place on the floor below. When he returned, only moments later, he found Gobuzo dead.'

'Thereby pre-empting my plans to interview him first thing in the morning. Look Annette, it's obvious someone is keeping a close watch on us, which is why I think you should have round-the-clock police protection,' he said walking her back to her ward.

'You're never going to be able to arrange that at such short notice!' she smiled up at him.

Smiling back at her, he pulled out his mobile, dialled a number and spoke briefly to someone at the other end. 'I'll just sit here until they arrive.' Less than five minutes later, two constables arrived from the Nelspruit police station. The female officer sat in a chair in Annette's ward, while the male constable stood outside the door.

'I'd give anything to know who you called?'

'I'm meeting him at the airport tomorrow morning and, if you behave, I'll bring him here to meet you.'

She looked at him and mouthed a rude reply.

———◆———

Andre stood in the waiting area of the Kruger Mpumalanga Airport watching the Airlink Embraer jet land and taxi up to the terminal. Twenty five passengers deplaned and walked into the terminal. Most were overseas visitors decked out in their idea of African safari chic. An Indian man, probably in his early sixties and wearing a light business suit, stood out from the arriving passengers. 'Colonel Banerjee?' Andre said extending his hand, 'I expected you to be in uniform, sir.'

'Detective Chief Inspector Andre Meyer, I'm very pleased to meet you. No, no uniforms. This is an unofficial visit. Off the record, as you Brits would say. Now is there a quiet place where we can talk?'

'I was about to suggest we take a short drive to the hospital and include Captain Fourie in any discussions. Providing that's OK by you, sir?'

'Excellent suggestion Andre, I prefer we use first names and please drop the sir and call me Garjan. Now, how is Annette Fourie doing; did you get the increased protection at the hospital you required?'

'Yes, we did; thank you for that.'

'Bad luck with that fellow Gobuzo. I don't suppose you had any opportunity to question him before his unfortunate end?' Andre shook his head negatively. As they pulled out of the airport parking lot, Garjan turned to face Andre, 'OK, fill me in on everything that has happened, right from the beginning; bearing in mind I hope to get the late flight back to Johannesburg.'

———⬦———

Suggesting the female police constable on duty in Annette's ward took a coffee break, Andre and Garjan pulled up chairs on either side of her bed. Introductions over, Garjan spoke first. 'As I see it, there's an obvious link between *Cavalo Marinho* operating out of Lisbon and the cartel's growing interest in Angola and, particularly in Mozambique, one of the fastest growing of the six former Portuguese colonies in Africa.'

'I had no idea the cartel was interested in Mozambique, let alone Angola,' Annette commented.

'And quite possibly the other four colonies as well,' Garjan continued. 'But first off, we need to establish the origin of the aircraft that crashed in the Kruger Park; bearing in mind this could be a contentious subject with the Mozambican authorities. To this end I've arranged for two crash investigators from the Civil Aviation Authority and one of our forensic pathologists to fly out to Phalaborwa tomorrow morning. Andre, I want you meet up with them and accompany them to the crash site along with that section ranger you mentioned, Phuti Mabuza.'

'I'll have to get in touch with Phuti to see how his leg is doing.'

'No need, I've spoken to him already. He's agreed to meet with you and our trio of experts at the airport tomorrow and will drive you all to Punda Maria camp.' Turning to Annette who was feeling a little left out, 'Your doctor tells me he'll agree to your conditional discharge in three days' time, leaving Andre sufficient time to get back before the two of you need to decide how best to proceed with this case.'

'I should remind you, Colonel Banerjee, I've been taken off this case by my superior, Major Baloyi,' Annette said.

'Not any more Captain Fourie. From now on, you're under my command. And it's definitely your case as much as it is DCI Meyer's.' Seeing Andre about to interject, Garjan quickly added, 'Before I left Johannesburg, I contacted DCS Bryson and, for the foreseeable future, you have been seconded to our police service as a Foreign Criminal Investigator at your present rank. Now Andre, I would appreciate it if you would drive me to the airport in time for the early afternoon flight.'

Taking advantage of the thirty-minute drive to the airport, Andre used the opportunity to quiz Garjan about something that had puzzled him since his arrival in South Africa. 'Colonel, please explain to me, if you can, the reason for the sudden increase in police interest in drugs being smuggled into South Africa from Mozambique.'

Garjan was silent for a moment before he finally answered, 'Mozambique is only the tip of the proverbial iceberg.'

'By that I take it you believe drugs are being smuggled in from other neighbouring countries as well?'

'You know, I can't think of anywhere on this continent, or offshore for that matter, where someone isn't trying to avoid or evade customs and border controls. Because this country is one of the most politically and financially stable democracies in the whole of Africa, it offers the best opportunities for innovative criminal enterprises. *Cavalo Marinho* is but one of a half dozen organizations attempting to exploit our *nuevo riche* population.'

'With all due respect Garjan, your problems are probably much the same as those we experience in the UK and other, so called, developed countries around the world.'

'Be that as it may; to us it's a new problem. One that's growing at an alarming rate and, frankly, a problem we don't seem to be able to get a handle on. Take my niece for example; a Rhodes scholar until a boyfriend, or someone close to her, introduced her to *TIK*.'

'If that's a drug, I've never heard of it.'

'No surprise there. Two years ago, I'd never heard of it either. Now it's only one of the three or four Class A drugs rapidly growing in popularity with hundreds of thousands of recreational drug users in almost all of the major population centres around this country.'

'What exactly is *TIK*?' Andre asked.

'It's a crystal methamphetamine drug, sometimes boosted with fentanyl and God knows what else. To make matters worse, it's readily available on the street with hits costing as little as a few Rand. As you can imagine, it's highly addictive causing paranoia and psychosis amongst its regular users, my niece being one of them.'

'Are you not able to get her into some sort of rehabilitation program?'

'No,' Garjan replied sadly, 'my niece died from a massive overdose before we were able to do anything to help her.'

'My God! That's awful news,' Andre said placing a consoling hand on Garjan's shoulder. 'Not that it changes anything,' he continued, 'but you do know the Class A drug we found in the crashed plane was heroin?'

'Yes, I do. However, according to lab tests on the bricks of heroin you dropped off in Phalaborwa, they also contained small quantities of synthetic opioids, including fentanyl and the granddaddy of them all, carfentanil! Quite a cocktail mix for unsuspecting users.'

'Bloody hell you say. What about the packages taken off the three *skelms* caught heading towards the Luvuvhu Gorge?'

'I haven't seen any of those test results as yet, but I can think of no reason why they'll be any different.'

Andre stopped the little Kia at the entrance to the airport terminal. 'I'll be in touch as soon as we have any results from the crash investigators and the pathologist,' he said as Garjan grabbed his bag and dashed into the terminal joining the last of the passengers boarding the flight. Once he was certain Garjan had made it onboard the aircraft, he turned the car around and headed back to Nelspruit.

❖

The three women were sitting out on the *stoep* - veranda drinks in hand, staring out over the Crocodile river. 'Are you sure you should be drinking so soon after discharging yourself from hospital?' he asked Annette as she looked up at him with Janet and Elsie sitting on either side grinning from ear to ear.

'You don't seem surprised to see me here,' Annette said raising her glass in a toast towards him.

'No, I'm not at all surprised. Ever since I first met you, I knew right away you were not the sort of woman who followed orders; even if they were from her doctor and for her own good,' Janet quickly rose to her feet and, in an effort to avoid any sort of unpleasantness that might arise, got Andre a whisky and ushered him towards a chair.

'Andre, do you think we should drive up to Phalaborwa tomorrow or should we fly?' Annette asked sweetly.

'Heavens no!' he replied with a chuckle, 'you only have to look at what happened to me the last time I drove! We're definitely going to fly!'

CHAPTER 20

CHIPANGA HILLS

THE TWIN-ENGINE CESSNA ANDRE HAD hired through Nelspruit Air Charter landed and taxied up to the Phalaborwa Airport terminal fifteen minutes ahead of schedule. 'Annette!' Phuti exclaimed out loud as they walked into the reception area, 'I thought Andre would be on his own.'

'No such luck Phuti; I'm here whether you like it or not.'

'That's not what I meant, and you know it. However, I'm glad to see you up and about.'

'Now you two, behave yourselves!' Andre said shaking Phuti's hand. 'How's your leg doing?'

'Recovering nicely, thank you. More importantly,' Phuti said hugging Annette, 'I see your burns are still covered by bandages; are you sure you're supposed to be here and not in a hospital?' He looked towards Andre for a response, but all he got was a smile and a wink. 'Well, you're a little ahead of schedule, our two accident investigators and the forensic pathologist aren't due to arrive for another thirty minutes, leaving us enough time for a pee or a cup of coffee.'

'It's a pee for me,' Annette said looking around for the ladies, 'please be a dear and arrange for our suitcases to be unloaded,' she said sweetly to Phuti.

The SA Airways Embraer jet settled down on the runway and taxied over to the terminal. Twenty seven passengers disembarked and made their way into the reception area searching the faces and placards held aloft by the numerous safari companies waiting to pick up their visitors. 'That must be them over there,' Phuti said nodding towards three men carrying heavy briefcases standing to one side. Consulting his notebook, he approached them. 'Good Morning gentlemen, I'm Phuti Mabuza, section ranger for Punda Maria. Perhaps you're looking for me?'

'We certainly are,' the apparent leader of the trio said shaking Phuti's hand. 'I'm Jim Dyson and this is Eric Khumalo, we're from the Civil Aviation Authority and this gentleman here is Doctor Hugh Forsyth, a forensic pathologist with One Military Hospital in Pretoria. In case you're wondering how we know each other; I should mention that we've worked together on a number of aircraft accidents.'

Phuti introduced Annette and Andre as he led the way out into the parking lot. 'We'll all ride in the Land Rover station wagon, while your luggage and equipment will follow along with the two police constables in the police *bakkie* provided by Major Baloyi here in Phalaborwa.'

'May I ask, where will we be staying tonight?' Dr Forsyth inquired.

'Everyone will be accommodated in Punda Maria camp for tonight while you get all your equipment sorted. However, for tomorrow night I've arranged for tented accommodation at the crash site, which will save us the trouble of having to drive to and fro every day. Of course, for medical reasons, Captain Fourie will stay each night in Punda Maria and will drive out to the crash site each morning.'

'I'll bet you had something to do with this,' Annette remarked the first opportunity she had to speak privately to Andre.

'Don't blame me; the order came directly from Colonel Banerjee. If I didn't agree, you wouldn't be here at all. Besides, given your injuries, it's in your own best interests to keep safe.'

━━━◆━━━

Phuti stopped the Land Rover station wagon a short distance from a circle of tents pitched close to a huge sycamore fig tree. 'This will be home for the next little while depending, of course, on how long it takes to thoroughly investigate the crash site which lies in a small valley just beyond the cleft in the rocks in front of you.' An African ranger carrying a rifle emerged from the cleft and approached the group as they climbed out of the station wagon. 'Ah! This is Ranger Hanyani. He, together with patrol rangers Isaac and Ngwenya, will be your eyes and ears while we're out here. It will be their job to keep everyone safe from any creatures that may take more than a passing interest in our presence. For the few of us who have already had the pleasure of visiting Chipanga before, you'll be glad to know the black mamba has been relocated to somewhere a long way away.'

'Always glad to hear that,' Dr Forsyth said, 'now, if there are no objections, I'd like to take a quick look at the human remains in the aircraft before we start work.'

'Yes, of course. Isaac will accompany you to the aircraft while the rest of us choose our tents and unpack our gear.'

Hanyani came over and shook Andre's hand and gently hugged Annette. 'I'm so glad to see you both, especially you Annette. I understand it will be my pleasant task to drive you to Punda each evening so our Doctor Swanepoel can change your dressings.'

'Wasn't my idea I can tell you,' she replied looking pointedly at Andre, 'I'd rather be out here with the boys playing around a crashed aircraft than being mollycoddled in camp. Come on, let's go and see what Dr Forsyth can tell us.'

<hr />

'Judging by the condition of the body, I'd say this gentleman died about two months ago. However, it will require a full autopsy for me to be more precise. Though I can tell you it appears as though a predator of sorts tried to chew his left arm off; a hyena I'd suspect.'

'Poor bugger! Couldn't he have driven it off or got away from it,' Andre wondered.

'No. It would have been quite impossible for him to move, let alone exit the aircraft. You see, when the aircraft hit the cliff face, the angle of the impact drove the engine into the right side of the cockpit area, crushing his legs and lower torso against the seat, trapping him in the aircraft. Give me a hand here,' Forsyth asked as he struggled to pull open the crumpled cabin door so he could get a better look at the floor in front of the pilot's seat. 'Bloody hell!' he swore as he reached in and retrieved a shoe from the dust and debris covered floor. 'This proves there were two people in this aircraft when it crashed.'

'OK!' Annette said taking charge, 'please all gather around. I want everyone to start looking for human remains other than those of the pilot. If the good doctor is right, it's very likely that one or possibly both of the people flying in this aircraft were attacked by a carnivore, likely a hyena.'

An hour into the painstaking search, the net result comprised a few slivers of animal bone, part of the dried carcase of a hyena, scattered debris from the aircraft and the well-chewed sole of a man's shoe; but nothing conclusive. 'Knowing the appetite and bone crushing ability of *crocuta crocuta*,' Forsyth remarked, 'it's unlikely we will find anything of the second person's remains.' Turning to Annette, he asked if he and the two police constables could be given permission to remove the body of the pilot from the wreckage with as much dignity as possible. Leaving the doctor and the constables to this grisly task, Andre asked everyone else to join him for a late morning coffee and rusks at the tables being set up under the sycamore fig tree.

'What are your first impressions of the aircraft itself?' Annette asked Jim Dyson as she sat down next to him at a table.

'Well, she's an old girl for a Cessna 172. Probably built around the late 1960s I'd say,' he replied exchanging a glance with Eric Khumalo who nodded in agreement. 'A brief look at the remains of the instrument panel over the doctor's shoulder suggests the aircraft was in serious need of upgrades and, more than likely, was not airworthy. Once Doctor Forsyth has completed the removal of the body, we can start looking for registration marks and serial numbers which could give us some clue as to the aircraft's origin.'

'Frankly, we're more interested in finding out where this particular flight may have originated,' Andre added jumping in.

'That's going to be a lot more difficult. The best we could come up with would be an educated guess based on the probable direction of flight.'

'Even that would be a huge improvement over what we have right now.'

Their coffee finished, Dyson and Khumalo picked up a knapsack, enlisted the company of patrol ranger, Ngwenya, and set out to climb some of the nearby hills. 'We should be back in an hour or two,' Dyson added.

It was early afternoon when Doctor Forsyth and the two police constables emerged from the cleft in the rocks carrying a black body bag. Placing the bag in the tent allocated to him, the doctor joined Annette and Andre sitting in folding chairs arranged in a circle under the shade of the sycamore fig. 'I'm always surprised by how hot it gets in the bushveld,' the doctor remarked, 'and the less said about the stifling heat in that small valley the better. I know it's a little early but, if you don't mind, I'd love to have one of those cold beers.'

'Of course. Sit down Hugh, I'm just about to get two beers for ourselves. What would you prefer, Castle or a Windhoek Lager?'

'Anything, so long as it's wet and cold.'

Andre returned in a few minutes and set down three Castles on the table. 'Cheers! Here's to a successful day.'

'Well Doctor Forsyth,' Annette said taking a sip of her beer, 'what can you tell us about the pilot?'

'First of all, please call me Hugh and secondly, I don't believe the body in the aircraft was that of the pilot; always bearing in mind pilots traditionally sit in the left hand seat.'

'So, what about the pilot?' Andre asked.

'I believe he killed the man in the passenger seat with a bullet in the back of his head.'

'My God!' Annette said in disbelief, 'I take it you're quite serious?'

'I'm afraid so. The deceased was shot by someone crouched behind him in the rear compartment. However, I don't believe it was wilful murder. I see it more as an act of mercy, given that that the poor man's legs and lower torso were crushed and jammed hard against the seat by the engine, which must have been very hot at the time.'

To make matters worse,' Forsyth continued, 'both the passenger's arms were broken in the crash due to the failure of his seatbelt to properly activate itself. I should mention we had to completely dismantle the seats in order to remove the body. Before we finished up, we searched the cabin for any personal effects. But, to our surprise, apart from a wedding ring, we couldn't find any other clues to the identity of the deceased, other than the badly worn inscription engraved around the inside of the ring.'

'May I look at the ring please,' Annette asked.

'Of course,' Forsyth replied taking a gold ring from his pocket and handing it to her. 'As best as I can decipher it without using a magnifying glass, the inscription reads Lil & Jim and appears to be dated 1992.'

'That's all? Just Lil & Jim, 1992. Nothing else?' Andre asked.

'Afraid not. Though I can tell you it almost certainly wasn't the dead man's wedding ring.' Seeing the puzzled expressions on their faces, he continued, 'When I found it, the ring was jammed onto his pinkie finger and not on his ring finger, which was far too large for the size of the ring. Someone obviously intended for it to be found hoping to encourage the erroneous conclusion that the body was that of Lil's husband, Jim, or her boyfriend, Jim, whichever you prefer.'

'I hope we're still in time for lunch,' Dyson said as he, his partner Khumalo and the patrol ranger walked back into camp, 'or for one of those cold beers I dreamed about all the way back here.'

'Of course, gentlemen,' Andre replied as he took another three beers from the cooler. 'A successful walk in the woods I hope?'

'Yes, I'd call it successful. I believe we can now give you some idea as to the aircraft's most likely origin and destination.'

'Well, you've certainly got our attention. Let me pull out a map so we can follow along with you,' Annette said reaching into her briefcase and taking out a well-used Michelin road map. 'I like using this map because it covers both Mozambique and South Africa on a scale of 1 / 4 000 000. Once we have established which area we are interested in, we can switch to a more detailed map later.'

'Sounds good; but first let me explain our idea. To begin with, we assumed the pilot had no idea of his height in relation to the terrain due to the fact that his altimeter was not working. By examining the trees along the higher ridges of the surrounding hills, it did not take us long to discover where the aircraft's landing gear had clipped the uppermost branches. Using that as our starting point, we used our lensatic compass to get a direct bearing to the impact mark on the cliff above the crash site.'

'I see where you're going with this,' Andre said helping Annette spread out her map on the table, 'all we've got to do now is follow that bearing back to an airfield in Mozambique.'

'Providing the pilot didn't make any major course changes during the flight,' Annette added. 'Phuti,' she said calling him over, 'I'd appreciate your help here; what can you tell us about this place called Zangeni?'

'I've only been to Zangeni once or twice. Though I've heard recently it is now an important diamond mining town on the banks of the Save River. It's not an easy place to get to and is probably not on the average tourist's bucket list.'

'What about airfields?' Andre asked.

'I know that Zangeni has a small dirt airstrip,' Eric Khumalo added to the conversation. 'I once investigated a helicopter accident there, but that was a long time ago and I'm afraid I can't remember much about the town.'

'What are your thoughts about a possible destination?' Annette asked looking at Dyson and Khumalo.

'Could we leave that discussion until after lunch and we've had an opportunity to thoroughly examine the aircraft. In light of Doctor Forsyth's discoveries, Eric and I may need to rethink some of our initial impressions.'

<hr />

It was shortly after four in the afternoon before the two Civil Aviation Authority crash investigators and their patrol ranger escort emerged, dripping with sweat, from the rocky cleft that led to the crash site. Waiting until they'd had a chance to pack away their equipment, the rest of the team sat patiently around the large table under the shade of the sycamore fig tree nursing their beers.

'I've never come across such a strange aircraft accident in all my twelve years as an investigator,' Jim Dyson said in his opening remarks. 'We couldn't find any sign of a flight logbook, personal papers, maps, or even a handheld GPS. Coupled with the fact that someone, most likely the pilot, tried, but failed to set the aircraft alight, demonstrates his determination that the origin and destination of this aircraft remains unknown.'

'Given that this aircraft was smuggling drugs into the Republic,' Phuti commented, 'would that be so unusual?'

'I suppose not,' Eric replied. 'But with no maps or a working GPS, how the hell did they expect to get to their destination?'

'Unless these items were removed after the aircraft crash,' Andre observed. 'In your opinion, what sort of condition was the aircraft in. I seem to recall one of you remarking that it was quite possibly not even airworthy.'

'I'd stand by that,' Jim Dyson replied, 'as best as we can tell most of the critical flight instruments, such as the altimeter for example, were not in working order.'

'Not a very good idea when you're flying at night over unfamiliar terrain,' Eric Khumalo added with a chuckle. 'Also, we are considering the idea that somewhere along the line, the aircraft may have been topped up with dirty fuel. Always a problem with small, remote airfields.'

'Going back to what you said about the pilot trying to burn the aircraft, do you have any idea why he did not succeed?'

'Yes. Quite simply the cloth fuse he stuffed into the port side fuel tank did not reach the fuel as he intended.'

'So, you're saying the fuel level in the tank was that low?'

'Practically empty. Obviously, he had forgotten, or he was not aware, that the fuel pump had been switched to the starboard tank. Based on the amount of fuel remaining in that tank, I estimate he would have had enough fuel for at least another half hour of flying time.'

'So, his final destination could easily have been somewhere in the area around Masisi,' Annette added. 'That's where the Masara brothers inadvertently came to the attention of that gang.'

CHAPTER 21

MAJOR BALOYI

ANNETTE AND ANDRE ACCOMPANIED PHUTI as he drove the two CAA investigators and Doctor Forsyth to the Phalaborwa Airport for their early morning return to Johannesburg. Satisfied the trio had connected with their flight, he dropped Annette and Andre off at the police station for a debriefing by Major Baloyi. 'So, what are your conclusions after this very expensive waste of our scarce resources in the game reserve,' Baloyi asked pushing back in his chair and staring at them.

'I saw our time in Kruger Park as an essential part of any thorough investigation into the smuggling of drugs into South Africa,' Annette said trying to control her exasperation with Baloyi's attitude.

'Major, please forgive me,' Andre quickly jumped in, 'I had no idea Colonel Banerjee expected your department to foot the bill for our investigation. This contradicts his assurance to me that his office in Jo'burg would pick up all the costs.'

'Oh! I didn't mean it to come out sounding like that,' Baloyi said shifting uncomfortably in his chair, 'my words just came out wrong. I was referring to the amount of time it took Captain Fourie away from her work here.'

'Fortunately, I'm on paid leave for the time being, so Major, you will just have to manage without me,' Annette said smiling sweetly.

'As your commanding officer, I insist you keep me fully up to date on any progress you make.'

'Of course, Major,' Annette replied giving Andre a nudge as she stood up preparing to leave, 'that goes without saying.'

⋖◈⋗

They picked up Annette's little Mahindra from the parking lot at the rear of the police station and drove to her home in the Luiperd's Vlei Wildlife Estate adjacent to the Kruger Park. 'I've really got to find a place to stay until we decide how best to continue our investigation.'

'That can wait until later,' Annette said pulling into the driveway of a surprisingly large, thatched cottage set back from the road and surrounded on both sides by bush. 'We should sit down and discuss what we've come up with so far. But first, I need to visit the local clinic to have my dressings changed; here are my keys, go in and make yourself comfortable, I'll be back within the hour.'

Andre unlocked the front door and stepped into the cool interior, a welcome relief from the growing heat of the late morning sun. Setting his bag down on the slasto-paved entrance hall, he walked into a living room tastefully furnished with a pair of sofas and a set of matching occasional chairs. He wandered over to the window which overlooked a well-kept garden surrounding a small swimming pool. Beside the window, in the corner, stood an antique writing desk decorated with an old-fashioned vase and a pleasing arrangement of flowers, presumably plucked that morning from the garden.

Wondering how Annette could afford such an obviously expensive home, he wandered into the kitchen. Searching around, he found an electric kettle, a packet of ground coffee and an open tin of condensed milk in the fridge. Brewing a cup of coffee, he walked out into the shaded area of the *stoep* overlooking the garden and settled into a comfortable chair.

He awoke with a start from a dreamless sleep when Annette placed her hand on his shoulder. 'I'm sorry, I didn't mean to wake you. You looked so peaceful sitting there, but it's almost lunch time and, like me, you must be starving.'

'Sit down,' he said reaching up and taking her hand, 'first tell me how things went at the clinic.'

'It's all good news, I'm glad to say. Look,' she said holding out her arms, the hydrogel bandages are gone and all I have to do for the next few days is keep the burn areas covered with what the doctor called an emollient cream. I filled the prescription at a local chemist and would appreciate your help spreading the goo around.'

'I'd be only too glad to help. Now, how about I fix us something for lunch; you give the directions and Chef Andre will do the rest.'

Relaxing on the *stoep* after lunch, Annette was anxious to get started. 'Right, Detective Chief Inspector Meyer, what conclusions have you arrived at after two days in the Chipanga Hills?'

'Well to begin with, we are going to have to track down Lil and Jim, 1992.'

'I take it, you too believe he was the pilot and that he survived the crash?'

'I can't see it any other way. Also, while we're impugning his character, it's my opinion that this man walked away from the crash carrying at least one, or possibly two canvas bags of heroin worth, by my best estimate, £372,000 per bag or 13.6 million Rand in total! Well worth the effort on his part.'

'And by putting a bullet into the head of his co-pilot, passenger or partner, or whatever he was, he eliminated any possible future repercussions,' Annette added.

'Hardly necessary I suppose given the extent of the second man's injuries. So, perhaps we should give him credit for at least one act of compassion, while ignoring the inestimable harm his bag, or bags of heroin, will eventually bring to hundreds of thousands of South Africans.'

Annette turned to face him. 'I agree with everything you've said so far, but it still leaves us with having to decide what we should do next.'

'True,' he replied, 'so may I ask what you think we should do next?'

'Go to Zangeni and make discrete inquiries?'

'My thoughts exactly! Let's have a drink to celebrate a decision we both agree on, then I must go and find a hotel for the night.'

'Nonsense,' Annette said going over to a liquor cabinet and pouring two Laphroaig single malt whiskies. 'After we've had our sundowners, I'll take two eland steaks out of the fridge and wrap some potatoes and veggies in tin foil, while you get the *braaivleis* – barbecue going. Then, once we've eaten, we'll worry about your hotel.'

Relaxing on the stoep nursing after-dinner drinks, they watched as the last reddish glow of the setting sun disappeared from the western sky. 'I can't get over how dark it gets here once the sun has set. In England, there's so much ambient light from streetlights, cars and nearby towns, that it never gets completely dark. Don't you feel a little nervous being out here on your own?'

'Sometimes I do. Especially if I've been investigating a brutal attack or a murder; that's when I keep my Z88 pistol close at hand and then, of course, there's always Xengelela.'

'He's a friend of yours?'

'More of an acquaintance really; though I wouldn't want to encounter him too often at night.' Seeing the puzzled expression of his face she explained. 'Xengelela is an enormous male leopard who's made our wildlife estate his home for the past three years.'

'What on earth does Xengelela mean?' Andre asked.

'In Tsonga it means lying in ambush; but in all the times I've encountered him, I never once felt threatened.' Taking a sip from her drink, Annette continued. 'One evening while sitting out here enjoying the sunset, I dozed off only to wake up and find him lying just the other side of the pool staring straight at me. We sat studying one another for what seemed like ages before he got tired of looking at me, got up, stretched and wandered off into the darkness. I've only seen him a few times since then, but I often hear his rasping cough at night as he patrols his domain.'

'Bloody hell, a leopard in the garden,' he said sipping his drink. 'Your nearest neighbour must be, what, a hundred yards away?'

'*Ja*, and it suits me just fine. Hell! If the mood takes me, I can swim *kaalgat* - naked in my pool and never have to worry about anyone watching.' Andre smiled at her confession, 'You don't believe me?' she said.

'The idea of you swimming naked intrigues me,' he chuckled, 'but

I'm sorry Annette, your claim just doesn't fit my perception of you as, and please forgive me for saying this, an uptight woman.'

'Is that your perception of me? Uptight? So, you think of me as being a strait-laced woman? A *preutse vrou*?' He started to apologise, but Annette had already jumped to her feet and rushed inside the house.

'Bloody hell!' he muttered, 'I had no idea she would be so sensitive.' He was about to go inside and apologise when she reappeared in the doorway with a towel wrapped around her upper body. 'Annette I'm sorry, you really don't have to do this.'

'Damn right I do,' she replied reaching inside the doorway and switching off the outside lights. 'If we're going to work together you've got to be able to believe anything and everything, I tell you.' Partly screened by the darkness, she walked past him and handed him her towel, 'You've got thirty seconds to join me in the pool.'

———◆———

The water was pleasantly cool and, he had to admit, quite refreshing. He swam over close to where she was holding onto the edge of the pool. 'I'm sorry I didn't believe you at first, but now I know better.'

'Apology accepted.' She pushed off from the side of the pool and, swimming up to him, put her arms around his neck and kissed him. Initially taken by surprise, he pulled her close to him and returned her kiss, enjoying the sensation of holding her naked body against him. His physical reaction was immediate and unmistakable. 'Well, what do we have here?' she whispered in his ear. 'OK, I think it's time to take our relationship to the next level,' she said taking his hand and leading him over to the steps out of the pool.

'Where are we going?' he asked, hoping he had already correctly guessed the answer.

'To where I would have liked to have gone on the very first day we met,' she replied, leading him to her bedroom door.

———◆———

The delicious smell of bacon frying drifted into the bedroom as Andre blinked awake to the sound of the curtains being opened. 'Good morning Madam, Master,' a black maid in a white uniform said smiling at the couple in the bed. 'Would you like your coffee in here or out on the *stoep*?'

'Thank you Thandi,' Annette replied, 'I think the master wants to sleep a little bit more. Let's have coffee on the *stoep* in, say, half an hour.'

'Half an hour?' Andre said as Thandi left closing the bedroom door behind her, 'not nearly enough time for all the things I have in mind.'

'There's always tonight, providing we don't exhaust your repertoire,' she said reaching out to him.

'Well,' Annette said pouring two coffees from the thermos flask Thandi had set out on the *stoep*, 'we've solved the difficulty of us travelling together as a couple on our holiday in Mozambique.'

'And in the very nicest way possible too,' Andre added taking a sip of his coffee, 'now to business. I think you'll agree tracking down Lil & Jim 1992 should be our first task, which means making discreet inquiries around Zangeni and its airport.'

'My little Mahindra is ready to go anytime we are, so I can think of no reason why we shouldn't leave first thing tomorrow morning. Of course, we're going to need camping equipment, a tent and so on as accommodation facilities are few and far between in that part of Mozambique.'

'How long do you think it would take us to get to Zangeni?'

'A day and a half, given good road conditions, or a month of Sundays if the roads are up to shit!'

'That long?' he said laughing, 'let's go and get our camping gear sorted.'

CHAPTER 22

ZANGENI

I T TOOK THEM THE BETTER part of two days travelling over end-less miles of dusty, red coloured, sand roads to reach the outskirts of the town on the banks of the Save River. As a destination at the end of a long journey, Zangeni certainly wasn't worth the effort. 'What a dump,' Annette remarked as they pulled into a roadside camping area further along the riverbank. 'Thank God we've brought enough supplies for the next few days or so,' she said as she stared in dismay at the rundown Bella Vista trading store and beer parlour.

'I'd better pop over there and see if I can get directions to the airport,' Andre suggested pulling over to the side of the road and getting out of their car. 'Please make sure you keep the doors locked,' he suggested as he walked towards the trading store. A pack of a half dozen mangy yellow dogs resting in the shade of a forlorn gum tree, watched his approach with interest.

Ten minutes later he was back. 'This is going to be a bit more difficult than we first thought,' he said getting back in the car. 'Most of the people in the store can't speak English and the proprietor, who could barely un-derstand what I was saying, apparently had no idea there was an airport nearby! Fortunately, he was able to pull a man out of the beer parlour who was sufficiently sober to understand what I was talking about. An officious little bastard, he began by asking a lot of questions and, at one stage, he even demanded to see our passports. When I told him I'd only hand them over to a uniformed customs officer, he backed off. Eventually, after handing him a few Rands for his trouble, he gave me directions to the airport which, I understand, is roughly seven miles south of where we are now.'

'So, what do you suggest we do next?'

'Head out in the direction of the airport and find somewhere around there to camp for the night. To be quite honest, having had a good look at the crowd in the Bella Vista, I don't think we'd be safe camping anywhere around here!'

As far as airports go, it was a disappointment to say the least. 'It's nothing but a stretch of relatively flat dirt with a windsock that's seen better days,' Annette remarked.

'At least there aren't any trees growing in the middle of the runway,' Andre replied trying to make light of the disappointing situation. 'There's an aircraft hangar and a couple of corrugated iron buildings over there, let's drive over and see if we can find anyone who can help us.' As they drove up to the larger of the two buildings, an elderly African man emerged and stood waiting for them. He was dressed in a threadbare dark suit, grubby white shirt and tie and was carrying an umbrella to shield him from the sun.

'Good morning,' he greeted Andre in perfect English as he climbed out of the car, 'I'm *Senhor* Aloisius, I'm in charge of this aerodrome. How can I help you?'

'I'm Andre Meyer and that is my wife Annette sitting in the car,' Andre replied shaking the mans outstretched hand. 'We're trying to find some old friends of ours who used to fly small aeroplanes in and out of aerodromes just like the one you have here.'

'If you have their names, I'm sure I can find them. Please come inside, the sun is already too hot.' The interior of the hut was pleasantly cool so, feeling sorry for Annette sitting in the already hot car, Andre called her inside. Aloisius greeted her and scurried about finding a clean chair for her to sit on. Satisfied she was comfortably seated; he went over to a cupboard and took out what looked like a collection of school writing books which he set out on a rickety table. Sorting through them he turned to Andre, 'Now sir, in what month do you believe your friends may have landed here?'

Andre looked at Annette before answering. 'I'd say about three or four months ago. Oh, and I should mention, they usually flew a Cessna 172.'

'Well that does help,' Aloisius remarked flipping back through the pages. 'I'm sorry, what were their names again?'

'We only knew them as Jim and Lil, but, for the life of us, we just can't remember their surnames.'

After a few minutes, Aloisius straightened up saying, 'I'm sorry, I cannot find any record of passengers going by those names landing here. The only Cessna 172 to refuel here in the last four months was flown by two men.'

'You wouldn't perhaps know their names, would you?' Andre asked hopefully.

'No. Neither the pilot nor his passenger filled out our landing forms properly. Unfortunately, I do not know the pilot's name, but I do recall that his passenger was a Colonel Lopes, a member of the *Policia da Republica da Mocambique.*'

'Do you have any idea of the origin of their flight or its final destination?'

'Had they filled out our forms correctly, I could have provided you with that information. However, what I can tell you is that the passenger, Colonel Lopes, was *Chefe de Policia* in Cimboa da Praia in Cabo Delgado Province.'

'That's to hell and gone in the northern most area of Mozambique! It's practically on the Tanzanian border,' Annette said as they sat in her Mahindra trying to decide what to do next. 'According to my Michelin, Cimboa da Praia is close to a thousand miles by road from here.'

'No wonder they had to refuel here,' Andre said thinking out aloud, 'and did you see the state of the fuel drums stored out in the open? It's no bloody wonder they had problems with dirt in the fuel lines.'

'Still doesn't help us though,' she replied. 'While we can reasonably assume the dead guy could be this Colonel Lopes that Aloisius mentioned, we're still no closer to finding out who Jim really is.'

'According to this,' Andre said pointing to the town of Cimboa da Praia on her Michelin map, 'there's an airfield there. It's reasonable to assume that's where our Cessna took off from. I suggest we drive to the city of

Beira and fly to Cimboa; you've got to admit, it would be a lot quicker than travelling all the way by road.'

―――――◄◄◈►►―――――

It took them the best part of a day to drive to Pande on the coastal road just south of the Save River. Then, despite vastly improved roads, it still took a full morning to reach the port city of Beira. Not wanting to waste any time, they went directly to the airport and booked two tickets on the Mozambique Espresso flight to Cimboa leaving early the next morning. 'You should be aware,' the ticket agent warned them, 'there's a lot of unrest in Cabo Delgado Province and particularly in Cimboa. You must be very careful where you go at night.'

'Doesn't sound very welcoming,' Annette remarked as they drove around looking for a motel close to the airport.

'With any luck, we may not even have to leave the precincts of the airport in Cimboa,' Andre replied hopefully.

CHAPTER 23

CIMBOA DA PRAIA

FOLLOWING THE COLLAPSE OF TOURISM in Beira after the Rhodesian War and the civil unrest that followed, the industry was struggling to get back on its feet. Nevertheless, Annette and Andre managed to find a reasonably priced hotel near the airport, which also provided a wooden lockup garage for the Mahindra.

The sparkling blue waters of the Mozambique channel appeared briefly beneath the wings of the Embraer jet as it circled out to sea in preparation for a landing at the Cimboa Airport. 'Our flight took just under two hours,' Andre said as they walked into the small terminal, 'sure beats the hell out of driving wouldn't you agree?'

Walking over to the single counter which handled everything from booking flights to ordering taxis, they asked whether it was possible to hire a light aircraft for a sightseeing flight over Cimboa. 'Not in here you can't,' the clerk replied. Andre slid a folded ten Rand note across the counter. 'You'll have to go out of here and take a taxi half a mile down the road to Amrit Singh's Aerial Tours. Someone there should be able to help you.'

'It's too nice a day to take a taxi for such a short distance,' Annette said, 'let's walk.'

Amrit Singh's Aerial Tours sign appeared above the main door of an old aircraft hangar at the far end of the airport. Annette decided to wait outside in the sunshine while Andre went in to make a few discrete inquiries. Walking into the cool of the hanger, he approached an Indian man working on the engine of a Cessna 172. 'Good morning,' Andre greeted him, 'is Amrit Singh around?'

'I'm Amrit,' the man replied with a friendly smile, 'can I help you?'

'I hope so. My wife and I just flew in from Beira and we're hoping to get in touch with some old friends of ours, Jim and Lil. When we last heard of Jim, he was flying an old Cessna 172 out of this airport; much like the one you're working on now.'

'How long ago would that have been?'

'Oh! About three or four months ago.'

'And where was he supposed to be flying to?' the man asked suspiciously.

'Down south somewhere, I believe.'

'As you can see a Cessna 172 is usually a two-seater aircraft. Who was his passenger?'

'I'm really not sure; someone high up in the police I think.'

'*Madre Dios*,' Amrit Singh exclaimed as he grabbed Andre by his arm and led him out of the hanger. 'Are you *loco*. Questions like that, *Senhor*, can get you killed around here.'

"We're not looking for trouble, we only want to get in touch with Jim. Do you know him?'

'We know him as Jimmy, Jimmy Erasmus. His wife Lil now lives somewhere in South Africa. We haven't seen Jimmy around here since he flew a policeman down south three months ago. Obviously, you don't know where he is now, otherwise you wouldn't be here asking about him. Are you from the police in South Africa? I know Jimmy had some problems there a few years ago, and, like most of the people living up here, he's trying to stay under the radar.'

'May I ask why you think it's so dangerous to be asking questions about a friend?'

'Problem is, I don't know who you are or why you want to find Jimmy. Perhaps, if you told me the truth, then maybe we could help each other.'

'OK. The truth is I'm a detective from Britain and the lady waiting outside is a police officer from South Africa. Together, we're investigating the crash of a Cessna 172 in South Africa's Kruger Park game reserve. The passenger in the aircraft, we have reason to believe, was a Colonel Lopes with the *Policia da Republica da Mocambique*. The policeman died in the crash, while the pilot, whom I now know to be your friend Jimmy Erasmus, survived. I should also add that a significant quantity of drugs, heroin to be specific, was found in the aircraft.'

'What do you think happened to Jimmy?' Amrit asked.

'We believe he survived the crash and, somehow, managed to make his way into South Africa, leaving the wreckage of his Cessna and its cargo of drugs lying undiscovered in the bush for close to three months.'

'Surely you don't expect me to believe that good ol' Jimmy walked away leaving a fortune in drugs lying in the jungle with no one to look after it?'

'He may have removed a bag or two for safekeeping,' Andre said with a smile, 'but, as I'm sure you must be aware, trying to sell heroin on the open market anywhere without the right contacts, can be a very dangerous undertaking.'

Amrit stood gazing out the hanger door, deep in thought. 'Well,' he said to Andre, 'now that you have discovered his name and the origin of the drugs, what do you plan to do next?'

'We're flying back to Beira tomorrow morning, then it's back to South Africa to hand in our report. Any further action will be up to the authorities.'

'You're not going after Jimmy?'

'Not as far as I'm concerned. He's not the problem here; it's the international cartels who are behind the drug trade that are the real problem.'

<hr />

Annette and Andre hailed a passing taxi and asked the driver to take them to a good hotel close to the airport. 'A friend of mine owns a very nice hotel not far away and I can get you a special price,' the driver promised.

They exchanged glances, but not feeling much like arguing, they agreed to his suggestion. As it turned out, they were pleasantly surprised to find that his friends hotel was clean, well-run and even had a garden with a pool. 'Well, I can see us spending the rest of the day relaxing around the pool,' Andre suggested, 'all we need now are a few beers. I'll go and see what the girl on the reception desk can suggest.' He was back in a few minutes. 'They don't have any beers, cold or warm, but she tells me there's a liquor store not too far away. All we have to do is go out through the rear of the hotel, turn right and it's a couple of hundred yards down the road. What do you say, are you up for a short walk?'

'Would you mind if I don't go with you? I'm still feeling a little queasy after the flight and all the rushing around, I think I'll just relax around the pool until you get back.'

Fifteen minutes later Andre, carrying half a dozen cold bottles of the local beer, Txilar, walked back up the road to the hotel's rear entrance gate. As he turned into the grounds, the girl from the reception desk ran up to him screaming and babbling in a language he couldn't understand. Struggling to calm her down, he tried his best to make sense of what she was saying. A passing guest, attracted by the commotion, stopped to see if he could help. 'She says four men came into the hotel looking for you and your wife. When your wife told them you had gone out, they grabbed hold of her and pushed her into their car before driving away. This girl says your wife was screaming out your name and crying.'

'Can you please ask her to call the police.'

'She says she has already called them, but she is not sure whether they will come.'

Turning to the guest, Andre asked, '*Senhor*, you live here, can I rely on the police?'

'It's much better if you can find some people to help you. This girl,' he said looking at the receptionist, 'thinks the four men who took your wife were probably police.'

Andre's immediate reaction was to blame Amrit Singh, the owner of the Aerial Tours business but, on reflection, he realized the man could not have known which hotel they were staying at. Aware he had no other options; he ran out of the rear of the hotel towards a taxi rank he had passed on his way to the liquor store. Waving down a taxi as it approached the taxi rank, he directed the driver to take him to Amrit Singh's Aerial Tours at the airport. Finding Amrit still at work on the aircraft engine, he threw caution to the wind and told him what had just happened.

'Who else knew you two were planning to travel up to Cimboa?' Amrit asked.

'The only other person I can think of is a *Senhor* Aloisius; he's the airport manager at Zangeni. He was the one who told us about this Colonel Lopes, the *Chefe de Policia* here in town. As I told you earlier, we believe this colonel was most likely the passenger who died in the Cessna flown by Jimmy Erasmus.'

'If that's the case, then you must have been followed all the way from Zangeni to Beira and on up to Cimboa. This is important, when you arrived did you take a taxi from the airport terminal to here?'

'No. After sitting for two hours on the plane, we felt like walking.'

'That's how they missed you. The *Policia* control all the taxis here in town and no one, especially white people, ever walk anywhere.'

'Oh shit! To get here now I took a taxi from near the hotel.'

'Then they mustn't find you here when they come looking. Quickly, climb in here,' Amrit said opening the hatch on the rear luggage compartment on the aircraft he was working on. 'Keep quiet and try not to move around too much,' he warned as Andre climbed up and squeezed into the tiny compartment. Amrit had just closed up the hatch when two cars pulled up outside and four men ran into the hanger. From his hiding place Andre could hear voices raised in anger, but he couldn't understand a word of what was being said. After a while the voices died down, but it seemed to him as though an hour had passed before Amrit opened the hatch and said it was safe to get out.

'I can guess what that was all about,' he said to Amrit as he stretched his cramped muscles.

'Your taxi driver called the police minutes after he had dropped you off. I told them you wanted a flight out right away but, as I pointed out to them, my Cessna isn't in flying condition at the moment. When I said you'd run back towards the airport terminal, they jumped into their cars and drove off in that direction. Not wanting to run the risk of a return visit, I waited an hour and a bit before letting you out,' he smiled apologetically.

'Not a problem. What I want to know is who the hell are these people and what do they want with Annette?'

'To answer your first question. The four guys who are anxious to get hold of you are, as far as I can gather, members of a local drug cartel made up of former Renamo fighters and corrupt members of the police force.'

'But what do they want from us?'

'This is only speculation on my part, but I think the Colonel Lopes who died in the Kruger Park crash was ferrying drugs on behalf of this cartel into South Africa. Raising money by any means available, is essential to this cash-strapped group.'

'So, where do you think they've taken Annette?'

'Well, certainly not to police headquarters! I've heard rumours that this drug cartel has a base of sorts somewhere out of town; it's possible they may have taken her there.'

'Please, can you think of anyone who may be able to help me?' Andre asked, desperation evident in his voice.

'How about an Islamic terrorist group?'

'You're not serious?'

'I'm quite serious. The group I'm thinking of is *Ansar al-Saleem*; while it's anti-Christian and anti-western, it's strongly opposed to the smuggling and distribution of drugs in any form. With some convincing, they might give you a favourable hearing.'

'I'm willing to try anything if it will get Annette back. How do I get in touch with this *Ansar al-Saleem* group?'

'I'll contact someone who may be willing to help us. In the meanwhile, I'll take you to a friend's house where you'll be safe until something can be arranged.'

CHAPTER 24

ANSAR AL-SALEEM

I T WAS CLOSE TO MIDNIGHT when Amrit Singh met Andre in front of the friend's house where he'd been in hiding for the past twelve hours. 'I've managed to arrange a meeting with one of the commanders of *Ansar al-Saleem*. He is Sheik Aboud Said Alawi, better known locally and to the police by his *nom-de-guerre*, Abu Alawi.'

'Is he here in town?'

'No. For obvious reasons, he's constantly on the move. However, he's agreed to meet with you later tonight at a trading store a few miles outside of town. In getting him to agree to this meeting, I had to tell him of the time you spent in the British Parachute Regiment. He's a great admirer of the British army, so it's an aspect of your past you would do well to promote.'

'How on earth did you know about that?'

'Google, my friend. We may be living in the back of beyond, but we're not entirely ignorant,' Amrit said as he parked his car around the back of a rural store that was in complete darkness. As they got out of the car, two men appeared out of the night and, at gunpoint, ordered them to raise their hands above their heads. They were thoroughly searched, and their mobile phones confiscated. Apparently satisfied, the two men led them to a small hut barely visible in bush a short distance behind the store.

'*As-Salaam-Alaikum*,' a bearded man dressed in a white kanzu greeted them as he emerged from the hut, light now streaming out of the open doorway.

'*Wa-Alaikum-Salaam*, Sheik Abu Alawi,' Amrit replied bowing his head in greeting as he introduced Andre.

'Come in my friends,' the Sheik said inviting them to join a group of men seated on cushions arranged around a small iron brazier heating a copper coffee pot. 'You must be the one who needs our help,' the Sheik said looking at Andre as small cups of coffee were passed around. 'Anyone who is willing to help us stamp out the drug trade in our country is indeed a friend of *Ansar al-Saleem*.'

'Thank you for agreeing to meet with me. You are correct, I'm the one who needs your help. I'm trying to find my wife who is being held prisoner by some people we believe are involved in the drug trade. I'm sure Amrit has explained my problem to you.'

'Yes, he has told us of your problem. We believe your wife is being held by a Portuguese-based drug cartel that calls itself *Cavalo Marinho*. I see from your expression you are familiar with these people.' Andre nodded in agreement. 'Good. Now you know who and what you are up against.'

'Sheik, do you have any idea where my wife is right now?'

Abu Alawi nodded. 'These people are holding her on a small island in the middle of the Rio Ruvuma, near the village of Nangade. This island, which is close to the mouth of this river, provides the cartel with a secure base for the unloading and storage of heroin smuggled into Mozambique by dhows sailing from ports across the Middle East.'

'This island sounds like a difficult place to get to, let alone to free someone being held there against their will.'

'*Ansar al-Saleem* fighters tried a few months ago to attack and destroy this place, but we were driven off with heavy losses. The cartel made use of a searchlight and rifle fire to sink our boats even before they could land on the island. You must understand the cartel did not choose this location as their base without giving careful thought to its security. This island, known locally as *Ilha de Crocodilos*, is notorious for its man-eating crocodiles and Zambezi river sharks. It goes without saying the only way on or off the island is by boat and, as you would expect, these are carefully guarded.'

'Unless I am very much mistaken,' Andre said, '*Ansar al-Saleem* must have come up with some idea as to how I can get onto this island?'

'As I said earlier, this is a task we've been unable to accomplish ourselves,' Abu Alawi replied. 'However, based on what Amrit here has told me, we believe we may have found a way that even the *Cavalo Marinho* cartel has never considered.'

'And that is…'

'Using your skill and experience as a paratrooper in the British Army,' Abu Alawi said with a smile.

'Sheik, it's been many years since I last used a parachute.'

'Six years, according to your record of jumps with the Thames Valley Parachute Club. Also, on Google!' Amrit added.

'That is true, but I don't have any of my gear with me,' Andre replied hoping he had nipped this idea in the bud. 'Unless, of course, you just happen to have all the gear I'd ever need safely tucked away in that hanger of yours,' he said looking at Amrit.

'Mister Singh was an instructor for many years with a skydiving club in Beira and has access to a variety of equipment,' Abu Alawi added, placing the ball firmly in Andre's court.

'OK. Fair enough, a night jump may just be possible. Then what do I do?'

'Our plan is for you to guide our fighters to a safe landing place on the upriver end of the island. Once they're ashore, you can leave everything to us. Rest assured; we'll help you find your wife.' Abu Alawi turned and held out his hand to one of the men seated behind him, '*Mapa.*' The man handed him a surprisingly detailed sketch map showing an island in the middle of a river.

'*Ilha de Crocodilos,* I presume,' Andre remarked. 'Just how big is this island?'

'It is roughly half a mile in length and three hundred yards wide. It is covered in riverine jungle, except for the downriver end where there are half a dozen buildings and a jetty. A dirt road runs from one end of the island to the other, alongside a makeshift airstrip in the centre. With your help, this is where our fighters will come ashore,' Abu Alawi said pointing to the upriver end of the island. 'We will be waiting further upstream for your signal of three quick flashes and three long flashes on your torch to confirm all is well. As soon as we see your signal, we will make use of the strong current to land, hopefully undetected, at the place of your choosing.'

'Sheik, forgive me for doubting you, but how sure are you that my wife is actually on the island? And, assuming she is, how do I get her away?'

'We have an informer who has assured me your wife is definitely being held on the island. In answer to your second question, once our fighters have taken control of the island, including this area here,' Abu Alawi said pointing to the buildings and jetty on the downriver side of the island, 'Amrit should be able to land his Cessna on the airstrip and fly both of you out.'

'Do we have any idea how many men the cartel has on the island, and are they all armed?' Andre asked.

'We believe they have around twenty former Renamo fighters on their payroll and, yes, they are armed with what you, in the British army would call small arms.'

'This building here,' Andre said pointing to a solitary structure on the upriver end of the island, 'any idea what it's used for?'

'Our informer says it's there to guard that end of the island; also, it's apparently used as a prison for people who have run afoul of the cartel.'

'Once your men have taken control of the island, how will my wife and I get away from the cartel which, as I'm sure you're aware, is still actively looking for me in Cimboa?'

'As I mentioned earlier, once we've secured the island, Amrit will fly you and your wife to Pemba where we will hide you until your midday flight to Beira.' Abu Alawi paused before asking, 'Well, what do you think of our plan?'

Andre looked at Abu Alawi and the men seated next to him. 'I can see only one major problem with this plan; despite having the element of surprise on my side, how on earth will I pull this off against twenty former Renamo fighters? I can't see them allowing me to take control of the upriver end of their little island without so much as by your leave...'

Abu Alawi threw his head back and laughed, 'Of course, we'll give you any weapons you require plus a few thermite and fragmentation grenades to distract them while you go about your business. Surely that would be enough for a former member of that famous Parachute Regiment!'

Andre, acknowledging this backhanded compliment, asked if the Sheik would mind taking a look at a photo of a man who may be behind the arrival of the *Cavalo Marinho* drug cartel in Mozambique. Abu Alawi gestured to one of his bodyguards who handed over the mobile phone confiscated earlier. 'This is the man I'm referring to,' Andre said bringing up the photo of Clive Rylston that Anand Banerjee had sent to his phone.

Abu Alawi looked closely at the photo before slowly shaking his head. 'I'm sorry, I've not seen this man before. But,' he said brightening, 'once we have control of the island you should show this to our informer; it's possible she may recognize him.'

⸻⬥⸻

'Do you really believe you can do this?' Amrit asked as he and Andre drove back to Cimboa.

'A lot will depend on what sort of equipment you have.'

'I have a good ram-air 'chute that I use whenever the skydiving club puts on a show for the locals. I can assure you my gear's in top-notch condition.'

'It had better be! If the 'chute fails to open, I'll want my money back.'

Amrit chuckled politely. 'OK, so back to my original question.'

'I plan to use the high altitude, high opening technique to jump at least four miles from the island as I don't want the sound of a low flying aircraft to alert anyone on the ground.'

'Talking about the island, any ideas on where you plan to land?'

'I thought the building on the upriver end, which the Sheik's informer believes to be a prison. I would assume this would be the most likely place to start looking for Annette.'

'That's not going to be very easy, given it'll be the middle of the night!'

'Hopefully by using the Sheik's sketch map, together with the reflection of the night sky in the river to guide my descent, I should be able to choose a landing zone close to that building.'

'Of course, you do realize you may find yourself in a situation where it could be your life or theirs.'

'Don't think I haven't thought about that! Naturally, should it come down to our lives on the line, I wouldn't hesitate to shoot.'

'And I'm sure Abu Alawi would agree with you wholeheartedly!' Amrit said as he turned off on a gravel road that led around the back of the airport. 'Our skydiving club rents a storage shed where we keep a lot of our less valuable equipment; you should be safe there from prying eyes until early this evening, when I'll drop off my 'chute and harness so you can make any adjustments you may want. Also, I'll bring the latest weather forecast.

Though I can tell you the moon will be moving into its third quarter and, despite some predicted scattered clouds, you should have enough light to see where you're going.'

Left to his own devices in the storage shed, Andre stripped and reassembled the folding stock AKS-74 rifle Abo Alawi had given him along with the American made M14 thermite and fragmentation grenades. He unloaded and reloaded the three 30-round magazines as he had done many times before while preparing for an operation with the Paras. Casting about the shed, he found a piece of canvas together with a stitching needle and thread used by the club for repairs to equipment. After a bit of cutting and stitching, he came up with a canvas sock about ten inches long which he filled with sand from a fire bucket. 'Just the thing for silencing the occasional guard,' he said hefting his makeshift cosh.

<hr />

Amrit arrived shortly after ten that evening to pick up Andre and drive him out onto the airfield where his Cessna 172 was parked. 'I've removed the passenger seat and door,' Amrit said as he helped Andre, wearing full harness, parachute, helmet and goggles, to climb into the aircraft. 'I'd be grateful if you would bring my parachute and harness back with you,' Amrit asked. 'It cost me a small fortune and I had to travel all the way to Johannesburg to pick it up.'

'I'll do my best to bring it back in one piece,' Andre promised strapping the AKS 74 rifle to his right leg. The engine noise through the open door limited further talk to shouted instructions as the Cessna lifted off into the night sky and headed out over the sea.

'I'm going to circle out here while we gain the height needed for your jump; that way we won't attract too much attention on the ground,' Amrit shouted over the noise in the cockpit. 'It'll take us at least twenty minutes to reach our ceiling of twelve thousand feet,' he added. Andre gave him a thumbs up to indicate he understood as the air temperature in the cockpit began to drop dramatically.

Shivering in the pair of mechanic's overalls Amrit had scrounged up for him in the hanger, Andre began to question whether it was necessary to go all the way up to their maximum ceiling. Leaning forward he looked at the altimeter. Grabbing Amrit's arm, he shouted over the noise in the cockpit, 'Seven thousand! That's high enough; let's get over the river, I'm ready to go!' Amrit nodded in acknowledgement and, throttling right back on the power, he banked the Cessna into a gentle descent crossing over the river mouth.

'You're about four miles from the island,' Amrit shouted, 'keep an eye on your altimeter. Good luck!' Andre edged his cramped legs over towards the open door. Struggling against the slipstream, he got his left foot on the wheel strut step and pulled himself out of the cockpit using the wing support. As he dropped into the void, the roaring noise suddenly disappeared, leaving him hanging peacefully in the air watching as the Cessna banked away and vanished into the darkness.

Manoeuvring into a stable, horizontal position as he had done a hundred times before as an active service paratrooper, he pulled the ripcord. After a few seconds, the sharp crack and sudden jerk on his harness confirmed that his main 'chute had successfully deployed. Checking the reading on the altimeter on his arm, he made a quick calculation and concluded he had around fifteen minutes before he would have to land. Looking up at the dark shape of his 'chute blocking out in the night sky above, he grabbed the two steering toggles and turned his attention towards the silvery ribbon of the Rio Ruvuma visible in the darkness below.

CHAPTER 25

ILHA DE CROCODILOS

As Andre drifted down towards the river, the moon appeared briefly through the scudding clouds giving him his first glimpse of the island. As he descended lower, he could see the lines of security lights surrounding the buildings and storage areas on the downriver end of the island, exactly as Abu Alawi had shown on his sketch map. Also, clearly visible and tied up alongside a floodlit jetty were two dhows, no doubt unloading their cargoes of illegal goods and drugs.

Looking towards the upriver end of the island, he could just make out the building Abu Alawi's informer claimed to be a prison holding people detained by the cartel and, quite possibly, where they could be keeping Annette. He decided to land as close as possible to this building, hoping to confirm whether Annette was actually on the island before he created a distraction for the cartel's security force.

Spilling air out of his 'chute, Andre steered towards the dark patch of ground that lay between the building and the river, now clearly visible in the moonlight. Slowing his rate of descent as he came in for a landing, he was puzzled by three tall posts standing in a row between the building and the river. Pulling hard on the left steering toggle on his 'chute, he narrowly avoided the first post and came in for a landing close to the river's edge. Pitching forward on his face in soft mud, he scrambled to his feet and spilled the remaining air out of the 'chute. As he was gathering it up, remembering that Amrit expected its return in good condition, he gagged at the appalling stench of rotting flesh and death that seemed to be all around him.

As the moon appeared briefly between scudding clouds, Andre stared in horror at a body lashed by its arms and legs to the post he had barely managed to avoid on landing. Realizing that the area between the building and the river served as a place of execution, he was terrified that Annette might be amongst those murdered in this killing field. Glancing up at the back of the building facing the river, he saw at once that the concrete block wall was unbroken but for four small barred windows set up high. Evidence which appeared to support Abu Alawi's informer's opinion that the building served as a prison for the cartel's enemies.

Unstrapping the rifle from his leg, Andre checked that the weapon was clear of mud from his landing and, removing a magazine from the pouch on his chest, he loaded and cocked the weapon. Cautiously, he made his way to the other side of the prison building, keeping to the deep shadows cast by the overhang of the roof.

The front of the building, its concrete block wall punctuated by four heavy doors, faced out onto a corrugated iron roofed *stoep* which ran the length of the structure. In the centre of each door, a small observation hatch at shoulder height further confirmed the Sheik's belief that building was indeed a prison.

Between the centre two doors, a solitary guard cradling an AK47 rifle across his lap, dozed in a chair. Three of the cell doors stood wide open while the door at the far end of the *stoep* was closed and secured by an outside bolt.

As Andre took in the scene, someone behind one of the open cell doors began shouting to attract the guard's attention. It took a few seconds for Andre to realize that the voice was shouting in French. *'Fais attention mon ami, faire le guet!* - Be careful my friend, be on the lookout!' the voice warned.

As the guard, alerted by the shouting, rose to his feet and walked over towards the open cell door, Andre ran up behind him and brought his cosh down hard on the man's head, dropping him to the floor. *'Je t'entends moi ami!* - I hear you my friend,' he replied in the best schoolboy French he could muster.

Andre was surprised by the sight of a European man dressed in a white kanzu, his hand extended in greeting, as he emerged from the open cell door. '*Merci Monsieur. Dou etes vous?* - Thank you, sir. Where are you from?' the man asked as an African woman dashed out from behind him and ran off into the darkness.

'*Angleterre,* - England,' Andre replied quite unsure on how best to respond. '*Mon ami,* do you speak English?' he asked. 'Do you know if there is a white woman being held in this place?'

'*Oui Monsieur,* there is such a woman. I've not seen her, but I've often heard her cry out. Perhaps she is in there?' the man replied pointing to the bolted cell door at the far end of the *stoep*. Andre ran over and, pulling back the bolt, opened the door. Shining his Maglite around the pitch black interior of the cell, he gave a cry of anguish as he rushed to the side of a woman lying huddled on a filthy blanket on the concrete floor. It was Annette.

Cradling her in his arms Andre carried her outside and gently laid her on a patch of grass. He called her name a few times but got no response. 'Perhaps she is sleeping off the heroin they give her,' the Frenchman said, 'they do this with all of us. They give all of us drugs to keep us quiet and, how do you say, docile,' he added.

'Bastards!' Andre cursed. 'I'll kill the fucking lot of them.'

'They are too many, *Monsieur.* You are only one.'

'For now, but soon many fighters from *Ansar al-Saleem* will arrive and then we will see!'

'Will they arrive by parachute like you? When I saw you through my little window, I thought you were *le Parachutistes d'Infanterie* come to rescue me!'

'Sorry to disappoint. I'm a British police officer and this woman is a South African police officer. I parachuted onto this island to find this woman and clear the way for Islamic fighters who will wipe this lot off the face of the earth.'

'And where do they plan to land, *Monsieur,* surely not on this end of the island?

'Why not? What can you tell me?'

'These people have reinforced an existing strongpoint on the riverbank and are busy installing a generator to power new searchlights all along this end of the island. A few months ago, a terrorist group launched a surprise attack from the far riverbank, but they were beaten back.'

'I will need your help to destroy this strongpoint and any searchlights they've set up. In exchange, I'll help you get away from this place. Tell me *Monsieur*, who are you and how did you come to be here in the first place?'

'My name is Claude Duval. I left Marseilles almost a year ago to sail my small boat down the east coast of Africa to Cape Town. Needing to earn more money to pay for my journey, I worked for six months as an electrician for *Médecins Sans Frontieres* in Dar Es Salaam.

Four months ago, I continued my journey down the coast, but my sailboat was badly damaged in a storm and was sinking when I was rescued by a dhow sailing from Pakistan to this island. Because of my skill as an electrician, I was allowed to live. Since I arrived on this island, I've seen them kill many people by tying them to the posts next to the river and shooting them. Their bodies are usually left next to the river for the crocodiles.' Duval paused for a moment, '*Monsieur*, you are indeed fortunate your lady policeman was not amongst them.'

—◄❖►—

Andre left it to Duval to lock the semi-conscious guard in Annette's old cell while he gently placed her on a bed in one of the other cells. 'Now, while it's still dark, please take me to have a look at this strongpoint,' he asked Duval, 'and then show me where they've set up this new generator for the searchlights.' Duval led Andre through the dark forest to a large cement bunker which looked out over the upriver approaches to the island. 'Where are the soldiers who man this strongpoint and what weapons do they have?'

'As far as I know, it's only manned when an alarm is sounded at the jetty at the other end of the island; as for weapons, I'm sorry, I've no idea.' Despite Duval's claim that the lookout was unmanned, Andre moved cautiously along the riverbank searching for a suitable gap in the vegetation where he could use his Maglite to signal to the *Ansar al-Saleem* fighters waiting upstream. Finding a place with a clear view of the river, he used his torch to signal three quick flashes, followed by two long flashes, the signals he and Sheik Abu Alawi had agreed on. Not seeing the recognition signal of two quick flashes, he repeated the signal.

He was about to repeat the signal for the third time when he spotted the reply; the *Ansar al-Saleem* fighters were on their way. Satisfied he had fulfilled his end of the bargain; he was staring out over the dark river when the unmistakable sound of a truck labouring along a rough track in low gear reached his ears. Turning to ask Duval what this could mean, he was not altogether surprised to find the man was no longer at his side. Before he could react to this changing situation, the sound of a generator chugging into life was followed almost immediately by a bright glare as half a dozen searchlights suddenly lit up the river.

Moving quickly, he made his way towards the sound of the generator at the same time taking out one of the M14 thermite grenades from his pocket. A glimmer of light shining between the wooden sides of a small shed, led him directly to the generator. Removing the pin, he pulled open the door of the shed and rolled the grenade underneath the generator. Scrambling away into the sheltering forest, Andre counted down the five seconds it took for the grenade to detonate, igniting the thermite core which instantly reached a temperature of over four thousand degrees Fahrenheit, effectively destroying the generator and cutting power to the searchlights.

Fearing that the sudden unexpected appearance of searchlights may have deterred the *Ansar al-Saleem fighters*, Andre made his way back to the riverbank and repeatedly flashed the agreed signal until he received a reply.

His concern now shifted to the threat posed by the truck he'd heard earlier. Making his way along the riverbank, he crept as close as he could to the bunker which faced towards the approaching *Ansar al-Saleem* fighters. The sound of voices and the careless use of a torch, confirmed that a number of men, presumably guards from the other end of the island, were intent on occupying the bunker. Realizing the need to discourage this from happening, he activated the remaining thermite grenade and the two fragmentation grenades and tossed them into the bunker. Fearing discovery by the approaching guards, Andre slid down the bank to the water's edge as quietly as he could. He need not have worried.

His grenades detonated the huge store of ammunition the cartel had carefully stockpiled to beat back any attack launched from upriver. The resulting blast not only demolished the bunker, it threw Andre into the river and so demoralized the approaching guards that those still capable of running, lost no time in heading back the way they'd come. Flashing the signal once more to reassure the approaching *Ansar al-Saleem* fighters,

Andre made his way back to the prison building to look for Duval and to be with Annette when the fighters arrived.

————◆————

The first pale pink blush of dawn coloured the eastern sky as Andre approached the prison building. He went straight to the cell where he had left Annette lying on a bed recovering from the heroin injections Duval claimed she had been given by members of the cartel. He found the door of the cell ajar and pulling it open, was surprised to see in the light of a flickering oil lamp, Duval sitting on the bed with his arm around Annette. He was holding what appeared to be a hypodermic syringe and needle up against her neck. 'Don't come any closer if you want her to live! This syringe contains a lethal dose of heroin, enough to kill an elephant!'

'Duval! Are you crazy? The *Ansar al-Saleem* fighters will be here at any minute. If you want to get out of this alive, I suggest you reconsider what you're doing. One word from me and you'll be lucky if all they do is cut your throat.'

Duval laughed, 'You'll do nothing of the sort. I swear I'll kill this bitch if you so much as hint to anyone that I'm not here as your partner. After we've all flown out of here and I'm safely back on the ground, I'll release her, unharmed. Do you agree?' he asked, pressing the tip of the needle firmly against Annette's neck.

'Yes, of course. Just don't do anything stupid,' Andre said backing away and standing just inside the door. 'So, I take it your story about being a lone yachtsman imprisoned by the cartel is a load of bullshit.'

'Not entirely,' Duval smirked. 'The truth is the cartel moved in on my very successful enterprise importing drugs from Pakistan. Sadly, success in this business either attracts the likes of *Cavalo Marinho,* or law enforcement people like you and this woman here.'

'If that's the case, I'm surprised you're still alive. I'd have thought they'd have got rid of you right away!'

'Hardly! I'm much too important to a lot of people in Marseilles for them to take that chance. That's the beauty of this business – it's never what you know, it's who you know.'

'I imagine being a big shot in the drug trade, you'd know many of the players?' Andre asked.

'Fuck you!' Duval sneered, 'if you think I'd give anything away, then you're more stupid than I thought.'

'Always worth a try,' Andre replied, holding his hands up in supplication.

A shout from outside drew Andre's attention to a line of camouflage clad men emerging from the jungle. Stepping out into the open, he carefully laid his weapon on the ground and raised his hands above his head. One of the men broke away from the line and approached him, 'Are you Meyer?' he asked, 'Andre Meyer?'

'Yes, I'm Andre Meyer.'

'Sheik Abu Alawi ordered me to find you and your wife and to make sure you're both safe. Is your wife with you? he asked in perfect English.

'Yes, she's here in this cell behind me with my partner, Claude Duval. Please thank the Sheik for his concern and tell him we are all glad to see you and your men have landed safely. Will I have a chance to meet with him before our aircraft arrives?'

'Of course. He still wants you to meet his daughter who has been our eyes and ears on this island since the cartel arrived.' Pointing to the weapon Andre had placed on the ground he said, 'Please, *Senhor*, you may keep your rifle with you until you are safely on the aircraft.' With that he turned and trotted off to join his men as they advanced along the track towards the downriver end of the island.

'Who is this woman who spied for these people?' Duval inquired from inside the cell doorway.

'I've no idea,' Andre replied, 'but I'm looking forward to hearing what she may have to say.'

The sound of small arms fire coming from the direction of the buildings and the jetty, was followed by a series of explosions and columns of fire and smoke reaching high into the air. 'I'd say that doesn't bode well for your lot – why don't you give up this nonsense and stop threatening Annette. In exchange, I'll do everything I can to see you safely off this island.'

'Not good enough! I don't trust you or this gang of terrorists you seem to be part of; this bitch of yours is my ticket out of here. Don't forget, one false move and she dies.'

CHAPTER 26

CLAUDE DUVAL

Amrit Singh brought his Cessna 172 down in a low pass over the airstrip watching carefully for signs that the island was now in safe hands. Seeing the aircraft turn for a second pass, Andre ran out in the open waving his arms to attract his attention. Amrit waggled his wings in recognition and turning once more, lined up for a landing. As he slowly taxied towards the end of the airstrip where Andre was waiting, a jeep raced up alongside the Cessna from the direction of the burning buildings with a dozen or so fighters and a young woman clinging to its sides.

'Amrit, welcome to the liberated *Ilha de Crocodilos*,' Abu Alawi shouted, come sit here beside me, I'll drive you to Andre and Annette.'

Andre walked to meet them stopping a little way from the former prison building. 'Sheik Abu Alawi, please forgive me, but I'm afraid I'll have to ask all of you not to go any closer. A man is holding my wife hostage and is threatening to kill her if I don't help him escape from this island, and the retribution he expects from your men.'

'So that explains it! One of my commanders reported that something was wrong when he stopped to speak to you earlier. If you will allow me, one of my sharpshooters could put two bullets in his head before he can blink.'

'Not a risk I would like to take. I would be grateful if you would allow me to deal with this man myself.'

'As you wish; our success today is due, in large part, to your efforts and courage.'

The young woman who was listening to their conversation, stepped out of the jeep and approached Andre. 'This man you speak of, is he the Frenchman, Duval?'

'Please forgive my daughter, A'isha for her forward nature,' Abu Alawi apologized. 'She has been living amongst these *shenzi* - savages for far too long.'

Andre smiled. 'Ah! I take it this young lady is also your informer when it comes to information on the cartel,' Andre said smiling as he turned to speak to her. 'Yes, he calls himself Duval. He claims he was importing drugs into this area for many years, long before the cartel arrived and took over his business. What do you know of him?'

'A man without scruples who has tortured and murdered on behalf of the cartel. However, what he has told you is quite true. When the cartel arrived in Cabo Delgado Province, they got rid of most of his people and made use of his base here on the island. They kept him alive because of his skills as a torturer and his connections to Renamo groups still operating along the Rio Ruvuma.'

'When you say the cartel, are you referring to the *Cavalo Marinho* – the Portuguese drug cartel?'

'The same. Do you know of them?' she asked.

'Do you recognize this man?' Andre asked taking out his mobile phone and scrolling down to the photo taken of Clive Rylston in London that DS Anand Banerjee had sent him.

'Yes, I recognize him. I never got to know his name, but he was clearly in charge. I only knew him as the man from Lisbon. A very dangerous man: he could have someone killed just like that!' she said clicking her fingers. 'Three weeks ago, he had a man tortured and shot behind the prison,' she said pointing to the building behind them.

'Do you know why?'

'I heard it said that months ago he had supplied heroin to a crooked policeman in Cimboa. Apparently, this policeman planned to set up his own drug operation in South Africa, flying in heroin and cutting out the cartel.'

'Any idea what happened?'

'The small aeroplane they were flying disappeared without trace. Then, a few weeks ago, the South African Police found the aeroplane and recovered the drugs. This so angered the man from Lisbon that he wanted all those involved killed.'

'A'isha, this man from Lisbon, do you know where he is now?'

'Shortly after the aeroplane was found, he disappeared from the island. Next, I heard it said that he was down south making plans for drugs to be shipped by faster, motorized dhows from the Makran Coast of Pakistan, bypassing the smaller, slower dhows the cartel relied upon in the past.'

'When you say, "down south," are you referring to Beira or Maputo?'

'Definitely Maputo. This Rylston, as you call him, prefers larger ports where there are a lot of places to hide and where customs officers and policemen are more likely to accept bribes.'

'What do you think he will do as a result of our attack on his base here?'

'Nothing.'

'Nothing? You don't think he'll take any action?'

'If I've read him correctly, he would probably have closed it down anyway. He's after bigger fish to fry!'

Amrit, who stood patiently listening to all of this, interjected, 'I've got to get the Cessna turned around and ready to go. Andre, give me a few minutes, then bring Annette and your so-called friend out to the plane.'

Andre walked over to the room where Duval was holding Annette, 'The plane is ready to go,' he announced. Duval, who had been preparing for this eventuality, pulled Annette to her feet and, slinging a blanket over their heads to confuse a possible sharpshooter, walked out to the Cessna holding her close to him.

Abu Alawi took Andre by his hand, 'Thank you for all you have done for the good people of Cabo Delgado.'

'No, I should be thanking you for helping me find Annette. I will always be in your debt.'

Sneering at this exchange, Duval ordered Andre to sit in the front seat alongside Amrit. 'Just in case you get any crazy ideas, Annette's sitting in the back with me. This *Monsieur Anglais détective,* is what we French call *Sauve Qui Peut*! - Every man must save himself!'

'Ladies first,' Amrit said forcefully, helping Annette into the rear seat behind the pilot. 'Make sure your seat belt is on securely,' he said to her. 'Pull it good and tight; there could be a lot of turbulence.'

'Andre are you here?' Annette asked fearfully from beneath the blanket Duval kept over their heads.

'Shut up you bitch, I said no talking,' Duval snarled.

'Leave it,' Amrit whispered in Andre's ear as he helped him into the passenger seat in front, 'same applies to you. Pull your seat belt tight.'

'Hard to believe this is the same aircraft I jumped out of not so long ago,' Andre remarked trying to lessen the tension.

'I can tell you I had quite a job getting the seats back in and the door re-attached in the little time I had. Right let's get going, I want to be in Pemba before word about the attack on the island gets to the so-called authorities.'

Amrit climbed into his seat and, quickly running through his checklist, started the engine. Waving to Abu Alawi, he eased the throttle to full power and commenced the bumpy run down the airstrip. Watching until the airspeed indicator passed the fifty-five knot mark, he slowly pulled back on the stick and the Cessna lifted off the ground. Passing over the still smouldering remains of the buildings at the end of the airstrip, he pointed out the two dhows, still burning fiercely alongside the remains of the jetty. 'I can see why the cartel won't be coming back here any time soon,' he said loudly, as much for Duval's information as for anyone else.

Keeping the engine at full power, Amrit remarked to Andre, 'I'm trying to get up to at least eight thousand feet to avoid being observed from the ground when we change our heading towards Pemba.'

Andre was a little puzzled by this announcement but decided not to say anything as he watched the hands on the altimeter crawl slowly around the dial until they indicated eight thousand feet.

Amrit turned to look at Andre, 'Well, as the Americans say, here goes nothing!' He rolled the aircraft into a steep bank to port, tightening the turn and increasing the engine power to maximum. The centrifugal force, combined with the spiralling descent, ripped open the starboard passenger door and would have thrown Andre out of the aircraft were it not for his tightly cinched seatbelt.

'My seatbelt is broken! Help me!' Duval screamed from the rear seat behind him. Andre was able to turn his head just enough to see Annette kicking out repeatedly at Duval's hands where he had managed to get a grip on the door frame. His scream of terror was whipped away by the slipstream as the centrifugal force of the tight turn flung Duval's body out of the aircraft.

'*Sauve qui peut* Monsieur Duval!' Andre said aloud as Amrit levelled off the aircraft and set a course for Pemba.

CHAPTER 27

BEIRA

A MRIT LANDED AND TAXIED THE Cessna up to the small Pemba Airport Terminal. 'Your flight to Beira leaves in about thirty minutes, just enough time for you two to get a cup of coffee.'

'Wait, I can't find my purse,' Annette said growing more and more anxious, 'I know I had it when I got on board. I've got to find it!'

'How about the mesh bag in the seat in front of you,' Amrit suggested.

'Yes, thank God! Here it is,' Annette said breathing a sigh of relief as she clutched her purse tightly to her breast.

'Now that's settled, won't you have a coffee with us?' Andre asked Amrit as he helped Annette down from the rear compartment.

'Thank you, my friend, but I must refuse; I'm anxious to get this aircraft safely back in my hanger in Cimboa before any authorities come calling. Oh! I nearly forgot. Here are your passports and your flight tickets to Beira. Also, Abu Alawi asked me to give this to you,' he said reaching into the rear luggage compartment and taking out a leather attaché case. 'The Sheik believes this once belonged to the man from Lisbon.'

'What's in it?'

'No idea, but Abu Alawi said you would find it very useful.'

Puzzled, Andre took the case and, shaking Amrit's hand said, 'I can't thank you enough for everything you've done for us, you've been a good friend.'

'Who knows, one day I might need your help,' Amrit replied hugging

Annette tightly before climbing into the Cessna, starting the engine and taxiing out onto the runway.

———— ⬥ ————

Their Mozambique Airlines Embraer 120 landed after a comfortable thirty-minute flight and taxied up to the Beira Airport Terminal. Annette, who had slept for most of the flight, seemed a little out of sorts as they made their way into the arrivals lounge. 'How about a cup of coffee before we get a taxi to the motel to pick up your Mahindra?'

'First, I've got to go to the lady's washroom,' she replied clutching her purse and looking anxiously about her.

Andre sat staring out of the window as their Mozambique Airlines flight, now leaving for Inhambane, taxied out onto the runway. The demanding ring of his mobile phone, which he had recharged on the flight in, interrupted his reverie. 'Thank God I've got hold of you,' Amrit said as Andre answered the call. 'I take it you're still at the airport?' he asked.

'Yes, we're still here. But after a cup of coffee, we'll be on our way to the motel where we left Annette's little car.'

'Don't go anywhere near your motel, the cartel is on to you! They'll have people there waiting to take you both out.'

'How the hell could they possibly know about the motel?'

'A'isha contacted me urgently. Apparently, they've just recovered documents from the cartel's base which seem to show that Annette, probably under pressure, told Duval where both of you would be staying on your return to Beira.'

'For the life of me, I find it most unlikely that Annette would be willing to give that sort of information to the likes of Duval. Nevertheless, Amrit, I truly appreciate your call and we'll stay well clear of the motel in question. Before you go, did A'isha make any mention of Annette's car which we left in a lockup garage near the motel?'

'Not that I recall; but if I hear anything, I'll get back to you.' Anxious to discuss changes to their plans, Andre stood and looked around the terminal for any sign of Annette. Seeing a branch of the Standard Bank close by, he went over and used the ATM to withdraw five thousand South African Rands. As he tucked the money into the inside pocket of his jacket, he noticed a sign reading *Banheiros* above a corridor leading out of the reception area. Walking down the corridor, he knocked on the door displaying the universal sign for the woman's washroom. Getting no response to his knocking, he stopped a female flight attendant about to enter the washroom. 'Excuse me,' he asked smiling pleasantly at her, 'please, would you mind seeing if my wife is still in there. Her name's Annette.'

Scarcely a minute later, the flight attendant burst out of the washroom. 'Come quickly, she may be dying!' she blurted out in obvious distress. He followed her into the washroom and was horrified to see Annette, apparently unconscious, lying back sitting on a toilet in one of the booths with the needle of a hypodermic syringe sticking in the crook of her arm. 'Call the police,' the flight attendant demanded, her voice becoming loud and shrill, 'she is taking drugs! The police must be informed.'

'No! no!' Andre said thinking quickly, 'my wife is a diabetic, she is having a bad reaction to her insulin injection.' Scooping up Annette's purse and the needle as it fell from her arm, he turned to the flight attendant, 'Please help me, call a taxi. I must get my wife back to our hotel.'

Minutes later, as he laid Annette on the back seat of a taxi, the flight attendant, still shaken by the experience said, 'I hope she is not flying today.'

'No, we're not flying today,' he assured her as he directed the taxi driver to take them to the Grand Hotel, whose ad he had seen on the wall of the arrivals lounge.

By the time the taxi pulled up in front of the hotel, Annette had recovered sufficiently to be able to take his arm and walk into the reception area. Settling her down in a chair, he went over to the desk and booked a room for the night, asking the desk clerk to place the attaché case in the hotel safe. Helping Annette up to their room, he laid her down on the bed where she promptly fell asleep. Covering her with a blanket, he sat down in one of the armchairs in the room and opened her purse.

He was horrified to discover a dozen disposable syringes, a blackened spoon, a plastic cigarette lighter, a length of surgical rubber tubing and over a dozen plastic baggies containing a white powder. Each baggie was prominently stamped with the blue seahorse symbol of the *Cavalo Marinho* – the Portuguese drug cartel they were hunting. 'My God, Annette!' he said going over to her and putting his arms around her, 'what have we got ourselves into?'

Satisfied Annette was asleep; he locked their room door and, going down to the reception desk, asked them to call him a taxi. Minutes later, a dilapidated taxi pulled up in front of the hotel. 'Coimbra Motel,' he said getting in and handing the driver a hundred Rand note, 'but I don't want anyone outside the motel to see me arrive. Do this well Holden,' he said reading the driver's name off his taxi license, 'and I've got a thousand Rands bonus for you.'

Holden entered into the spirit of things and drove past the motel, close enough for Andre to spot the two thugs sitting in a car in an alleyway watching the motel entrance. 'Bad mens, *Senhor*?' Holden asked.

'Very bad,' Andre confirmed. 'Now, do you see those wooden lockup garages over there, drop me out of sight behind them, lend me a screwdriver and keep a sharp lookout for me. If you see anyone coming, call me on my phone,' he said exchanging mobile numbers with the taxi driver. Getting out of the taxi, Andre approached the rear of the garage where their Mahindra was stored. Using the screwdriver, he carefully prised open a rear service door. Checking carefully around Annette's Mahindra for any signs of tampering and, finding nothing, he cautiously opened the driver's door and looked under the seats. He was about to insert the key and start the engine when, acting on an impulse, he reached underneath the dashboard.

His hand encountered what he hoped he wouldn't find, an oblong object six inches long and two inches in diameter, connected by two wires to someplace under the dashboard. Reaching over and opening the glovebox, Andre took out a small Maglite torch. Carefully, he got out of the car and, kneeling down next to the driver's door, he used the torch to examine the bomb more closely.

'Not a bad job,' he remarked as he traced the wires to the ignition switch and a small battery wedged up underneath the bomb. Carefully, he disconnected the wires to the battery and, after checking for a secondary device, he pulled the bomb out from under the dashboard. 'You'd never get a job with the Provisional Wing of the IRA,' he said referring to the bombmaker who had built the bomb, 'and, believe me, I'm bloody grateful for that!' Carefully, he placed the bomb on the back seat to be disassembled later and the components thrown into some convenient crocodile-infested river.

After searching around and underneath the car more carefully than on his initial inspection, he concluded it safe enough to continue with his hastily concocted plan to retrieve the Mahindra from under the noses of the cartel's thugs. Using his mobile phone, he called his taxi driver, 'Holden, I'm getting ready to drive out; follow me just in case I need a ride in a hurry. But keep a safe distance, just in case there's shooting!'

'I'm ready for much excitements, *Senhor*,' Holden replied. Andre started the engine and, engaging low gear and four-wheel-drive, drove the Mahindra slowly forward until the front bumper came into contact with the rear wall of the wooden garage. With his foot jammed down hard on the accelerator, the Mahindra broke through the wooden slats at the back of the garage and out into the open, dropping bits of wooden slat as it raced away into the suburbs.

<hr />

Parking in front of the hotel behind Holden's taxi, Andre walked up to the driver's window and gave him the thousand Rand bonus he had promised. 'I've one more favour to ask Holden, where can I get this car repainted in a great hurry?'

'No problem, *Senhor*. Give me keys, I get it spray painted and back before morning.'

'Thank you, Holden,' he replied removing the bomb from the backseat of the Mahindra and handing the keys to Holden.

As he was walking into the hotel, Holden shouted after him, 'What colour you want, *Senhor*?'

'Any colour, as long as it isn't white!'

CHAPTER 28

PRACA DE INDEPENCIA

Using his pass card, Andre opened their room door, walked in and saw right away that Annette was no longer asleep on the bed. Calling out her name, he checked the bathroom and finding it empty, looked around the room. All the desk drawers had been pulled out and cupboard doors left ajar, just as though someone had ransacked the room. 'Oh Shit!' he swore as he dashed into the bathroom and felt around behind the cistern where he had hidden Annette's purse and the drugs it contained. It was gone.

Dashing downstairs, he went up to the reception desk. 'Did you see my wife leave the hotel?' he asked the young woman on duty.

'I'm sorry, *Senhor*, I do not know your wife. There are many ladies staying in this hotel.'

'Of course. But someone may have noticed her leaving. She would have appeared to be very anxious, a little scared perhaps.'

'I've only just come on duty; let me ask the lady who was on the desk before I arrived.' Expressing his appreciation for her efforts, he waited in a state of panic for the receptionist's return. She was back in less than a minute with another woman in tow. 'I saw her leave about fifteen minutes ago; she looked distraught. Is she ill, *Senhor*?'

Ignoring the question, he asked, 'Did she walk, or did she take a taxi?'

'I saw her speak to a taxi driver, but I do not know if she got in his taxi.'

Thanking the women for their help, Andre dashed out of the hotel and, to his relief, he found Holden sitting behind the wheel of his taxi. 'Thank God you're still here,' he said, 'my wife has gone missing; the women on the desk think she may have taken a taxi. Could you please ask the other drivers if they picked up a woman who appeared to be anxious or upset?'

'Of course, *Senhor*,' Holden replied as he got out and spoke to the taxi driver in front. '*Senhor*, he says a woman, very sick, did speak to him, but she did not want a taxi, only the way to the beach. Do you wish me to take you to the beach?'

'Yes, please; but please drive slowly. If she is walking, I may be able to spot her.'

It took them all of ten minutes to reach the beach area, but without catching so much as a glimpse of Annette. 'Thank you Holden, please let me out here, but stay close by. If I find her, I will need you to take us back to the hotel.'

Andre walked slowly along the beachfront following the Avenida Mateus Muthemba. He stared intently at the occasional white face he saw amongst the crowds attracted by the restaurants, beer parlours and hotels lining the avenue. As he neared the Praca de Indepencia circle, he noticed a small crowd gathered on the beach staring at something happening at the water's edge. Looking in the same direction, he saw two men carrying someone out of the surf and laying them on the beach. 'What happened,' he asked the people standing nearest to him.

'A white woman tried to drown herself,' the man next to him replied to his question. 'I call already for *ambulancia* and *policia*,' but Andre was already running across the beach towards the two men laying the body of a woman down on the sand.

'Oh My God! Annette,' he sobbed in fear and anguish as he recognized the top she was wearing. Kneeling beside her, he checked her breathing and pulse and finding neither, immediately began CPR.

'*Por favour, Senhor. Ambulancia,*' someone said placing a conciliatory hand on Andre's shoulder. He looked up as two men in white jackets carrying a Red Cross bag, took over the task of trying to revive Annette. The older medic drew his partner's attention to her blue lips and the small amount of vomit dribbling from her mouth. 'Naloxone,' he ordered, '*rapidamente!*' The medic unzipped a small bag and handed his partner a syringe which he immediately injected into Annette's thigh. The older medic continued giving her CPR for a few more minutes when, to Andre's indescribable relief and joy, Annette stirred and, within another minute, tried to sit up.

Looking up at the people standing around her, she burst into tears the minute she recognized Andre's face. 'I thought you had left me,' she sobbed, 'please don't leave me, I can't live without you.'

'It's OK, my darling,' he said, tears streaming down his face, 'I'm here now; I will never leave you.'

One of the medics, receiving a call on his phone, said something to Andre and then to his colleague who responded by packing up their gear in a great hurry.

'They go now to big crash on highway,' a voice explained to Andre, who looked up to see Holden emerge from the crowd now gathered around. 'Come, *Senhor*, we must go, policemans come soon. Not good,' he warned.

'Thanks Holden, that sounds like good advice. Give me a hand and we'll get her to your taxi.' Telling the crowd of bystanders that they were taking her to hospital, they half walked, half carried Annette across the beach to his taxi parked illegally on the sidewalk.

'To hospital?' Holden inquired pulling out into the road.

'No, absolutely not. Take us back to the hotel please,' Annette ordered sitting up in the back seat, 'I'm fine. I just need a good bath and a change of clothes.'

'OK Holden, you heard the boss,' Andre confirmed, 'it's back to the hotel as quick as you can.'

⟨◆⟩

'I've got beach sand in my hair and all down my top,' Annette protested as Andre helped her upstairs and into their room.

'I can soon fix that,' he said taking her into the bathroom and running the shower. 'Arms up,' he ordered pulling her wet top up over her head and removing her bra.

'I've got sand in here as well,' she smiled as she unbuttoned her jeans and hooked her fingers into the elastic top of her knickers. She steadied herself leaning on his shoulder while he knelt down and removed her jeans and panties. 'Please shower with me,' she said reaching out and undoing his belt, 'I don't want to shower alone.'

'That's a request I could never refuse.' Stripping off his shirt and pants, he stepped into the shower and put his arms around her. His physical reaction was immediate and unmistakable. She reached down for him but, to her surprise, he turned away. 'First, let me get your hair washed, then we will attend to our other needs.' He rubbed half of the small bottle of shampoo into her hair then, rinsing it out thoroughly, began soaping down her body. She leaned back against him, running her bottom against him as he gently washed her breasts.

'You don't have to be gentle; I won't break. You can be as rough as you like.'

'Is that right?' he said, pulling the shower curtain aside and, lifting her in his arms, sat her on the edge of the vanity.

'Oh yes!' she said opening her legs wide and pulling him to her. He entered her as she lay back laughing, 'Fuck me as hard as you can. Oh Yes! Oh Andre! It feels so good.' The stimulating sight of their frantic coupling reflected in the vanity mirror, combined with her erotic gyrations brought them almost simultaneously to the climax they both needed so badly.

CHAPTER 29

THE BORDER

'I THINK WE SHOULD DO SOME shopping,' Andre suggested as he towelled her hair dry, 'we can't have you arriving back in Phalaborwa looking dishevelled and badly dressed. People would think we haven't had a wonderful and relaxing holiday!'

Holden was more than happy to drive them to the best clothing stores in town, given the generous incentive Andre offered. On their return to the hotel, Andre confirmed with Holden that the repainted Mahindra would be ready to go the next day. 'Of course, *Senhor*, I have it ready for morning.'

As Annette and Andre passed by the reception desk, he stopped to confirm that they would be checking out in the morning. '*Senhor* Meyer,' the receptionist called out, 'please do not forget the attaché case you left with us for safekeeping.'

'Thank you; I had almost forgotten about it. Perhaps I should take it now, I may no longer need to keep it.'

'Where on earth did you get that?' Annette asked as she began to unpack and try on the clothes they had bought, 'it looks very expensive to me.'

'Apparently Sheik Abu Alawi gave it to Amrit to pass on to me when we landed in Pemba.'

'And you've no idea what's in it?'

'Other than it may have once belonged to Clive Rylston. But we may never find out,' he said struggling with the lock, 'it seems to be jammed. I'd hate to have to break it open; you've got to admit it's a beautifully crafted piece.'

'C'mon, pass it over here,' she said taking a nail file out of her new cosmetic bag. 'I've opened more luggage searching for contraband than you've had hot breakfasts.'

'Well, what's in it?' he asked from his side of the room, 'not a bomb I hope!'

'*Liewe God Andre! Kom kyk hierso*! - Come and look at this! Did you know about this?' she asked tossing aside a white towel that covered dozens of tightly stacked bundles of American Dollar bills.

'Bloody hell! There must be quite a few thousand in this lot.'

'By my guess, there's a hell of a lot more than that; and look what else I've found,' Annette said unwrapping a yellow dust cloth around a Glock G19 pistol and spare magazine. 'The pistol was packed fully loaded,' she said expertly unloading and clearing the weapon. 'I'd say someone was expecting trouble; so, what do you suggest we do with all this?'

'The only person who would know anything about this is Amrit in Cimboa,' Andre said taking out his mobile and dialling the number for Amrit Singh's Aerial Tours. There was no answer, so he left a brief message asking Amrit to contact Abu Alawi and find out why he had been given the attaché case and to call him back with his answer. 'Meanwhile, why don't we find out just how much money we have here.'

Spreading the money out over their queen-size bed, it took both of them almost an hour to sort out and count all the tightly stacked bundles of fifties and hundreds. 'By my calculation, we have close to twenty seven thousand in American Dollars here,' Annette said, 'I can't wait to hear what Amrit has to say about this.'

'Andre, I'm sorry it took so long for me to get back to you,' Amrit apologized when he finally called back, 'but Abu Alawi first wanted to speak to his daughter A'isha about the case.'

'And what did she say?'

'She confirmed that the case belonged to a *Senhor* Clive Rylston, also known on the island as the man from Lisbon. Apparently, it was meant for his personal use should he ever have to flee the island in an emergency. We can only assume he didn't have time to take it with him when he left in a hurry during the attack by *Ansar al-Saleem*. Abu Alawi says he wants you to use the money in your fight against the cartel.'

Andre shared the gist of this conversation with Annette. 'I'm not sure it would be strictly legal were we to do that,' Annette replied, 'but I won't tell anyone if you don't.'

'My lips are sealed,' he replied with a wink. 'Now, while I think of it, I'd better give my sister Janet in Nelspruit a call to let her know we're still alive.'

'Well little brother, why has it taken you so long to respond to my emails!' Janet complained answering his call.

'Sorry about that; you could say we've been out of circulation for a while.'

'You can make your excuses later, but first please call Colonel Banerjee in Jo'burg; he's been trying to get in touch with you for the past two days; apparently its urgent.'

Andre scrolled through his contacts and placed a call to Garjan Banerjee. His call was answered promptly. 'Banerjee.'

'Good afternoon colonel, I'm sorry I've taken so long to get back to you, but things have been a little hectic over here.'

'Andre! Good to hear from you. Now look, I've a meeting that I'm already late for, so I'll have to make this brief,' he said drawing a breath as he marshalled his thoughts. 'We've had a massive increase in the amount of heroin being smuggled into Mpumalanga and Gauteng over the last few weeks. Problem is, we've no idea how it's getting into this part of the country. I've doubled and trebled border security at all border crossings and, despite the fact that drug seizures are way down, we haven't seen any decrease in the quantity of drugs available on the street. My superiors are holding my feet to the fire on this one; please tell me you have something I can give them?'

'How about giving them this to chew on,' Andre replied. 'Clive Rylston, who now heads up the southern African branch of the Portuguese drug cartel, *Cavalo Marinho*, is now operating in Mozambique. We've managed to shut down his base in Cabo Delgado Province, but in doing so, we may have forced him to move his operations into southern Mozambique, which may account for the spike in heroin traffic you're experiencing. There's not much else I can tell you other than we'll be back in Phalaborwa in the next few days and would like to meet with you to discuss ways to put these people out of business permanently.'

'We have plans to do that?' Annette asked, struggling to keep a straight face.

'Well, we will have by the time we get to Phalaborwa,' he said packing their belongings into a large holdall along with the attaché case. 'By the way, I've taken out five hundred as a bonus for Holden; he's been a big help to both of us over a difficult two days. I'll explain in detail when we're on the road.'

Once Annette got over the shock of seeing her little Mahindra sporting a coat of black paint and, once she had heard the story of the bomb under the dashboard, together with the incident involving her at the beach, she was of the opinion that five hundred was an insufficient reward for all that Holden had done for them. 'Glad to hear you say that, seeing as I upped his *bonsela* – tip to seven hundred,' Andre said as he manoeuvred her little car through the outskirts of Beira and onto the coastal highway retracing their route back to the Kruger Park - Mozambique border post of Giriyondo.

'I've made things very difficult for you over the last few days,' she said after a long silence, 'I wouldn't blame you if you wanted nothing more to do with me after we reach Phalaborwa.'

Pulling over to the side of the road, he took her in his arms. 'Nothing that has happened was in any way your fault. It's just how things turned out. I love you Annette and I would rather die before I allowed anything bad to happen to you.' He kissed her and wiped away the tears that rolled down her cheeks, 'Now, let's put our heads together and figure out what we can do to put Rylston and his lot out of business.'

'Looking at it logically,' Annette began, 'if large quantities of drugs are still getting into the country while seizures at controlled border crossings are way down, it stands to reason the cartel has found some other way of getting them across the border. Which leaves flying them in, or using irregular border crossings, as their only other options.'

'As we well know, flying drugs in has its own problems. This leaves us then with irregular border crossings.'

'The only areas I can think of that are suited to irregular border crossings,' Annette said, 'are Kwa Zulu Natal, Swaziland, Kruger Park and Zimbabwe. The Kruger Park, given its proximity to Inhambane, being the most likely. I should give Major Baloyi at Phalaborwa a call, perhaps he could add something to our ideas.' Identifying herself to the desk sergeant who answered her call, she was told the Major was away at the moment. Asked if she wanted to leave a message, she had an idea. 'Sergeant Ngoveni, perhaps you can help me. What is the situation in and around Phalaborwa when it comes to drugs, particularly heroin?'

'No big problems here at all Captain, it's been quiet for the last few weeks.'

'Are you sure? No heroin or other drug seizures?'

'Well, not here in town; but the police in Gravelotte did stop a car carrying six suitcases packed with over three hundred pounds of heroin. Biggest seizure around here in years.'

Thanking the sergeant for his help, Annette turned to Andre, repeating what the desk sergeant had told her. 'What makes the town of Gravelotte so important to us?' he asked.

'Only the fact that Gravelotte is on the R71 highway connecting the central area of the Kruger Park to Pietersburg on the N1, the most direct route to Gauteng and its population of close to fifteen million.'

'I take it you're suggesting this drug seizure the sergeant mentioned came through the Kruger Park?'

'Stands to reason doesn't it?'

'Except that Banerjee assured me they had increased inspections at all border crossings, and that must surely include Pafuri and Giriyondo.'

'I hardly think the cartel would risk smuggling such a valuable quantity of heroin through any border crossing that's on the alert for illegal drugs,' Annette countered.

'Good point! If that's the case, then the drugs would have to be carried through or under the border fence before being transferred to a waiting vehicle. From that point, it would be easy to carry them out through one of the Park gates and onto whatever destination they've chosen.'

'And, given that there are no customs checks on vehicles leaving the Park, my idea makes good sense,' Annette said.

'I think I'll give Phuti Mabuza at Punda Maria a call and run this idea by him.'

━━◄◆►━━

'Glad you're both back safe and sound!' Phuti said answering his phone. Not wanting to spend a lot of time recounting the details of their trip to Mozambique, Andre got right down to the reason for his call. 'I suppose it's possible,' Phuti conceded, 'there are a few areas in the Park where one of our tourist roads comes close to the border. Pafuri, Giriyondo and N'wanetsi come to mind. This car filled with drugs detained near Gravelotte; if you can get me the license number, I can find out where they entered and exited the Park and how long they were here.'

'Excellent idea! That would go a long way towards proving or disproving our theory. I'll get back to you as soon as I get that information.' Getting Annette to call the sergeant at Phalaborwa for the car's license number, he was back on the line to Phuti within fifteen minutes. 'Now all we have to do is wait for Phuti to get back to us.'

━━◄◆►━━

It wasn't until the following morning before Phuti called Andre back. 'Sorry it took so long, but we're not really set up for this sort of inquiry. Though I think it is something we may be doing a lot more of,' he added. 'Well, you were right. The vehicle in question entered the Park through the Phalaborwa Gate at midday on Friday. The male and female occupants spent the night at Letaba and exited the Park, mid-afternoon, again through the Phalaborwa Gate.'

'Thank you for going to all that trouble Phuti,' Andre said, 'however, you may have hit the nail on the head when you said this was something we may be doing a lot more of.' Andre went on to share with Phuti the gist of his conversation with Colonel Banerjee and the alarming increase in drugs showing up in major centres, despite increased vigilance at regular border crossings.

'When do you think you'll be back in Phalaborwa?' Phuti asked.

'Barring any problems on the road, we should enter the Park through the Giriyondo Border Crossing around three tomorrow afternoon.'

'Actually, that works out very well. I'll meet you both at Giriyondo tomorrow; perhaps we can discuss this new problem with some of our border guards and customs officers. With a bit of luck, we may collectively come up with a solution or at least a way forward.'

CHAPTER 30

BLUE HORIZON

'PHUTI, WOULD YOU MIND IF I asked you to give Andre a lift back to Phalaborwa when you're done here?' Annette said to both men shortly after they arrived at Giriyondo Border Post.

'I thought you'd want to sit in on this,' Andre said to her, 'surely there's no rush to get back.'

'Look, I just want to get back to my own home. I've had enough of camping out and just want to have a hot bath and sleep in a real bed. Please Phuti, I'd appreciate this.'

'Of course,' he replied, 'I'll bring him back to you tomorrow; that's a promise.'

'I'll see you both then,' Annette said kissing Andre before climbing into her Mahindra and driving off to Phalaborwa.

'If you don't mind me saying so,' Phuti observed, 'she seems to be a little pissed off. Did the two of you have a disagreement?'

'Not to the best of my knowledge. Though thinking about it, Annette's been on tenterhooks since we broke camp this morning; so, I'd appreciate it if we could get through our meetings as quickly as possible. Between you and I, I'm a little concerned about her. We encountered a bit of a problem while we were on that bloody island in the Rio Ruvuma. While it wasn't of her doing, I'm a little worried she might do something totally out of character.'

To Andre's disappointment, their meetings with the South African and Mozambique border guards and customs officers did not come up with any new ideas on how shipments of drugs were getting into the Kruger Park. However, just before they were about to leave, one of the Mozambique customs officers took Andre aside and suggested he got in touch with a Father João Pires in Massingir. 'Father Pires is a Jesuit priest who has dedicated much of his life to stamping out the drugs destroying the people of this country. If you want to know who's behind the smuggling of this poison through the Kruger Park, and how they're going about it, Father Pires would be your man.'

'You do realize what this means?' Andre said to Phuti as they drove from Giriyondo towards Phalaborwa Gate.

'Yes,' he replied, 'the fact that drugs are being smuggled through the border fence with Mozambique for pickup up by couriers masquerading as visitors, is a major problem. But, to be quite honest, I've absolutely no idea how we could possibly stop it without seriously damaging our tourism industry.'

'What about this Jesuit priest in Massingir? Do you think it's worth following up?'

'You're the detective; you tell me,' Phuti replied.

<hr>

They were only a few miles from the Phalaborwa Gate when Andre's phone chirped into life. 'Andre Meyer,' he said answering it.

'*Meneer* Andre, is that you? This is Thandi; I am housekeeper to *Mevrou* Annette.'

It took him a few seconds before he remembered that Thandi was the housekeeper Annette employed at her home at Luiperd's Vlei. 'Hello Thandi, is everything OK?' he asked fearing the worst.

'*Nee Meneer, alles is nie reg nie. Mevrou is baie siek en ek weet nie om wat te doen. Asseblief Meneer, kan jy gou by die huis kom?*'

'Phuti,' Andre said handing him his phone, 'my Afrikaans is not up to it; please translate what Thandi is saying.'

Phuti spoke briefly to Thandi before turning to Andre. 'She says Annette is not well and asks that you return home as soon as you can.'

'Please tell Thandi I'm on my way and that she should call an ambulance immediately for a possible heroin overdose.'

❖

The ambulance was just leaving Annette's house in the Luiperd's Vlei Wildlife Estate when Phuti dropped Andre off. 'Would you like me to stay?' he asked Andre.

'I appreciate your offer, but no thanks. You've done more than enough for me today. Annette and I can handle this; you carry on home and I'll get in touch with you tomorrow.'

Thandi met him at the door, '*Meneer* Andre, the doctor says she will be OK after a good night's sleep. I was very worried when I came to work and found her lying on the bathroom floor; I thought she was dying.'

'You did very well Thandi, thank you for everything. You should go and rest, I'll look after her now.'

As he walked into the house, he found the doctor waiting for him in the lounge. 'Good evening, *Meneer* Meyer,' he said shaking Andre's hand, 'I've a feeling you know what happened here tonight?'

'Yes, I'm afraid I do.'

'Now I know *Mevrou* Fourie is a serving police officer and I have no wish for this incident to go any further. However, I strongly recommend that you seek help for *Mevrou* Fourie without delay.'

'I give you my word, together we will both make sure this never happens again.'

'I will give you a referral and the address in Nelspruit of the Blue Horizon Centre for Addiction Treatment. I often recommend this facility to patients who have fallen prey to this dreadful plague which seems to be growing by leaps and bounds.'

As soon as the doctor left in his car, Andre called his sister, Janet, in Nelspruit and, as succinctly as he could, explained the situation. 'Just bring her down here to us, Elsie and I will look after her. I'll make all the necessary arrangements with the Blue Horizon Centre first thing in the morning. I'm familiar with this place and you're right, it does come highly recommended, but I should warn you, it's not cheap!'

'Not a problem,' he replied, 'the people who are responsible for this are going to pay for everything, and I don't just mean in dollars and cents.'

―――――◆―――――

As they were about to drive to the airport to catch their early morning flight to Nelspruit, the front doorbell chimed. Thandi answered the door then came and called Andre, 'It's a policeman,' she said breathlessly, 'he wants to speak to Annette.'

Andre found the uniformed officer waiting in the lounge. 'Good morning, sir, I'm Sergeant Ngoveni, I'm the desk sergeant here in Phalaborwa.'

'Good morning Sergeant, I'm Andre Meyer. Annette has often mentioned you. What can I do for you?'

'It's a delicate matter, sir.' Taking a deep breath, the sergeant continued, 'sometime yesterday, the evidence locker at the station was broken into and a small quantity of drugs, principally heroin, was stolen. Now, I'm aware that Annette, Captain Fourie, would want the matter investigated and the culprits punished but, unfortunately, the video surveillance tape showing the break-in has been destroyed and we have had to close the investigation due to the lack of evidence. I know the Captain takes matters such as this very seriously, which is why I thought the Captain should be made aware of that.'

After the man had left, Andre went through to the bedroom where Annette was waiting, 'I suppose you heard who it was?'

'Yes, I did. Andre, I'm so sorry,' she said wiping away tears, 'I don't deserve you and the people around who want nothing more than to save me from myself. I know you phoned Janet last night about this addiction centre in Nelspruit, you should know I'm ready to do whatever you think is best.'

―――――◆―――――

The Blue Horizon Centre for Addiction Treatment stood on the side of a hill overlooking the Crocodile River as it flowed lazily past acres of citrus trees in the De Kaap valley. 'It's one of the best in the country,' Janet said as she drove Annette and Andre up to the imposing entrance and the two staff nurses awaiting their arrival.

'Oh, how nice,' Annette said, 'a reception committee to make sure the drug addict doesn't try to make a break for it.' Andre touched her arm lightly. 'I'm sorry,' she said kissing him on his cheek, 'I'm just a little nervous that's all.'

'You'll be fine,' Janet said, 'we're just down the road; call us any time you want supportive friends.'

'Six weeks you say,' she said to Andre, 'I'll hold you to that. Please don't come in with me, it will be upsetting enough to have to say goodbye. I love you both!' They watched as Annette, carrying the small suitcase Andre had packed, walked over to the nurses and, without a backward glance, went inside with them.

CHAPTER 31

JOÃO PIRES

I T TOOK ANDRE AN HOUR to drive from Phalaborwa to the Giriyondo Border Crossing and a further hour and a half to the outskirts of Massingir. Having given a great deal of thought on the long drive as to the best way of tracking down Father Pires, he decided to call at the first church he saw on entering the town. The day was already heating up and the cool temperature inside the church, the result of stone walls and a solid timber roof, was a welcome relief.

'Good morning, can I help you?' a voice said from behind him.

Turning around, Andre saw a bald, heavyset man emerge from a small office just inside the main door. Returning the greeting, he answered the man's question, 'I'm hoping you may be able to tell me how I could find a Jesuit priest who goes by the name of João Pires?'

'I have two questions; who are you and what do you want of him?'

'My name is Andre Meyer and I would like to talk to this Father Pires.'

'I am Pires,' the man said taking Andre's hand in a powerful grip. 'Who told you about me?'

'It was suggested to me that you may be able to give me some advice.'

'In what respect?' Pires asked, a quizzical expression on his face.

'Your name came up while I was looking into reports of drugs, principally heroin, being smuggled into South Africa through the Kruger Park boundary fence

'I think its late enough and hot enough for us to continue our discussion over a few beers.' Pires must have noticed the surprised expression on

Andre's face because he quickly added, 'By my book, Jesuit priests are allowed a certain amount of freedom of opinion and expression. Is that your little black car outside?' Andre said it was. 'Good,' Pires said, 'let me lock up first, then we can go to a quiet place where we can discuss everything in a more congenial atmosphere.'

Although only mid-morning, the beer garden was already half full. Taking a table at the back under the shade of a tree, Andre went up to the bar and ordered two bottles of Manica Lager which he carried over to their table. 'You may sound English,' Pires said taking a sip of his beer, 'but mixed in there I hear a bit of a South African accent.'

'It's a long story.'

'Good. I've nothing else to do today,' Pires added.

'That's certainly quite a story! I don't believe I've ever met a real detective from Scotland Yard before. Anyway, that's not the reason you're here today. What do you want to know?'

'Anything you can tell me about drugs being smuggled through the Kruger Park and into South Africa.'

'At the moment, nothing. I'll have to start asking around town, but this sort of information doesn't come without a price.'

'I expected that,' Andre said passing an envelope under the table to Pires, 'Here's five hundred Rands in ten Rand notes; there's more if you need it. In the meantime, I think I'll head down to Maputo and follow up on one or two leads Annette and I managed to come up with.'

Finishing off their beers, Andre drove Pires back to the mission. As the Jesuit priest got out of the car, he turned to Andre, 'I like you Detective Chief Inspector Meyer, but you must be careful, Maputo isn't London. Sometimes it's hard to tell the difference between the crooks and the police!'

Driving to the outskirts of town, Andre searched in vain for directional signs to the highway leading to Maputo. Giving up, and as it was now getting dark, he stopped at a small hotel and took a room for the night.

The following morning, with scrawled directions from the hotelier clasped in his hand, Andre soon found the highway leading to the city of Maputo. Following the directions he'd been given, he turned off at Marracuene and continued south onto the Costa do Sol Highway, entering Maputo via the Avenida Julius Nyerere. Checking into one of the luxury hotels on the Marginal, he took his bag up to his room and placed his recently acquired Glock G19 automatic pistol and spare magazine into the room safe. Using his mobile phone, he looked up the Escudos Shipping Agency and pinned it to his digital map. Following the suggestion of the young lady behind the reception desk, he took the Marginal all the way around to where it joined the Avenida 25 de Setembro.

Parking close to the four-storey building housing the shipping agency, he consulted the concierge on the front desk who directed him to the third floor. The shipping agency could best be described as a hole-in-the-wall operation working out of a two-room office with an elderly woman on the reception desk. Luckily for Andre, she could speak a little English.

'Good day, *Senhor*, can I help you?'

'Good day. I'd like to speak to *Senhor* Rylston; is he in?' he asked glancing at the closed office door behind her.

'Oh no,' she replied, flustered, 'I don't believe he is in today. Are you sure you have the right name?'

'Quite sure,' he replied spelling it out, 'Rylston, Clive Rylston, from Lisbon.'

'I don't believe I've ever heard of him. Are you sure you have the right address?'

'Quite sure. How about a *Senhor* Gobuzo,' Andre continued referring to the name on the business card he got off the man who died of his burns after the incident at the aircraft crash in the Kruger Park. 'Have you ever heard of him?'

'Oh! Yes of course, I've heard of him; he is a customs agent in Moamba, on the highway to Komatipoort.'

'So, you've heard of him, but not of Clive Rylston.'

'No. I've already told you that.'

'How about *Cavalo Marinho*. Ever heard of them?'

She replied with a shake of her head, 'All these questions! You must speak to *Senhor* Gobuzo.'

'OK. How can I get in touch with *Senhor* Gobuzo?'

'I will call him for you,' she said picking up the phone on her desk and dialling a number. Her call was answered almost right away. Andre couldn't be sure, but it sounded as though the call was answered in the closed office behind her. The woman spoke rapidly in Portuguese to the person who answered the call, before handing the phone over to Andre.

'May I know who I'm speaking to?' a modulated voice asked in English.

'Meyer, Andre Meyer.'

'And what can I do for you Mr. Andre Meyer?' the voice asked.

'I have a few questions I would very much like to ask you *Senhor* Octavio Gobuzo.'

'Ah! You confuse me with my brother Octavio; I'm his elder brother, Ernesto. Octavio, I'm sad to say, was murdered in South Africa some time ago. You know, Mr Andre Meyer, people sometimes tell me Maputo's a dangerous city and that South Africa is far safer. But we know that to be untrue; Maputo is only dangerous if you don't know the rules.'

'And what would those rules be *Senhor* Gobuzo?'

'These things are best discussed in person Mr. Andre Meyer. I have some free time this evening; may I suggest we meet for a drink at the Manica Bar sometime around eight. I will see you then,' Gobuzo said terminating the call abruptly.

The Manica Bar and Lounge was on Avenida 10 de Novembro overlooking the Maputo waterfront. Parking his car a few streets away, Andre arrived at the bar right on eight. The bar area was fairly crowded, but he managed to get a booth along the back wall that afforded a good view of everyone entering or leaving. Ordering a Manica Lager and two packets of chips from the waiter, he settled down for what he hoped wouldn't be a long wait.

Two hours and two bottles of Lager later, the only person who had approached his booth was the waiter. The crowd in the bar had thinned out considerably, leaving three men still standing at the bar. Their raucous, drunken voices convinced him that they were not connected with Ernesto Gobuzo then, just as Andre was about to get up and leave, two men entered the bar and took a table near the door. Ordering another beer, he decided to wait in the hopes that eventually one of them would approach him. The newcomers ordered brandies, downed them and, without so much as a glance around the bar, got up and left.

'Bugger this!' Andre muttered as he paid his bill and, leaving a tip for his waiter, got up and made his way out onto the Avenida. It was now quite dark and there weren't many people about, as he struggled to remember exactly where he had parked the car. As he walked along the waterfront, he heard the sound of footsteps close behind him. Pretending to look in the window of a small store, he watched out of the corner of his eye as a man approached him. Bracing for a possible mugging and annoyed with himself for leaving the Glock in his room safe, he breathed a sigh of relief when the man, whom he now recognized as one of the two brandy drinkers from the bar, continued on without so much as a backward glance.

Finding the narrow lane which led to the Rue Marques de Pombal, where he now remembered parking the car, he was dismayed to see that the streetlights in the lane were not working. The lane, while quaint and charming in daylight, was now dark and laden with menace. Quickening his pace, Andre found himself catching up with the brandy drinker from the bar who had walked past him earlier. As the lane neared the Rue Marques de Pombal where the streetlights were working, he saw the brandy drinker standing in a doorway looking at him. Thinking he may be Ernesto Gobuzo, Andre approached him and asked, 'Are you wishing to speak to me?'

The blow to the right side of his head, which came from someone behind him, was powerful and vicious and was intended to do maximum harm. Dropping to his knees, Andre reached out to steady himself on the edge of a doorway, anxious not to fall down and expose himself to what could be a good kicking. A painful lesson he had learned the hard way as a young paratrooper in Northern Ireland when he foolishly stopped for a beer in an IRA bar on the Falls Road.

Pulling himself to his feet, he staggered towards the end of the lane, hoping to get to the street beyond where he could hear cars and see movement. Before he took two steps, a powerful pair of arms encircled his body, pinning his arms to his side. The brandy drinker from the bar, who had been standing quietly in the doorway, now stepped in front of him and drove his fist hard into Andre's unprotected stomach. Doubled over in pain, but held upright by the assailant behind him, the man from the doorway redoubled his efforts to inflict as much punishment as he could before Andre lapsed into unconsciousness.

Someone was shaking him and shining a torch in his face. He heard voices around him as he was helped to his feet and carried out onto the street. Still fearful of a further beating, his panic subsided when he noticed the badges on the uniforms of the two men holding him upright. 'Thank God you got here in time,' he said chuckling through cracked and bleeding lips, 'you've just saved two men from a severe beating!'

'Hospital?' one of the policemen asked.

'No, no!' Andre said as he touched his hand to the right side of his head. It came away covered in blood. 'OK, *obrigado*, thank you,' he said exhausting his one word knowledge of Portuguese, 'hospital.' The policemen bundled him into the open back of their bakkie, presumably to stop him from bleeding all over their seats and dropped him outside the *emergencia* entrance of the Hospital Central Maputo on Avenida Eduardo Mondlane.

Three hours later, Andre made his way to where he had parked his car and drove back to his hotel on the Marginal. Getting back to his room, he walked into the bathroom to take a look at himself in the mirror. Only now could he understand the horrified expressions on the faces of the two women working the late shift on the hotel's reception desk. Gingerly touching the four stiches in his right cheek, he opened the bottle of painkillers the hospital had given him and, shaking out three tablets, he downed them with a mouthful of Manica Lager from the bottle he took from the minibar in his room.

CHAPTER 32

YASSIN DIQUE

'My God, Andre!' João Pires said opening the door to his determined knocking, 'please tell me the other guy looks a lot worse!'

'Actually, there were two of them and I regret to say, their only injuries are confined to their fists.'

'It looks to me as though they intended to kill you,' Pires remarked as he ushered Andre inside.

'I've had worse beatings, and at the hands of truly hard bastards. Though, to be fair, I must give credit to the timely arrival of the *Policia da Republica da Mocambique* for saving my bacon.'

'Come in and sit down; can I get you anything?' Pires asked.

'A Manica Lager would not go amiss while I recount my tale of woe.'

Pires opened two beers and set them down on the table. 'Right, apart from developing an obvious taste for Manica Lager, what else did you accomplish in Maputo?'

'I confirmed that Clive Rylston is not only alive and well but is also actively involved in the operations of *Cavalo Marinho* in Maputo. He's supported in his activities by a man called Ernesto Gobuzo. It turns out he's the brother of Octavio Gobuzo who, as you may recall, was murdered in hospital by the cartel before he could be questioned.' Andre paused and took a swig of his beer, 'Now, please tell me you have better news.'

'Well, unlike you, I managed to avoid a beating from the bad guys, but I did come up with an interesting titbit of information. A few months ago, a local poacher and career criminal, Yassin Dique, was wounded in a clash with an anti-poaching patrol in the Kruger Park. Due to his injuries, Dique lost his job with some local worthy who employed him as an enforcer escorting illegal aliens through the Kruger Park and into South Africa.'

'I take it you're of the opinion that this Dique's skills could have turned to the art of moving illegal shipments of contraband and drugs under or over the border fence?'

'Something like that,' Pires agreed.

'So, how do we go about finding this Yassin Dique?'

'My sources tell me he lives just south of here in an informal settlement called Mapulanguene. In fact, if we left right now, we may catch him in the local bar. I understand he's something of a serious drinker now that he can't walk anywhere without a cane.'

There wasn't much to Mapulanguene outside of a scattering of houses, a wider collection of shanty dwellings, hundreds of mud huts and, of course, a beer garden where they hoped to find Yassin Dique. João ordered a couple of beers from the makeshift bar and carried then over to a not very clean table near the door, 'Apparently he hasn't come in yet, but the barman expects he will be here shortly. Ten Rand of your money guarantees the barman will give us the nod when he shows.'

They were halfway through their second round, when the barman, perhaps for the first time in his long career, came over and wiped off the top of their table. 'He's just come in,' he whispered, 'that's him over there trying to find someone who'll buy him a drink. The young woman with him is his long suffering wife, Ana.'

'Thank you for that,' João said passing the barman a ten Rand note, 'please ask him if he would like to join us for a drink.'

Yassin Dique made his way over to their table, closely followed by his wife who sat quietly at an adjacent table. 'Brandy,' Yassin said aggressively, 'brandy and I'll tell you my story; no brandy and you can fuck off!'

'Not a problem my friend,' João said signalling the barman who brought a glass of brandy over to their table, Yassin's wife having refused a drink.

'OK Yassin, but first we have a few questions for you,' he said moving the brandy just out of his reach.

'What sort of questions?' Yassin asked, his eyes fixed on the amber liquid in the glass.

'Tell me, how easy is it to get things through the border fence and into the Kruger Park game reserve?' Andre asked.

'For me, it very easy. I help you get rhino horn, lion bone, also *miereneter*.'

'Pangolin scales,' João whispered, 'the new gold in the illegal wildlife trade.'

'How about getting heavy suitcases or boxes across the border?'

'Easy for me, I do good job! Then no more work for Yassin. Fucking peoples! Now they use *ndege*. You give me drink now, yes?'

'First Yassin, you must tell us all you can about this *ndege*. Which I know from past experience is an aeroplane of sorts,' Andre said in an aside to João.

'No! Drink first,' Yassin demanded, 'then I tell about *ndege*.' Relenting, Andre pushed the glass of brandy in front of the man, who downed it in two gulps.

'*Ndege* come in back of truck,' Yassin told them, accompanying his description with a high-pitched, whining noise as he raised his hands up above his head. 'Box gone over border, quik quik, then *ndege* come back for more box.'

Andre signalled to the barman to bring another brandy to their table. 'Where does this *ndege* come from and who does it belong to?' Andre asked him, 'answer my questions and you can have this brandy.'

'Big boss; fucking Aloisius Zama. He too much rich man. Big farm on Rio N'wasweni. *Ndege* come with him, now he not want me. Tell Yasin to fuck off. Yassin not like Zama, he too much bad man, will kill Yassin if he find I talk to you. Please you help me; you have much Rands. You give me fifty Rand.'

'OK Yassin,' João said jumping in, 'but we are giving your fifty Rand to your wife, if only to stop you from spending it all on brandy in one night!'

'He wasn't too happy about that,' Andre chuckled as they got into his car for the short drive back to Massingir.

'You've got that right,' João said. 'Now what do you think he was talking about, all that business about an *ndege* which, as you apparently know, refers to a bird or an aeroplane.'

'I know it's a crazy idea, but I got the impression he was describing a small aerial drone with enough power to carry a substantial weight over the border and drop it in the Kruger Park.'

'Surely there's no such thing as a powerful drone!' João replied. 'Remember, we're talking about hundreds of pounds in weight for the quantity of drugs you have in mind.'

'Before we dismiss Yassin's claims out of hand, I think we should first do some checking. João, would you mind taking over the driving while I fire up my mobile.'

Five minutes later, Andre gave a loud snort. 'You won't want to believe this, but such a machine not only exists, it's actually in full production in Norway and also in the United States. Apparently, it can carry up to five hundred pounds of cargo and costs around a quarter of a million American dollars; well within the financial capabilities of the cartel. And, get this, it's about the size of the cargo bed of a large truck.'

'OK! OK! So, Yassin was telling the truth. All we have to do now is find out where this Aloisius Zama has his base on the N'wasweni River. A river, I might add, I've never heard of in all my years living in this part of the country!'

<hr />

Andre was awakened by a loud knocking on the door of the room he was renting two doors down from João Pires's mission church. 'I'm coming!' he shouted as the knocking continued. Opening the door, he was surprised to see Yassin Dique's wife, Ana, standing there with her now sober husband hovering sheepishly in the background.

'Yassin tell you about *ndege*,' she said looking around cautiously, 'Zama take boxes over border tonight. You want to see?'

'Yes, we would very much like to see,' Andre replied. 'Where is this going to happen?'

'Must pay first,' she said, 'five hundred Rand.'

'OK. Half first, then after we have seen this *ndege* working, I will pay you the rest.'

'Yassin will come find you and priest when sun is there,' she said pointing high in the sky.

'Good. We will be ready,' Andre said returning with two hundred and fifty Rand which he handed to her. After watching Ana and her husband head straight towards the local beer hall, Andre, hoping he'd made the right decision, made his way over to the church to rouse João. Bringing him up to speed, Andre's second thought was to contact Phuti Mabuza at his new Skukuza headquarters. 'Phuti is our newly appointed police liaison officer in the Park,' Andre explained to João, 'we'll need to coordinate surveillance of the drop-off sites with him the moment we have some idea of their locations.'

<hr>

'I've been wondering when I would hear from you,' Phuti said to Andre as his call was patched through.

'Sorry I've taken so long to get back to you, but I seem to have a lot more on my plate these days. Taking a deep breath, Andre told Phuti about the meeting with Yassin Dique and his wife Ana. 'They're disgruntled former employees of the cartel who were recruited to carry drugs through the border fence for pickup by couriers posing as visitors.'

'I've heard reports of similar activities all along our eastern boundary, particularly wherever a road open to visitor traffic passes close to the border fence.'

'Unfortunately, I have more bad news, 'Andre continued, 'the reason our informers are unhappy with the cartel is because they're being replaced by a new type of aerial drone capable of carrying large quantities of drugs deep inside the Park, thus doing away with their jobs.'

'Bloody hell! How far into the Park can this thing fly?'

'Right now, we haven't a clue; but I suppose it would depend on the weight it's carrying, the state of its batteries, or even how the whole bloody setup works!'

'Whatever happens Andre,' Phuti said, 'we've got to get hold of one of these things to find out its capabilities.'

'My thoughts exactly! Now for some good news! We've been offered an opportunity, thanks to these former employees now turned informers, to get a look at one of these drones in action. I'm hoping to plant a tracking device on the truck that will carry this drone back to its base which, according to the informers, is somewhere on the N'wasweni River. Incidentally, a river Father Pires tells me he's never heard of before.'

'N'wasweni is probably a local name for our N'wanetsi River after it flows into Mozambique. Now, how can I help?' Phuti asked

'We're going to need a couple of vehicle tracking devices.'

'Not the sort of things I usually have in my toolbox,' Phuti replied. 'If you can get Colonel Banerjee to have a few dropped off here in Skukuza, I'll see that you get them as soon as possible.'

'I'll get onto Banerjee right away; given the urgency, I'm sure you'll have them within the hour. Later today, Pires and I are off to meet up with our informers in Mapulanguene where we are hoping to get a closeup look at this cross-border drug smuggling enterprise in operation. I'll keep you informed by mobile as soon as we know in what direction the drone is flying the moment it heads towards the border. Hopefully, this will give you enough time to organize surveillance teams to cover all possible drop-off sites.'

'Roger that,' Phuti replied. 'Mapulanguene you say! How come you get to go to all the nice places!' he added with a laugh.

CHAPTER 33

MAPULANGUENE

THE DISTANT THROB OF ROTOR blades alerted Andre and João to the approach of a South African Police Bell 206 helicopter, as it flew in low over the trees and settled on the grassy field behind Pires's mission church in Massingir. Andre waited for the pilot to shut his engine down before he and João walked over to greet Phuti as he climbed out of the machine. As they shook hands, a police officer emerged from the rear compartment and handed a box and a laptop computer to Andre. 'Four magnetic GPS tracking units and a laptop programmed to follow each unit individually or collectively,' he said. 'All the batteries are fully charged and ready to go. Any questions?' Andre and João shook their heads negatively.

'Good; if you have none, we'd better get going; we're not even supposed to land in Mozambique,' Phuti said as he and the policeman walked back towards the helicopter. 'Anyway, I want to be high in the sky ready to track this drone well before it crosses into South African airspace.' As he climbed back aboard the helicopter Phuti turned and called out to them, 'Good luck to you both!'

'I'll phone through the GPS coordinates of the launch site the moment we confirm its location,' Andre shouted back as the pilot started the engine. 'It's just our bad luck the cartel has chosen a dark, moonless night for their second attempt to use this infernal machine,' he added, although Phuti could no longer hear him.

While João familiarized himself with the operation of the tracking units, Andre drove them to Mapulanguene, where they had arranged to meet up with Yassin Dique and his wife Ana. 'Do you really think you should be coming along with Yassin?' João asked Ana, 'this could turn out to be quite dangerous!'

'No,' she replied, 'my troubles is what Yassin do if you give him money you promise.'

Andre and João exchanged grins. 'OK Yassin,' Andre said breaking the uncomfortable silence, 'where do we go now?'

'Zama call two mens to help with *ndege*; he say they meet *caminhões* - trucks where road goes over N'wasweni River.'

'This place for Zama is on other side of Mapulanguene,' Yassin's wife, Ana, confirmed. 'Soon sun sleep. We find trees to hide car then we wait for Zama's *caminhões* to bring *ndege*.'

'Ana means the trucks that will probably be carrying the drone and the drug shipments,' João explained. 'Judging from your map, the road bridge over the river is about three miles as the crow flies from the Park boundary.'

'Good. As soon as Zama's trucks stop and we are sure they are preparing to launch the drone, I'll call in our GPS coordinates to Phuti so he can track the drones' route into the Park.'

<hr />

Unable to light a fire for fear of giving away their position, the four of them huddled together against the unseasonable cold and fought a losing battle with the hordes of mosquitos that rose from the floodplain of the nearby N'wasweni River. 'I hope this is close enough to their launch site that we will hear their trucks arrive,' João confided to Andre in a whisper. 'Of course, we've got to hope we'll be able to hear their trucks over the whine of these cursed mosquitos!'

'Be careful what you say, João,' Andre said smiling in the darkness, 'are they not all God's creatures?'

'*Caminhões,* they come.' said Ana rising to her feet and pointing to the distant flashes of headlights through the trees. The four watched as two double-cab trucks turned off the track and stopped in a small clearing leaving their lights on. As the vehicle doors opened, four men jumped out and began untying and removing the tarpaulins covering the backs of the trucks. These men, now joined by two others, gathered around one of the trucks and began lifting off a large black object which they placed on the ground using one of the tarpaulins as a groundsheet.

'Would you look at that!' João remarked as the men began unfolding and extending four long arms, each carrying two sets of propellers mounted vertically to one another. 'So that's what the drone looks like!' he said in awe.

'OK, we're in business,' Andre said calling Phuti in his helicopter and giving him the GPS coordinates of the launch site. 'I'll get back to you the moment they launch this thing with a rough estimate to its direction of flight.'

'Roger that! We're about a thousand feet above you now and are looking forward to alerting Baloyi's policemen and our Park rangers who will organize the surveillance of the drop off sites.'

'So that's how they do it,' João said as some of the men spread out a cargo net on one of the tarpaulins and began stacking suitcases and boxes onto the net from the back of one of the trucks. 'Ordinary looking travel suitcases and boxes,' João remarked, 'just the sort of luggage every visitor to the Kruger Park would have in the boot or on the back seat of their car.'

'Except that each case or box probably holds forty to fifty pounds of heroin, fentanyl, MDNA, crystal methamphetamine or whatever else the market demands. Ana,' Andre said turning to Yassin's wife, 'ask Yassin if he knows the name of the man working on the *ndege*.'

She conferred quietly with her husband before whispering in Andre's ear, 'He *Senhor* da Silva, Zama's man. He make *ndege* fly.'

'da Silva's definitely someone we will need to speak to when the time comes,' Andre said quietly to João. 'When they start packing this lot up, we've got to make sure we get at least one of our vehicle-tracking devices onto one, or preferably both, of their trucks.'

<hr />

As the eight rapidly spinning propellers lifted the drone and its cargo of boxes and suitcases off the ground, the machine rapidly gained height and flew, surprisingly quickly, in a south-westerly direction.

Using his Maglite concealed under a blanket, Andre checked his map and called Phuti right away. 'The drone has taken off and if it stays on course, I'd say it was headed towards the Trichardt Road, probably crossing it somewhere south of the Sweni Hide,' he said softly.

'We've got it on our scanner and are tracking it as we speak,' Phuti acknowledged. 'It's not moving very fast, which my pilot thinks, could be due to the weight it's carrying. Did you see them load it up?'

'By our best estimate, they loaded at least ten suitcases and boxes into the cargo net which attaches somewhere underneath the machine itself. You'll have to keep a close eye on its progress, as it wouldn't take more than a few minutes for any waiting handlers to unload the cargo and get the thing on its way back.'

Fifteen minutes later, Phuti called back. 'You were right; this load was dropped a hundred yards short of the Trichardt Road where two men were waiting in the bush to unload the cargo. Clearly a pre-planned destination. Rangers and police now have the site under surveillance with strict orders not to move in until the cargo is picked up, most likely by pseudo tourists sometime tomorrow.'

'Roger that,' Andre replied. 'The gang here is already loading up another cargo net, no doubt in readiness for their next delivery when the machine returns. I'll keep you posted.'

Fifteen minutes later, the high-pitched whine of the drones eight motors heralded its appearance over the trees followed by its gentle descent onto the waiting tarpaulin. Andre watched with no small degree of admiration, as da Silva and his crew went about the business of readying the machine for its next flight.

'It looks like he's replacing its batteries,' João remarked as he watched da Silva take two small boxes out of the cab of the truck that carried the drone to the launch site.

'By my rough calculation, that would give it an average flight time of around three quarters of an hour to cover a distance, there and back, of roughly twenty five miles. Bearing in mind, we don't know for certain whether the first set of batteries are fully exhausted,' Andre added. 'Of course, he could be replacing them simply because the next flight is longer.'

As it turned out, Andre's guess was correct. 'The load was dropped in a clearing one hundred yards off the Lindanda Road, just south of its junction with the Trichardt Road,' Phuti confirmed in his call to Andre. 'This flight was a little further than we thought this machine was capable of. Hopefully, this is its last flight of the day,' he added, 'our helicopter is getting a little short on avgas.'

———◆———

Phuti's worst fears were realized when Andre reported that the drone was preparing to make a third flight. 'We've no choice but to break off our surveillance and return to Skukuza for refuelling,' he reported to Andre. 'I'm told it will be at least an hour before we can return, so any ideas you may have on the drone's direction of flight will, at least, give us some idea where to start looking for the drop-off site.'

João and Andre watched with dismay as another cargo net was filled with suitcases and boxes, while da Silva was seen to be replacing the drone's batteries yet again. 'I'm going to move around to the other side of their launch site so I can get a better idea of the it's direction of flight as it passes over head.'

'I'll come with you,' João suggested.

'Thanks, but I'd rather you stayed here and kept an eye on Yassin and Ana. I'll be back once it's taken off; then we can concentrate on hiding a GPS tracking device on one, if not both, of their trucks.' The sound of the drone's propellers starting up, sent Andre scurrying as quickly and as silently as he could to get underneath the machines likely flight path.

It was obvious right from the start that one or two of the drone's eight motors were not functioning properly. As the machine began lifting into the air, it appeared to falter and the cargo net, instead of clearing the trees, was dragged along the ground. Reacting almost instinctively and, as he would admit later without any intelligent plan, Andre jumped forward and grabbed hold of the cargo net, perhaps hoping to bring the machine and its cargo crashing to the ground. His error was immediately apparent when the drones eight motors suddenly kicked into high gear and he felt himself being lifted high in the air. Too afraid to let go in case he was higher than he realized, Andre gripped the ropes of the cargo net and hung on like grim death.

As the drone and its cargo picked up speed following its predetermined route, Andre was forced to seriously consider his limited options. First, he knew he had to climb higher up the cargo net in search of some sort of foothold, as the thin nylon ropes he was clinging to were already cutting into his hands and fingers, making it even more difficult to support his weight. After what seemed like ages, he was finally able to climb higher up to where he could gain some sort of toehold on one of the suitcases or boxes in the net and relieve some of the strain on his hands and arms.

Andre considered climbing even higher, thinking to disable one or two of the drone's propellers, now spinning only inches above his head. However, sober second thought brought home the realization that, disabling even one or two motors could easily bring the drone crashing to the ground, which lay somewhere in the inky blackness far below. The cold night, made worse by the drones forward motion and the downdraft from its propellers, began to affect his hands, causing his grip on the nylon ropes to slip. His very real fear of falling drove him to climb higher up the net until he was finally able to force his arms between the uppermost strands of the cargo net and relieve the pain radiating from his cut and bleeding hands.

Andre was not a religious man, but he felt himself hoping and praying they were nearing the drop off point for this shipment of drugs. Unable to see his watch, he estimated he had been clinging to the drone's cargo net for close to twenty minutes which, based on his estimates of time and distance, meant they could have covered close to twenty miles as the crow flies.

As he struggled to conjure up a picture in his mind of the terrain and road systems in the area south of the Satara rest camp, he had to admit to himself that he hadn't a clue where they were headed other than that they were flying in a westerly direction.

A slight change in the high-pitched whine of the drone's motors, together with a sinking feeling in his stomach, were obvious indicators that the drone was about to land. Suddenly, he was now faced with a new problem. In Phuti's previous calls, he had reported there were at least two men at the drop-off site whose job was to unload the cargo net and see the drone off on its return journey. The strong likelihood that these men would be armed, was uppermost in his mind as the drone continued its descent into the darkness below.

As the cargo net brushed against the branches of a tree, Andre decided to act before the waiting handlers realized there was an unwelcome addition to the load the drone was carrying. Freeing his arm from the cargo net, he let go of his hold on the ropes and dropped into the night.

CHAPTER 34

NKAYA PAN

THE CRACKING SOUNDS MADE BY the cargo net and its load of suitcases and boxes as it was dragged through the treetops, masked the noise Andre made as he dropped into the uppermost branches of a Tamboti tree. Hanging on for dear life again that night, he watched as two men, using shaded torches, untied the cargo net and began offloading its contents. It took them barely ten minutes to unpack and stack the suitcases and boxes before one of them, using a mobile phone, spoke to someone on the receiving end of his call, prompting the drone, now relieved of its cargo, to easily lift off into the night sky.

Andre watched as the flickering lights from the cargo guards' torches showed him where they were bedded down for the rest of the night. Allowing them fifteen minutes to settle down, he slowly and as quietly as he could, climbed down from the upper branches of his Tamboti tree.

The distant grumbling roar of a lion gave him cause to consider the wisdom in climbing down from his treetop perch, safely out of reach of lions which he knew were well represented in the area south of Satara rest camp. Regardless of his concerns about lions, he knew the arrival of dawn in a few short hours, would bring with it even greater dangers, not the least from the cargo guards watching over the load of drugs awaiting pickup.

Despite walking headlong into trees in the dark, he put as much distance as he could between himself and the hopefully sleeping cargo guards before he thought it safe enough to switch on his mobile and call Phuti.

'I've been calling you for the last half hour!' Phuti said answering right away. 'Have you had your phone switched off?'.

'It's a long story that will have to wait,' Andre replied as he went on to give Phuti the GPS coordinates for this latest drug drop-off.

'Bloody hell!' Phuti replied as he marked the position on his map. 'That's within a hundred yards of the turnoff to the Nkaya Pan on the main north-south road through the Park. How the hell did you get there?'

'I'll tell you about that later. Right now, I urgently need a helicopter ride back across the border to the clearing near the N'wasweni River. I had to leave João Pires, Yassin and Ana there to keep an eye on this Aloisius Zama and his drone crew. To be honest, I'm more than a little concerned about their welfare.'

'Give me the GPS coordinates for your position and I'll see what I can do.' Thirty seconds later, Phuti called back, 'OK, we've got you. Walk three hundred yards directly east of your position and you'll eventually cross the main north-south road; its tarred so you should have no difficulty finding it in the dark. When you get to the road, follow it in a southerly direction.'

'I can't believe you actually did that,' Phuti said as Andre climbed into the police helicopter just as the sun was rising.

'To be quite honest, I find it difficult to believe myself; but on the positive side, we now have the location of their third and, hopefully, final drop-off site.'

'Yes, and thanks to you, a hastily cobbled together surveillance team of police and rangers are moving into place as we speak,' Phuti said. 'Now, why this concern about this João Pires and the two informers you left at the drone launching site. Surely, they wouldn't do anything foolish enough to risk their necks?'

'I would hope not; this thug Zama who's running the show, is a dangerous son-of-a-bitch and, I'm reliably informed, not someone to be taken lightly. However, I had impressed on João and the informers, the urgent need to place at least one of our tracking devices on either of the trucks carrying the drone or the drug cargo. Without that to guide us, it'll be very difficult for us to locate Zama's base on the N'wasweni River.' Turning and looking out of the windscreen, Andre pointed out the clearing to the pilot, 'That's the launch site down there. Fortunately, it looks like the trucks have gone, so it should be safe enough for us to land.'

The helicopter flared as it began its near vertical descent into the small clearing, its rotor blades narrowly missing the branches of the surrounding trees. Carrying the R5 assault rifles passed to them by the pilot, Andre and Phuti separated as they searched around the edges of the clearing for any signs of João, Ana and her husband Yassin.

'Andre! Andre! *Here God!*' Phuti shouted, his voice breaking, 'I've found them! Those fucking bastards have murdered them!'

Andre rushed over to that side of the clearing and stared in horror at the bullet riddled body of Yassin and, hanging by her neck from a tree nearby, the body of his wife Ana. 'That bastard Zama will pay for this,' he said to Phuti as he moved from one body to the other. 'Rigor mortis hasn't set in yet; so, I'd say they were both killed one to two hours ago, probably not long after the drone returned from the Nkaya Pan. Come and look at this,' he said softly.

Phuti came over and stared at Ana's body. 'Judging by the bruises and razor slashes to her face and body, I'd say she was tortured before they hanged her.' Peering more closely at her injuries, Phuti reached up and pulled an object from her mouth, '*Here God*! It's one of the tracking devices!'

'They must have discovered it under one of the trucks, or worse, caught her in the act of placing it. We've got to find João! With a bit of luck, he may have escaped these murderous swine.'

'*Kerels*!' shouted the pilot from his seat in the helicopter, '*Asseblief, gaan help vir die man, hy is erg beseer*! - Guys! Please go and help that man, he's badly injured!'

Andre looked in the direction the pilot was pointing and saw a man, covered in blood, stagger out of the bush and into the clearing. It was João Pires. 'João,' he yelled as he rushed over to help him. 'Thank God you're alive!' Together, Phuti and Andre helped him over to the helicopter as the pilot jumped out carrying a first aid kit.

'Lay him down here,' the pilot ordered, 'I'm a police medical officer as well as a pilot.' He took one look at João's injuries, 'This man's been shot: twice by the look of it. Once in his right upper arm,' he said examining João more closely, 'and again in his right shoulder. Lots of blood, but neither wound is life threatening, but obviously quite painful. Luckily for you my friend,' the pilot said to João, 'your shooter was a shit shot!'

The pilot medical officer got to work on João, giving him an injection against infection and bandaging up his wounds. 'Can he travel?' Andre asked the officer, 'we've got a long drive ahead of us back to Massingir.'

'Are you sure? Can't we just fly him to a hospital?' the pilot asked.

'Unfortunately, we can't,' Phuti interrupted. 'As it stands, we're violating Mozambique sovereignty, not to mention getting involved in a murder scene where we have absolutely no jurisdiction.'

'Phuti's right,' Andre agreed. 'Not too far from here, we've got Annette's old Mahindra stashed in the bush. Before you go, I'd appreciate a hand placing the bodies of Ana and Yassin into the car. We can't leave them here for the jackals and hyenas. Besides, their families need to be informed and they both deserve a proper burial.'

'Are you sure?' Andre asked, turning to look at João as he drove back to Massingir.

'Absolutely! I made bloody sure by sticking it inside a rust hole in the chassis. The bastards may have found Ana's tracking device, but I'm certain they never found the tracker I placed on their other truck. Nor would Ana have told them anything about it, no matter how much she was tortured. She was an incredibly brave woman.'

They drove in silence for a while, each with his own thoughts.

'What happened to the laptop programmed to follow each tracking device?' Andre asked breaking the silence.

'Oh! Yes, the laptop. Poor Ana knew she had to give Zama something if she and Yassin were to live. Unfortunately, it wasn't enough. Of course, once those thugs found the laptop, they smashed it to pieces, perhaps not realizing how easily it could be replaced.'

'On the positive side, your tracking device will enable us to move against these people and destroy that accursed machine of theirs. But we're going to need a lot more firepower than what you and I can provide.'

'And I don't think your friend Phuti would be too interested in joining us in an invasion of Mozambique,' João added with a smile.

'You're quite right,' Andre said, 'he wouldn't. But I do know some people who would have no qualms about it at all!'

CHAPTER 35

N'WASWENI RIVER

A NDRE'S CALL TO AMRIT AT Singh's Aerial Tours in Cimboa da Praia was answered right away. 'Good morning my friend, I was wondering when I'd hear from you again?'

'I'm sorry not to have been in touch earlier,' Andre apologised, 'but, as you'll hear, the situation down here has been rather hectic. Before I go any further, I must ask whether you are still in contact with Sheik Abu Alawi?'

'Well, not on a regular basis, but I'm able to get a message to him. Is that what you wanted to hear?'

'Yes, that's exactly what I wanted to hear. OK, then this is a good time to bring you up to date with everything that's happened since we last spoke.'

———◆———

'I'm sorry to hear about Annette,' Amrit said, 'please, when you do see her, express my wishes for her quick recovery. Now Andre, just to be clear, am I correct in assuming you're in need of some backup for a foray against the *Cavalo Marinho* cartel's drone base.'

'That's it in a nutshell. As I'm sure you'll understand, I can't expect any support from the police or any other semi-official group in South Africa and, as you well know the *Policia da Republica da Mocambique* may have been infiltrated by elements favourable to the cartel.'

'Diplomatically put,' Amrit laughed. 'I do know that Abu Alawi considers the cartel to be a major threat to this country. I tell you what, I'll put your request for assistance to the Sheik and we'll see what he comes up with.'

⊰◆⊱

Amrit called Andre back the following day. 'Sheik Abu Alawi says you can have as many *Ansar al-Saleem* fighters as you require; but he insists it will be up to you to get them down there and, of course, to get them back to Cimboa. Now, I can fly three men down to Massingir in my Cessna, providing you pick up the tab. The only other way would be for a larger number to use a civilian airline for their travel arrangements; that would also require you being able to arm and equip them your end. What do you think?'

'I'm more than happy to take you up on your offer. I'm looking for backup, not to start a small war. Can I leave it to you to impress on Abu Alawi that these three men must be able to speak a little English and be proficient in the use of small arms and explosives?'

'I thought you said you weren't planning on starting a small war?' Amrit replied with a laugh. 'Yes, of course, leave it with me. Give me twenty-four hours and I will call you back with details on the arrangements.'

⊰◆⊱

Amrit called back later that evening. 'Sheik Abu Alawi said I should tell you the three men he's sending are some of his best fighters and, if possible, he would like them back in good health.'

'Of course. Please pass on my thanks and tell the Sheik I'm not a believer in needless sacrifices. Did he mention anything about weapons and explosives?'

'He said to assure you that his men were always equipped with the finest weapons available; though he did add that one of them would be bringing along a number of demolition charges to make sure nothing of any value is left for the cartel to salvage.'

'What more could I possibly ask for!' Andre said thanking Amrit for his efforts. 'My last question; how soon can I expect you?'

'We plan to take off at about five tomorrow morning with refuelling stops in Quelimane and Massingir. All in all, it's about nine hundred and fifty miles in total which should take us, factoring in time on the ground for refuelling, about eight hours. Barring unforeseen circumstances, I hope to land at the Massingir airstrip around lunch time.'

'Have a good flight my friend, I'm looking forward to seeing you.'

———◆———

In recounting to Amrit the unfortunate series of events which led to Annette's heroin addiction, Andre was reminded that it had been more than a few days since he had last spoken with his sister Janet and inquired about Annette's progress at the Blue Horizon Centre.

'Oh God Andre! I'm so glad you called,' Janet said, 'I've been dreading having to call you; we've been hoping she'd turn up somewhere safe and sound.'

'Are you talking about Annette?'

'Yes, I'm sorry; I should have called you earlier. Two days ago, she checked herself out of the Blue Horizon Centre without telling anyone where she was going.'

'Can she do that – just check herself out?'

'Yes, she can; Blue Horizon Centre isn't a prison you know,' Janet replied. 'Elsie and I have been calling everyone we can think of, but no one has seen or heard from her.'

'Have you tried her home in Phalaborwa? She may have gone there. You should talk to her housekeeper; I think her name is…'

'Thandi,' Janet said completing his sentence. 'Unfortunately, she's not heard from Annette either. I really don't know what else we can do. Please Andre, how soon can you get back here?'

'I simply can't at the moment; I believe we're on the verge of striking a major blow against the cartel and I've set things in motion that I cannot walk away from. Janet,' he said urgently, 'If you haven't already done so, please call Major Baloyi with the police in Phalaborwa; tell him what you've told me and that I believe she may be in grave danger.'

'Do you really think so?'

'No, not really. But it should motivate the police to start looking for her. Please, will you call me if you hear anything?'

'Of course, I will. You're very fond of her, aren't you?'

'Yes. I suppose I am,' he said ending the call.

—◁◈▷—

Amrit's Cessna 172 touched down shortly after two in the afternoon. Taxiing up to the rear of the small terminal, Amrit shut down the engine as his three passengers, extricating themselves from the aircraft, stood around stretching cramped limbs. 'Not a very comfortable flight after the first hour or two,' Andre observed, extending his hand with a smile. 'I'm Andre Meyer.'

A tall man with a dark, full beard stepped forward and took Andre's hand. 'My *Ansar al-Saleem* name is Alabi and my two comrades are known as Ayman and Kashif; these are our fighting names and the only names we will use while we are here.'

'You're all very welcome. Come with me and I'll show you where you'll be staying. I'm sure you'd all like an opportunity to get something to eat and rest after your journey.'

That evening, Andre, João, Amrit and the three bearded fighters from *Ansar al-Saleem* were huddled around a table discussing plans to eliminate the cartel's drone operations. 'According to this map,' Andre said spreading out an aerial map on the table, 'the N'wasweni River, which flows from the Kruger Park into Mozambique, eventually joins the Massintonto River. As you can see, the map shows only one road, likely nothing more than a dirt track, running from the settlement of Mapulanguene to the area where we believe the cartel base is located.'

'This tracking device,' Alabi, the leader of the trio asked looking directly at Andre, 'is it still transmitting a signal?'

'As far as we can tell it's still working.'

Alabi stroked his beard as he stared thoughtfully at the map. 'I don't like maps,' he said finally, 'they are often wrong and almost always out of date. How soon can we carry out an aerial reconnaissance?' he asked looking at Amrit.

'Tomorrow morning,' Amrit replied. 'I don't know about all of you, but after flying for nine hours, I need a good night's sleep.'

'Of course,' Alabi agreed rising from the table, 'we can all use some rest.'

As Amrit and the other two *Ansar al-Saleem* men headed off to the accommodation João had arranged, Andre took Alabi aside. 'Your accent is familiar to me; I would say you were from somewhere in the English Midlands.'

'You're spot on; I'm from Leeds, to be precise,' he replied, 'ex British forces. Unfortunately, I cannot tell you anything more than that. No names, no pack drill. I'm sure you understand.'

'No problem; I'm just glad to have you on board,' Andre replied shaking the extended hand.

'I'd like us to approach this area from the east,' the man from Leeds suggested to Amrit as he, Andre and one of the other *Ansar al-Saleem* men climbed aboard the Cessna. 'Always keep the sun in their eyes,' Alabi said winking at Andre.

Amrit climbed steadily until they reached five thousand feet. 'I'll throttle right back so our engine noise isn't obvious to anyone on the ground. OK' he said to Andre, 'get your camera ready, we're crossing the location shown by the tracking device.' Andre opened the window on his right side and, leaning out, focussed his Nikon on the ground as Amrit, flying a little to the left of the target area, glided silently above.

'Keep shooting,' Alabi said as they passed over the target, 'try to get as many pictures as you can of the river upstream. I believe it will be the key to getting onto this base unobserved.'

'I'd like us all to take a good look at your photos while the images in our heads are still fresh,' Alabi said as they prepared to watch Andre's photographs on a computer in the basement of João's mission.

'Do you know what this place reminds me of?' João asked rhetorically. 'An army base built during the Rhodesian War by the ZANU forces of Robert Mugabe. Look at those shallow ditches lining both sides of the track leading into the camp. If I'm not mistaken, those were once trenches and the odd looking holes were foxholes and mortar pits. Believe me, I should know; I was once a member of the Rhodesian special forces which raided a base exactly like this one.'

'I fully agree with João,' Andre said, 'as I think my friend here does too,' he added looking at Alabi who nodded his head in agreement.

'Where can we get hold of two-man kayaks at short notice?' Alabi asked looking around the group watching the photos.

'Massingir Dam,' João replied. 'There's a tourist camp next to the dam that rents out canoes and suchlike to visitors. Two-man kayaks you say, I'll give them a call right away and see what they can suggest.' Five minutes later he re-joined the group. 'I explained that four friends of mine are planning to kayak down the Komati River where it flows into Mozambique from South Africa. I picked this river as it's sufficiently far away from our actual objective so as not to raise any suspicions.' Looking at the questioning faces around him, he continued, 'Their answer was yes. They can supply us with two kayaks and paddles but, in view of the dangers they believe we will face on the Komati River, they want us to buy the kayaks up front.'

'I'll look after that side of things,' Andre volunteered, 'also, I'll get prints made of some of my photos to carry with us. Now the sooner we get going on this venture the better, so, may I suggest we drive up to the dam and pick up our kayaks.'

'How much time will we have to practise paddling a kayak?' one of the fighters asked Alabi.

'Consider it training on the job,' he replied. 'Tonight, we clean weapons and prepare for an evening departure tomorrow. How about you Andre,' he asked, 'do you have a rifle?'

'Actually, I'm planning on taking my 9mm Glock pistol. It was a gift from Clive Rylston, the man whom we believe heads up the *Cavalo Marinho* cartel here in Mozambique.'

'Don't you think your Glock would be a little light on stopping power at a distance,' Alabi commented. 'But don't worry, Abu Alawi thought you may not have a weapon available so, on his instructions I packed a spare R4 assault rifle in our baggage. As you probably know, it fires a standard 5.56mm calibre round so, if the need arises, we can exchange ammunition amongst ourselves. Regretfully, I could only scrounge up a single pair of night-vision goggles,' Alabi continued, 'and as you're probably more familiar with the wildlife along the rivers around here, I suggest you take them with you in the lead kayak along with Kashif, you'll find his English is reasonably good.'

As the setting sun threw long shadows across the darkening waters of the N'wasweni River, the four men pushed their two kayaks out into the slow flowing current. They had spent most of the afternoon packing lightweight sleeping bags and food for four days into the waterproof spaces on the kayaks. For their protection while on the river, they kept their rifles close at hand, tucked just beneath their spray covers.

As agreed, Andre's kayak took the lead, keeping well within the dark shadows thrown onto the river by its high banks and overhanging trees. His biggest concern was them paddling into the midst of a pod of hippos, common in the swampy, reed beds growing along most of the lower reaches of the N'wasweni. He was aware, through conversations with Phuti, that hippos were responsible for more deaths amongst Africans living alongside rivers than any other animal, including the much-feared crocodile.

Their progress on the first night was slow. Made doubly so because so many of the channels leading off the main river ended in a dead-end or were blocked by debris swept downstream by last year's floods. Andre's nerves were kept on edge by the occasional splash as their passage disturbed a crocodile lying in wait for an unwary animal close to the bank. All the while he struggled in the green glow of the night-vision goggles, to watch for the tell-tale line of bubbles that might betray the underwater movements of a bull hippo intent on challenging their passage.

As a pale glow in the eastern sky announced the arrival of dawn, Andre signalled a turn towards the closest bank where a dense stand of trees promised a secluded campsite for them and their kayaks. 'Will we be safe camping here?' Alabi asked as he helped Andre pull the kayaks out of the river and high up onto the bank.

'If we're careful,' Andre replied as he covered the kayaks with branches and bundles of reeds, 'we should be. Hopefully, any fisherman paddling up or down the river won't be able to see them up here,' he added. Unpacking their sleeping bags and one-man mosquito nets, the four men settled down for the day in a small clearing close to a large African Fig tree. 'If we're going to boil water for coffee,' Andre suggested, 'we should do it now before traffic on the river increases. We don't want any local villagers smelling the fumes given off by our Hexi-stoves or, for that matter, the aroma of coffee being brewed.'

Sitting in a huddle with their cups of coffee, they discussed their first night on the river. 'It's a bloody maze of channels, most of which look promising but turn out to be cul-de-sacs. What I'm most concerned about is running into hippos,' Andre said opening the conversation.

'Surely hippos aren't all that dangerous?' Alabi said, 'we often sat on the banks of the Rio Ruvuma watching them in the water floating around and sleeping most of the day. Didn't look like much of a threat to me.'

'Hippos are extremely territorial, and a bull hippo will go to great lengths to defend his females and his stretch of the river. Believe me,' Andre continued, 'they're real killers when they take it into their heads to go after you. Even on land, they can probably outrun you and are not slowed down by bushes and small trees!'

'Fair enough; but surely being so large, they're easily seen.'

'Unfortunately, it's not so easy at night and if one is going for you, it usually approaches under water. All you can do is watch for a stream of bubbles as it comes for you.'

'Shit! If you'd told me all of this before, I would never have offered to take the lead kayak tomorrow night,' Alabi laughed, 'but don't worry old man, I won't let the hippos bite.'

CHAPTER 36

THE FIGHT ON THE RIVER

ANDRE SPENT MOST OF THE day worrying about Annette. He felt an overwhelming sense of guilt because he wasn't back in Nelspruit doing everything he could to find her. His greatest fear was not that she was in danger from the cartel, but rather that she had given in to the siren call of her heroin addiction. For him the night couldn't come soon enough. At least if I'm on the river, I have other, even more pressing problems to keep my mind occupied. 'Come on guys, it's getting dark,' he said shaking the others awake. If we push hard, we should arrive at the outskirts of their base just before sunup.'

'What do we do then?' Alabi asked, 'hit them right away while we have surprise on our side.'

'I suggest we play it by ear. Let's keep the base under surveillance and make that decision based on what we see and not go off half-cocked,' Andre replied as he handed the night-vision goggles to Alabi.

'Spoken like an experienced paratrooper,' Alabi replied grinning as he helped Ayman carry their kayak down to the water's edge.

The first hour of their journey downriver was uneventful. Alabi appeared to have mastered the technique of using the night-vision goggles and had managed to avoid taking too many wrong turns and dead-end channels. By the start of the second hour the river had widened, and the current had increased in strength. As they came around a bend, they were swept into a large pool and in amongst a pod of hippos. The hee-hawing and grunting sounds alerted Andre to the danger they now faced. 'Alabi, watch out for the bull,' he shouted loudly, throwing caution to the wind. 'Paddle closer to the bank and get ready to bailout if you have to.'

'Don't worry, I can't see any hippos near us,' Alabi called back. The next instant an enormous bull hippo surfaced right alongside him, its mouth agape as it attacked his kayak, biting it almost in half.

'Paddle over to them as fast as you can,' Andre shouted to Kashif, 'we've got to help them to get to the bank; if the hippo goes after them in the water, they're dead men.' Andre, who was in the forward cockpit of their kayak, reached down and grabbing Alabi by his jacket, pulled him alongside. 'Hold onto our kayak, we'll help you get to the bank. Kashif, can you see Ayman?'

'No, it's too dark,' Kashif replied, 'but I can hear him struggling in the water, I don't think he knows how to swim!'

'Take these,' Alabi said handing up the night-vision goggles to Andre.

Without time to put the goggles on, Andre held one lens up to his eye as he frantically searched the surface of the river for Ayman. 'Oh Christ!' he screamed, 'it's a fucking crocodile! Swim Ayman try to swim towards us! Kashif, paddle you bastard, paddle,' he yelled in helpless frustration as he watched a large crocodile rise out of the water and clamp its jaws around Ayman's torso. The reptile violently shook its victim to and fro before it sank beneath the water, leaving only a few ripples to mark the spot.

The three men huddled around the small fire Andre had got going in a dry watercourse, screened from the river by a dense patch of tall reeds. He passed around a small bottle of brandy he'd retrieved from his pack. 'What do we do now?' Alabi asked, his hands still shaking as he handed the bottle back to Andre.

'We go on,' Andre replied. 'By my reckoning we're only a few miles at the most from the base.' He looked around for their response.

'Too damn right. We've lost one man and we owe it to him to see this thing through. I say we leave that fucking river behind and carry on like the foot soldiers we are!' Kashif said forcefully.

'Don't tell me,' Andre said looking questioningly at Kashif.

'You got me,' Kashif smiled. 'My real name is Josh Winslow, Sergeant,

82nd Airborne. I served in Anbar Province, Iraq,' he said holding out his hand.

Andre took his hand, 'Andre Meyer, Parachute Regiment. I served in the Gulf War and Northern Ireland, I'm very pleased to meet you. Ayman, was he…'?

'No,' replied Alabi, 'Ayman was a genuine jihadi from Somalia, a very brave man.'

'That goes without saying,' Andre replied. 'Now what about you?' he asked turning to the man from Leeds that he only knew as Alabi.

'Andrew Carter, 40 Commando, Royal Marines. I served two tours in Helmand Province, Afghanistan. Court marshalled and discharged for striking a superior officer. Josh and I met while working for Blackwater in Baghdad, an experience that eventually led us to join *Ansar al-Saleem* and our conversion to Islam. But that's all in the past now.'

They set off in staggered column down the rough, rutted track that led towards the old ZANU military base the cartel now used to house its drone drug-smuggling operation. Andrew Carter took the point position, Josh Winslow the mid-point while Andre brought up the rear. All were separated by a minimum of thirty feet to compensate for the dense vegetation lining both sides of the track.

Breaking formation every fifteen minutes to rest the point man, they huddled in a thick patch of bush to discuss their progress. 'You know,' Andrew began, 'it's obvious this track isn't used much, yet from the aerial photographs we took, there don't appear to be any other roads leading into this place.'

'Have you considered they may be using the river to bring in the drugs?' Josh suggested. 'The stretch of river where Ayman was taken by that crocodile was wide and deep enough to be navigable by a barge or shallow draught boat.'

'You've got a point there,' Andre agreed as he unfolded a map of the area he took out of his pack. 'I see the N'wasweni flows right past the town of Magude, which lies less that twenty miles from the main north-south road which runs from one end of Mozambique to the other.'

'No matter,' Andrew said rising abruptly to his feet. 'If my judgement of distance is correct, we should be getting close to this base of theirs around sundown. It's time we got going; Josh it's your turn on point.'

They had scarcely travelled two hundred yards when Josh, raising his right hand, signalling a halt as the track led into an open grassed area with a cluster of wooden buildings visible at the far end.

'It looks like we've made better time than I had expected,' Andre said producing one of the aerial photos of the base he'd printed off João's computer. 'Looking more closely at this photo, I can see traces of another track leading off through the trees to our left, no doubt it's headed towards the river. Josh, I'd say your idea of them bringing in the drugs by river is probably spot on.'

'I can't see any signs of activity around those buildings,' Andrew said, 'I hope they haven't decided to close this place down.'

'Don't worry, they're still here,' Andre said as a truck appeared out from behind a roller door in one of the larger buildings and headed in their direction. 'We'd better get further away from this track,' he suggested, 'we can't afford to be seen by anyone riding in that vehicle.'

'No need!' Andrew said, 'they've turned off towards the river. A shipment of some sort must have arrived. Andre, could you see how many men there were in the truck?'

'I saw two, both were sitting up front in the cab,' Andre replied. 'This could be our chance to get amongst those buildings without being seen,' he continued. 'If we can get to the river, we can hijack that truck, take care of its occupants and drive into their base, hopefully catching them off guard.'

Josh was right about the cartel using the river to transport drugs. A small barge was tied up alongside a jetty while its crew passed up boxes and suitcases to the men who'd arrived in the truck. 'Another load of drugs,' Andre whispered to his two companions, 'same sort of boxes and suitcases João and I watched the drone carry into the Kruger Park.'

'So, what do you want us to do?' Andrew asked, 'hit them now, or carry on with your idea of surprising them in the camp.'

'I've got a handful of flex-ties in my pack,' Andre replied. 'Let them finish loading up then, once they leave the jetty and are out of sight of the barge crew, we stop the truck before they get out in the open.'

Leaving the two occupants of the truck flex-tied and gagged in the bush at the edge of the clearing, Andre drove the vehicle back along the track towards the buildings at the far end of the open area. Andrew sat with him him in the cab while Josh hid amongst the boxes and suitcases in the back. As they got closer, Andrew drew Andre's attention to a large building with an open roller door and the man standing just inside the door waving for them to come over. 'I think he wants us to drive inside,' Andrew said, 'let's hope he doesn't realize we're not the same guys who drove out.'

Hunched down in their seats, they avoided looking at the man waving them into the building. Staring straight ahead, Andre drove in through the roller door just as it began to close. 'It's a bloody warehouse for drugs,' Andrew remarked as Andre stopped the truck at the far end close to familiar looking stacks of boxes and suitcases. This move obviously angered the man on duty at the roller door who now strode towards them, screaming a torrent of abuse in Portuguese.

Suddenly, the rear window of the truck exploded into a crazed patchwork of shattered glass as the booming sound of a shot from a large calibre handgun echoed through the building. It was followed immediately by two rapid shots fired by Josh from his hiding place amongst the boxes and suitcases in the back of the truck. As Andre and Andrew jumped from the cab, rifles at the ready, Josh climbed down off the back of the truck and joined them. 'The moment he realized you two weren't the men he was expecting,' Josh remarked as he approached the body of the man he'd just shot, 'he foolishly decided to take matters into his own hands.' Bending down, he picked up the man's weapon, 'A Ruger Blackhawk .44 calibre, a serious gun and look what good it did him!'

'I think we've got ourselves into a bit of a pickle here,' Andrew observed as they took stock of their situation. 'By now, it must have dawned on those outside that we're not cartel employees, which means they're probably making plans to forcibly remove us from their warehouse as we speak. What's worse, we've no idea of their numbers or the types of weapons they've got.'

As if in answer to his thoughts, the staccato rattle of a machine gun broke the silence and a long line of holes appeared in the clapboard wall above the roller door they'd just driven in through.

'That's an RPK, Mikhail Kalashnikov's 7.62mm light machine gun; I'd recognize that sound anywhere,' Josh said. 'I think they're just trying to scare us into giving up!'

'Hopefully, we won't have to,' Andre said, 'providing we take the initiative and do what they least expect.'

'And, pray tell, what might that be?' Josh asked.

'Drive the hell out of this place.'

'What? Back through that bloody roller door? Surely, not while they've got a fucking machine gun set up out front!' Andrew protested.

'Of course not, but I'll bet you they've got nothing set up out the back; and that's the way we'll be going out!' Andre replied. 'OK, let's get the truck ready. Josh, I need you to make a small hole in the petrol tank, just big enough to fill up a bucket or two of petrol to splash around their stacks of drugs and perhaps a little to spare for the load on the back of this truck.'

'What exactly do you have in mind and how can I help?' Andrew asked.

'Well, I'm going to need a length of rope or wire to lash the steering wheel in place so it can't move. Also, I'll need a brick, or something equally heavy, to keep the accelerator flat to the floor while we set this bloody place on fire.'

'Oh, I get it! Crash the truck out through the roller door we came in and let them shoot up their own vehicle. But what are we going to do while this place burns down around us?'

'Good point Andrew. We're going to need a small demolition charge placed against the back wall to blast a way out. Once we're outside, I suggest we split-up and make our way around to the front of the building and give the gunmen outside the surprise of their lives.' They set about their tasks moving as quickly as possible, knowing full well the cartel gang outside was also busy making plans to evict them from the warehouse.

'Gentleman, good timing is essential if we're going to pull this off,' Andre said as he started the truck and, pulling on the handbrake as hard as he could, placed the shift in low gear. 'Andrew, hold the driver's door open and get ready to pull me out when I release the clutch.' Taking a deep breath, Andre let go of the clutch and, as the rear wheels screamed and smoked on the concrete floor, he released the handbrake. He felt Andrew grab his jacket and pull him free of the cab as the truck accelerated towards the roller door. With excellent timing, Josh flicked a lighted match into the stream of petrol splashing along the floor as it poured out of the punctured fuel tank. With a mighty whump the fuel ignited as the truck raced towards the roller door.

Falling to the floor as Andrew pulled him from the cab, Andre watched in horror as the truck, deviating from its intended course, looked increasingly likely to collide head-on with the edge of the roller door.

'No! Andrew leave it!' Andre shouted as Andrew ran after the truck struggling to open the driver's door and turn the steering wheel to avoid crashing into the side of the roller door.

Against all odds, Andrew succeeded and the truck, now fully engulfed in flames, punched through the roller door to be greeted by a hail of gunfire, punctuated by the staccato rattle of the RPK machine gun.

The sound of the fuel tank on the truck exploding, drowned out the muffled thud of the small demolition charge Andrew had placed against the wooden back wall of the warehouse. 'Right, let's get going,' Andre yelled above the din of the gunfire out front, 'no point in giving them time to think about what we may do next.' He led the way out through the jagged hole in the rear wall, 'The two of you go around to the left and I'll take the right, shoot any bastard that even thinks of pointing a weapon at you.'

Andrew and Josh grinned back at him, 'You got it boss,' Andrew shouted, 'we'll get this lot sorted in no time at all!'

Josh covered Andrew's back as they rounded the corner and prepared to carry the fight to the cartel gunman grouped around the front of the now fiercely burning warehouse. 'I'm more concerned about running into the RPK,' Josh whispered to Andrew, 'I can't forget the time in Afghanistan when I was pinned down by it's frightening rate of fire.'

'Head for those buildings,' Andrew shouted firing short bursts at positions where he thought a gunman may be hiding. Bobbing and weaving, they dashed across a stretch of open ground and, ignoring the few poorly-aimed shots fired their way, reached the relative safety of the nearby buildings.

'That took them by surprise!' Andrew grinned as they worked their way through the cluster of apparently derelict buildings, searching for a vantage point which offered a clear field of fire to the front of the building. The shattering sound of dozens of RPK rounds smashing into the wall just above his head, wiped the grin from Andrews face. 'Fuck! That was close,' he swore as he dropped to the ground and scooted back around the corner of the derelict building, brushing off the splinters of wood dislodged by the impact of the high velocity rounds.

'The bastard carrying the RPK must have figured out we'd try to out-flank them using these old buildings,' Josh whispered. 'I'm betting he hasn't seen me yet, so you stay put while I try to flush him out.'

'Now don't go getting yourself shot!' Andrew replied softly, 'this isn't a fight worth dying for.' Josh gave Andrew the finger as he leopard crawled towards the doubtful protection offered by the few rows of a brick foundation supporting a small shed. Careful to keep his head below the top of the last row of bricks, Josh eased his way to the end of the shed and carefully risked a quick look around the corner. To his disappointment, the area between the derelict buildings was empty; there was no sign of the machine gunner.

'Right you cunning bastard,' Josh muttered to himself, 'let's see if I can figure out where you've gone to ground!' Making good use of the shelter provided by the foundation and a thick patch of weeds, he watched the nearby buildings for any signs of movement. Seeing nothing and unable to figure out where the RPK gunman may be hiding, he was considering what to do next when the sound of gunfire erupted from the front of the burning warehouse. 'Sounds like Andrew and Andre are mixing it with the cartel's men out front, I can't let them have all the fun!'

As Josh was about to stand up the gunman, carrying the RPK machine gun, suddenly emerged from the dark interior of a nearby building and, in a crouching run, headed towards the sound of the gunfire. Realizing the man was unaware of his presence and reluctant to shoot him in cold blood, Josh rose to his feet hoping he may be able to take him prisoner. 'Drop your weapon!' he ordered, levelling his rifle at the man's back. The gunman stopped in his tracks and turning around, stared in surprise at Josh. 'Drop you fucking weapon and put up your hands or I'll shoot!' Josh warned, gesturing with his left hand for the man to raise his hands above his head.

Time seemed to stand still as Josh waited for the gunman to react to his threat. He did not have long to wait. His face distorted by a sneer, the gunman raised the RPK and pointed it at Josh, his intention quite obvious. Josh shot him twice in the chest and again in the head. The gunman pitched forward, the RPK machine gun clattering against the brick foundation.

CHAPTER 37

NICOLAU DA SILVA

ANDRE COUNTED FIVE BODIES LYING scattered around the front of the warehouse. He'd personally accounted for one of them and was now searching for another gunman he'd fired at without success. Assuming the man had sought cover in the tangled undergrowth surrounding one of nearby derelict buildings, Andre cautiously approached the building. He carefully examined the ground for any signs that his last two shots may have wounded his quarry before he reached cover. Spotting the barrel and magazine of an AK47 rifle jutting from beneath a bush, together with a large splash of blood, confirmed that his quarry was wounded and hiding in the undergrowth.

'You are wounded and need medical attention,' he shouted loudly, hoping the man could understand English. 'If you give up now, you have my word you will not be harmed, and your injuries will be attended to. One of my men is a skilled battlefield medic, he will treat you as we would one of our own.'

'How do I know you won't shoot me the same way you shot the others?' a voice replied.

'Those men were shooting at us; all we did was defend ourselves.'

'No! Not true! You shot the two men at the dock and threw them to the crocodiles. Those men were unarmed!'

'The men you speak of are lying tied up in the bush near the dock. We did not shoot them; we only took their truck, which you and your gang shot up as we tried to escape your warehouse.'

'Who are you? Who sent you here? Why do you attack us?'

'Whoa! One question at a time; come out now with your hands up and I guarantee you will not be harmed.'

'You sound too English to be from the *Policia da Mocambique.*'

'You are quite right. I'm a police officer from London and I'm only interested in finding Clive Rylston. Is he here?'

'No, he's not; he never goes anywhere there's any danger,' the man replied, a note of resentment in his voice.

'Come on, you're wounded, give up now before we have to take you out of there by force.'

'OK! I'm coming out. Don't shoot,' the man said as he rose to his feet from amongst the bushes and walked slowly towards Andre holding out a handgun by the barrel. Andre stepped forward and took the revolver as he helped the wounded man out into the open. Despite two obvious bullet wounds, one in the chest and one in his shoulder, he was able to walk a short distance until Andrew arrived in response to Andre's call for him to bring his medic bag.

Andrew bandaged the wounded man up as best he could with his limited supplies, giving him a morphine injection for the pain. Together he and Andre carried the man into the shade of a nearby building while they waited for Josh to finish gathering up the weapons lying in front of the warehouse.

'You're going to love what I've just found,' Josh said to Andre as he approached them dragging a half dozen AK47 rifles by their slings and carrying an RPK machine gun.

'And what might that be?'

'Come and take a look. Your friend over there doesn't look as though he's about to run off,' he said nodding in the direction of the wounded man lying in the shade. They followed Josh across a wide grassy area and into one of the buildings obviously used by the cartel. 'Don't worry,' Josh said, 'I've checked around, there's no sign of anyone about. Come on in,' he said opening a side door.

'This was probably the motor pool where they serviced their trucks. Is this all you wanted to show us?' Andrew asked.

'Oh! Ye of little faith. Wait until you see what I found in the back of this truck,' he said pulling aside a tarpaulin and smiling at their expressions.

'Bloody hell!' Andre shouted, 'it's the drone! Well done Josh!' he said clapping him on his back. 'This find will please Phuti, and the whole of the South African police force, no end.' Walking over to a pair of work benches set up against the back wall, he was delighted to find the laptop computer used by the man Ana said was Nicolau da Silva, to operate the drone. 'Let's get all this equipment into the double cab on the back of this truck – without it, our people may have a problem figuring out how the drone is operated. Anyway, we'll leave that to the experts.'

'I see they have quite a few jerrycans of petrol in reserve,' Josh observed. 'I'm sure there'll be enough left over after we've gassed up this truck to set the rest of these buildings well and truly ablaze. What do you think?'

'You and Andrew go to it while I haul the weapons you've collected down to the jetty and dump them in the river. Also, while I am down there, I may as well free the two men we left tied up in the bush. Although, if they'd had any initiative, they'd be long gone!'

'Easy with him,' Andre said on his return as they loaded the wounded man into the back of double cab of the truck carrying the drone.

'Friend of yours, is he?' Josh asked.

'Well, I wouldn't describe him as a friend, but he may have been the one flying the drone which carried me halfway across the Kruger Park.'

'So, you know who he is?'

'I'm not absolutely sure, but I've a strong suspicion our prisoner is the cartel's resident drone expert. A valuable prize to our sponsors.'

'That's him alright; Nicolau da Silva. Well done!' João Pires said as he watched Andre and Andrew carry their prisoner into the small hospital in Massingir. 'What about Zama? Did you get him?'

'We honestly don't know,' Andre admitted. 'But I tell you what, I gave Josh my Nikon to take photos of the five men who died during the exchange of gunfire. While they won't make pleasant viewing, you might be able to recognize this man Zama, providing he's amongst them.'

Andre and João walked outside the hospital and sat on a bench in the shade of a tree. 'Well,' João, 'what's next?'

'First, I've got to call my sister Janet in Nelspruit and Major Baloyi in Phalaborwa, to see if either of them has any news about Annette. I may not have mentioned this before, but it was largely due to the brave persistence of this remarkable woman, Annette Fourie, that we've been able to make any progress against this murderous cartel.'

'Now my friend, you should go and find out what's happened to Annette, a woman you are obviously in love with.'

'I never said I was in love…'

'You didn't have to; it was plain to see in your eyes and on your face. Go now and make your calls, and good luck!'

<hr />

'Andre! Every time the phone rings I hope it's you. Are you OK? The last time we spoke you were off to some jungle hideout looking for the people behind the smuggling of drugs into the Kruger Park. But you can tell me about it another time; more importantly, have you heard from Annette?'

'No, I haven't. I was hoping you had news of her whereabouts.'

'Nothing since I got the call from the Blue Horizon Centre. Elsie and I have called everyone and every place we can think of, including Major Baloyi and her housekeeper, Thandi, in Phalaborwa. The truth is Annette doesn't want to be found; at least not yet.'

'My heartfelt thanks to you and Elsie for all that you've done; I really appreciate it,' Andre said, his voice breaking with emotion.

'I forgot to ask, where are you calling from?' Janet went on, hoping to change the direction of the conversation. 'Are you back in South Africa?'

'No, I'm still in Massingir. But, providing I can get in touch with Phuti, I should be back in the Kruger Park within the next day or two. I've got a little "gift" for Phuti and Baloyi which I know they're going to appreciate.'

'You and your cloak and dagger enterprises! You should be more worried about Annette!' Janet scolded him.

'Of course, I am. Once this "gift" is safely in the hands of the right people, I'm off to Phalaborwa to have a talk with Thandi. She's worked for Annette for many years and, I suspect, knows far more about her than anyone else.'

'Ah! At last the Scotland Yard detective emerges! Good luck my little brother and please give us a call if there is anything we can do to help.'

⊰⊱

'Our prisoner didn't seem to be particularly happy when Andre placed him under your care,' João remarked smiling at Josh and Andrew. The trio were at the Massingir airstrip, waiting for Amrit Singh to complete the refuelling of his Cessna in preparation for their return flight to Cimboa de Praia.

'I must confess I'm at a loss to understand why,' Josh replied. 'I thought *Senhor* da Silva understood that the discomfort of waterboarding would stop the moment we had the information we required.'

'Not a particularly difficult premise to understand I would have thought,' Andrew added. 'By the way, the *Senhor* was able to confirm that the guy wielding the RPK was none other than Aloisius Zama, the one-time *Chef de Camp* on the N'wasweni River.'

'That bit of news must have pleased our boss no end.'

'It certainly did; but not nearly as much as what the *Senhor* had to say regarding the likely whereabouts of the elusive Clyde Rylston,' Andrew continued.

'Obviously information you passed on to Andre?' João confirmed.

'We certainly did. But I must confess, we had hoped he would want us in on that part of the operation.'

'It was not to be my friend. Amrit told me that Abu Alawi wants both of you back in the fold as soon as possible; I suspect it's because the Sheik's still a little upset over the death of Ayman due to that bloody crocodile. Besides, Andre has his own problems with the disappearance of his girlfriend, so whether you like it or not, it's back to being Alabi and Kashif, fighters serving *Ansar al-Salaam*.'

Andre's calls to Major Baloyi in Phalaborwa and Phuti in Skukuza, drew the response he'd expected. Early the following morning, after sincere thanks and envelopes of financial appreciation were handed to Andrew, Josh and Amrit, he left Massingir driving the truck carrying the drone to a prearranged location on the border fence with the Kruger Park. Following close behind in an ambulance borrowed from the local hospital, was João Pires and the patient temporarily in their care, *Senhor* Nicolau da Silva.

A section of the border fence had been neatly removed to allow easy access to a small clearing where a Kruger Park Land Rover and two South African police vehicles were parked. Phuti was the first to greet Andre as he got out of the truck he was driving. 'So, this is the *hommeltuig* that has caused us so much trouble?' he said using the Afrikaans word for a drone as he walked around the truck inspecting the machine. '*Here God* Andre! Is this the bloody thing you flew on all the way to Nkaya Pan?'

'Believe me, I'm very glad you did!' Major Baloyi said walking up to Andre holding out his hand. 'Had you not had the courage to take that awful chance, the third load of drugs would never have been recovered; and God alone knows how many lives they would have destroyed.'

'Seemed like a good idea at the time,' Andre laughed, 'but, given sober second thought, I wouldn't do it again.'

'And who or what do we have here?' Baloyi said nodding in the direction of the ambulance as it drove into the clearing.

'A very good friend of mine, João Pires from Massingir. He's doubling as an ambulance driver to deliver a *Senhor* Nicolau da Silva, the *Cavalo Marinho* drug cartel's former drone expert. João and I believe you'll find his input most informative.'

'What happened to him? Why the ambulance?' Baloyi asked looking at Andre.

'I think it would be safe to say he ignored repeated calls to surrender to the authorities.'

'Who are these authorities? Please tell me you refer to the *Policia da Republica da Mocambique!*

'Unfortunately, I cannot. However, I'm sure you'll find the *Senhor* is also wanted by the Portuguese and French authorities, not to mention Interpol itself. His capture is a credit to the vigilance and efficiency of the South African Police Service, a success that, I've no doubt, will not go unnoticed by Colonel Banerjee in Johannesburg. Now Major,' Andre continued, 'I have a favour to ask; I would very much appreciate a ride back to Phalaborwa.'

CHAPTER 38

LUIPERD'S VLEI

T HANDI ANSWERED THE DOOR TO Annette's house in the Luiperd's Vlei Wildlife Estate on the first ring of the bell. '*Meneer* Andre!' she exclaimed, her eyes wide and questioning, 'have you found Annette?'

'No Thandi, unfortunately I haven't; and I can see from your disappointment you haven't heard from her either.'

'Please come in *Meneer* Andre. Can I make you tea?'

'Thank you Thandi, I'd like some tea, but please do not call me *Meneer*, just call me Andre. But first let me explain why I'm here.' Stepping aside to allow him inside, Thandi led him to the lounge where she stood looking expectantly at him. 'I believe,' he began, 'as does my sister Janet in Nelspruit, that Annette has gone somewhere to recover from the terrible experiences she suffered because of her addiction to heroin. I'm sure you remember when, not so long ago, Annette got very sick and you called me to come and help her?'

'I remember. That was the time Sergeant Ngoveni from the police came to this house and Annette had to go to hospital in Nelspruit. But she did not stay there. I know because *Mevrou* Janet phoned me to ask if I knew where Annette may have gone.'

'Which brings me to the reason why I'm here,' he said. 'I need to look through all her papers and documents for any clue as to where she may have gone. Perhaps you may know of a friend or a relation she may have decided to visit?'

'*Mevrou* Janet asked me the same question but I could not help her.' Backing out of the room, Thandi said she would go and make the tea.

Andre followed her into the kitchen. 'Thandi,' he began, 'I think you should know that I'm on Annette's side in all of this; all I want to do is find her and bring her home safely. If there is anything you can think of that may help me find her, I would be grateful.'

Thandi turned to look at him, her eyes glistening with tears, 'I promise I will do all I can to help you find out where she may have gone.'

***

After Thandi had left for the night, Andre poured himself a whisky from the bottle of Laphroaig he found in the liquor cabinet in the lounge. Carrying the bottle and his glass out onto the *stoep*, he sat in one of the chairs looking out over the garden and the pool. As the sky darkened in the east with the approach of evening, his thoughts went back to the last time he and Annette sat in this very spot, watching the sunset steal over the bushveld. In remembering how he and Annette had made love that evening, an over-whelming sense of loss and sadness swept over him, bringing tears to his eyes. 'I will find you my darling and bring you back to me,' he promised, his emotions overwhelming his usually reserved nature.

Exhausted, Andre dozed off in the chair. He woke with a start and was about to go inside, when he suddenly had the feeling he was not alone. With no idea what was the cause, he rose to his feet staring intently into the dark shadows behind the pool. His sudden movement caused the leopard to growl a warning as it leapt to its feet and disappeared into the darkness that lay just beyond the reach of the light spilling from the open lounge door. 'Xengelela!' he smiled. 'Of course; it's that leopard of hers keeping an eye on the house. I only wish you could tell me where your mistress is now,' he said to the dark shadows in the bush as he slowly backed towards the lounge door.

Pouring himself another whisky, Andre sat down at her antique writing desk in the lounge and began to sort through the drawers searching for any clues as to where she may have gone to escape her demons. Feeling a little like a detective combing through the private papers of a suspect, he managed to overcome his reservations, believing that what he was doing would ultimately bring the two of them back together again.

Two more drinks later and with his eyes burning from the strain, he came to the reluctant conclusion that whatever answers he was looking for, he would not find them amongst her personal papers. Turning out the lights and feeling a little drunk, he decided not to use his rented car and drive around looking for a motel; instead, he went into her bedroom and, pulling back the covers and kicking off his shoes, he lay down on the bed. The same bed where they had made love not that long ago. The subtle scent of her perfume on the pillows comforted him as exhaustion overcame him and he slipped into a dreamless sleep.

❖

The sound of the curtains being opened and the rattling of the coffee cup Thandi placed on the bedside table woke him. 'Good morning *Meneer* Andre. Breakfast will be ready in half an hour.'

'Thank you Thandi, I must have dozed off. I trust I've enough time for a shower and shave?' She smiled in agreement. He was in the middle of shaving when he heard the telephone ringing and Thandi answering.

'It's *Mevrou* Janet in Nelspruit,' she said through the bathroom door. Hoping for news on Annette, he wrapped a towel around him and went straight to the phone

'Andre, I'm so glad you're back in Phalaborwa,' Janet said as he picked up the phone, 'perhaps now we can get on with finding Annette!'

'That's what I've been trying to do since I arrived. Last night, I spent hours going through all her personal papers and, I must admit, I feel like a bit of a sleazebag delving into her private affairs.'

'That's understandable; but did you find out anything useful, any clues as to where she may have gone?'

'Nothing; not a damn thing.'

'I've just had a thought! 'How about looking through her photo albums? I'm sure she must have a few lying around. Who knows, you may find something; a photo of her favourite place or a resort she's fond of visiting.'

'I'll have a word with Thandi; I'm sure she'd know where Annette keeps such things.'

As it turned out, there were only two albums. The first was filled with old black and white photos of elderly adults and young children. Andre thought he could recognize Annette in a few of the photos but, seeing nothing likely to help in his search, he moved on to the second album. This album, while now mostly in colour, proved to be almost as unenlightening as the first, but for two photos. One was of an old house with an elderly woman sitting on the *stoep* looking out over a garden; the second was a photo taken from a high point of a small town with a white church prominent amidst the houses. Unfortunately, there were no captions on the front or the back of either photos.

Hoping to ask Thandi about the photos, Andre went through to the bedroom where she was looking through a chest of drawers. 'Here it is,' she said handing him a small leather-covered album, 'it's Annette's wedding photos. They were so happy before that *dronkgat* – drunk crashed into Japie and killed him,' she said opening it to the first photo.

Andre took the album from her and looked down at a photo of a smiling, happy couple standing arm in arm in a garden. At a loss for words and struggling to keep his emotions in check, he walked through to the lounge and sat down as he paged through this sad record of two lives destroyed by the thoughtless actions of one man. Closing the album, he left it on a side table and walked out into the garden.

Standing and staring out over the pool, he couldn't shake that old, niggling feeling that he was missing something right in front of his eyes. Acting on an impulse, he went back inside and, picking up the wedding photo album, he compared the photo of Annette and her husband in the garden with the photo from the second album of the old woman sitting on a *stoep* looking out over the same garden. 'Thandi,' he said carrying both albums through to the kitchen where she was cooking, 'do you know where this house is?'

The homeowner, a Mrs van Jaarsveld, was home as Andre drove up to the house clutching both photo albums. 'Of course, I remember her,' she said, annoyed he was questioning her memory. 'Annette rented a room in my boarding house for many years after she was transferred to Phalaborwa police station; that is, until she and Japie Fourie got married. If I remember correctly, Annette's maiden name was Hilditch and the old lady you see sitting on my *stoep* is her grandmother, Emma Deacon, who came up for their wedding from Prince Albert in the Western Cape.'

'Did Annette ever visit her grandmother; I think you said her name was Deacon?'

'Every time she got leave, off she'd go to Prince Albert. She was very fond of her Granny Deacon as she called her.'

'Do you recognize the town in this picture?' he said showing her the photo of the small town with the white church.

'Of course; that's Prince Albert and that's the Dutch Reformed Church in the middle of the town. Granny Deacon used to live nearby on Church Street. I once travelled with Annette to Prince Albert to visit her granny. I was with her when she took that picture from the hill just outside town; it was their favourite place to go for a walk before the old lady passed away a few years later.'

<hr/>

Switching on his phone as he walked back to his car, Andre called Janet. 'I think I may have found where Annette has gone,' he said as she answered his call.

'Andre!' she shouted, 'don't you ever answer your fucking phone?'

'I've been busy,' he replied, annoyed at her outburst.

'Oh Andre,' she sobbed, 'they've found Annette; she's been murdered.'

CHAPTER 39

ANNETTE FOURIE

THE SA AIRWAYS EMBRAER JET carrying Andre and Major Baloyi, Annette's commanding officer, taxied up to the terminal of the Kruger Mpumalanga Airport near Nelspruit. Walking into the arrival's area, Andre saw Janet coming towards them in the company of two uniformed policemen. 'Andre, I'm so dreadfully sorry it has come to this,' she said hugging him. 'If you and Major Baloyi would come with us, I've arranged for a private meeting room where we can talk.'

Overcome with grief, Andre put his arm around Janet as they followed Baloyi and the two policemen down a corridor and into an empty office. 'How sure are they that it is Annette?' he asked her.

'No one is certain; but all of the circumstances point to it being Annette.'

'Surely you were able to identify her yourself?' Andre asked. Janet, tears welling in her eyes, turned and nodded to one of the policemen accompanying them.

'Unfortunately, sir, the body is badly decomposed,' he said, 'and this, combined with a botched attempt to burn the body using an accelerant, makes visual identification all but impossible.'

'Christ! 'When and how was she found, if it's actually her?' Andre asked the policeman, 'and where is the body now?'

'After our initial investigation at the crime scene, the body of the deceased was taken to the state mortuary in Nelspruit to determine cause of death.'

The second policemen, a sergeant by the stripes on his sleeves, anxious to assert his part in the investigation, answered Andre's first two questions. 'Two farm labourers sent to unblock a drainage ditch on a farm adjacent to the Blue Horizon Centre property discovered the body. I was on call at the station and was dispatched by the duty officer in response to a phone call from the farmer.'

Urged to carry on by Baloyi, the sergeant continued his report. 'After securing the crime scene, I sent uniformed officers to canvass all the properties in the immediate area, including the rehabilitation centre. The duty nurse at the centre informed one of my men that a female patient, registered under the name of Annette Fourie, had discharged herself, without formal permission, from the centre about a week ago. It appeared to us that, based on height and physical size, the body roughly resembled that of the missing woman.'

Baloyi jumped in. 'Thank you Sergeant for your report. Andre, I've brought samples of Annette's blood type and her DNA for comparison to that of the deceased woman. We should know within a matter of hours whether this is Annette or not.'

'With your permission Major,' Andre said, 'I'd like both Janet and I to accompany you to the Blue Horizon Centre to interview their staff and inspect Annette's room, given that Janet has visited her there on a number of occasions.'

'Thank you for that,' Janet said taking Andre's arm as they walked to the police vehicles in the visitor's parking area, 'I too am not totally convinced the body is that of Annette.'

***

Obviously upset and concerned over the police presence at the Centre, the Program Director met them at the entrance to the main building. 'I'm Mrs Khumalo, I understand you would like to have a look at the room Mrs Fourie occupied?' she said with a nervous smile.

'If that would be possible,' Major Baloyi smiled back, 'we would appreciate it.'

'Of course, please come this way. Mrs Fourie was staying in Chalet Six,' the woman said leading them out of the main building and over towards a row of bungalows.

'I'd always imagined Mrs Fourie would be housed in the main building?' Andre remarked.

'Oh no!' the Director confirmed, 'Mrs Fourie was not considered a high risk patient and certainly not in need of close supervision.'

'I can't help noticing that the Chalets are easily accessible from the visitor's parking lot. I assume this area is covered by CCTV?' Baloyi asked. The Director confirmed it was. 'Of course,' Baloyi continued, 'we would need to see all the tapes starting from the time Mrs Fourie discharged herself from the centre.'

'Here we are, Chalet Six,' Mrs Khumalo said pushing open the door. 'I'll go and make arrangements for you to view the CCTV tapes. Please pull the door closed after you've finished; we have a lot of trouble with Vervet monkeys getting into rooms.' The woman turned on her heels and headed back towards the main building.

'Excuse me!' Andre called after her, 'are these chalets kept locked when they are not occupied?'

'Of course not! This is not a secure area,' she replied.

'So, anyone could have been staying in Chalet Six from the time Mrs Fourie left the centre?'

'It's possible; but it would have been highly irregular,' the Director confirmed as she walked away.

Thinking over what he had just learned, Andre joined the group in the Chalet. 'Do you think,' he asked Janet, 'the handful of clothes left in the wardrobe belonged to Annette?'

'From what little I know of hers tastes; I honestly don't believe they're hers; but I couldn't swear to it.'

Opening up a bedside drawer, the police sergeant drew their attention to two packs of cigarettes, a lighter and an ashtray filled with cigarette stubs. 'We'd have no problem getting DNA off these stubs,' he remarked.

'Annette doesn't smoke!' Janet interjected, 'those must belong to someone else.'

'Then why hide them in a drawer?' the sergeant asked.

'Because smoking is strictly forbidden in any of the buildings or on the grounds of the Centre!' the Program Director, Mrs Khumalo said returning to the room. 'Anyone breaking this rule would be in for a lot of trouble.'

'I've worked closely with Captain Fourie for many years and I can assure everyone that she does not smoke,' Baloyi added.

'So, it would appear someone else occupied Chalet Six shortly after Annette discharged herself,' Andre said. 'I think, Mrs Khumalo, we need to take a look at those CCTV tapes right away.'

Andre, Janet and Major Baloyi were joined by a Major Xhusa from the Nelspruit police station to view the CCTV tapes in a small office just off the main entrance to the Blue Horizon Centre. 'There are six tapes; it's all we've got,' Mrs Khumalo said placing the tapes on the table next to a small video player. 'Each tape covers a two to three day period in the visitor's parking area. OK, I'll leave you to it,' she said leaving the room.

The CCTV footage was of poor quality, making it difficult to identify persons or to read car licence numbers. 'They've been re-recording over old tapes just to save a few Rands,' complained Major Xhusa, 'which makes one wonder why they bothered installing CCTV cameras in the first place.'

'Still, it's better than nothing,' Andre remarked.

They were halfway through the second tape when Janet pointed to a figure getting into a taxi, 'That looks a lot like Annette; can anyone read the name of the taxi company?'

'It's a Mpisa taxi,' Xhusa said, 'they're an efficient company; we shouldn't have too much trouble establishing the destination of the passenger. 'I'll go and get my sergeant onto it right away,' he said leaving the room.

'It's a pity this CCTV camera covers only the visitor's parking lot and not the Chalets,' Janet remarked. 'It's not going to tell us if anyone else occupied Annette's room after she left. Perhaps I should try and get hold of a member of the cleaning staff; it's always possible something's going on that even the formidable Mrs Khumalo knows nothing about.'

They had just started on the third tape when Andre spotted it. 'Go back,' he said, 'what the hell is going on in the bottom right of the screen?'

'It looks like two people dragging and carrying someone across the far corner of the parking lot. I'd say they were aware of the camera and were making every effort to avoid being seen,' Baloyi confirmed.

'It's obviously quite late at night, as there are very few cars in the parking lot,' Andre commented. 'If you ask me, I think we are seeing someone being abducted from the Centre!'

'I'm seizing these tapes,' Major Xhusa said gathering them up, 'and sending them up to our forensic people in Jo'burg. If we can get them enhanced, we may be able to make a case here.'

Walking out to the police car, Andre and Baloyi encountered Janet on her way back up to the main entrance of the Centre. 'Any luck talking to the cleaning staff?'

'Not at first. It appears our Mrs Khumalo wields a lot of clout around here. But, as in every chain, there's always a weak link and I found it in an unhappy little girl from Zimbabwe. She's quite sure that on the day after Annette left, Chalet Six was secretly made available to a female friend of a white member of staff, until such time as Annette returned.'

'Not a very good deal for the friend,' Baloyi said shaking his head. 'From what we've just seen on one of the CCTV tapes, it would appear she was kidnapped and then murdered!'

'Oh my God! You know what that means?' Janet said to Andre.

'It means Annette's in grave danger,' he replied, 'I've got to get to the airport as fast as possible. I'll explain why on the way.'

CHAPTER 40

PRINCE ALBERT

THE AIRLINK JET LANDED AT George Airport two hours after it departed from Johannesburg's Lanseria Airport. Clutching his overnight bag, Andre went over to the car rentals counter to talk to them about the vehicle he'd reserved while waiting for his flight in Johannesburg. A fellow passenger he got talking to on the flight to George, had warned him about taking a small car over the Swartberg Pass through the Swartberg Mountains. 'While the Pass is the more direct route to Prince Albert,' he cautioned, 'it can become treacherous in bad weather!' Heeding that advice, Andre changed his booking at the car rental counter to a more substantial Land Rover Defender.

Leaving the airport, he followed Highway 12 to the town of Oudtshoorn, where he joined a Highway which led through the Swartberg Mountains and over the famous Pass to the town of Prince Albert. Fortunately for Andre, the weather cooperated and by not allowing himself to be distracted by the magnificent scenery, he arrived four hours later in Prince Albert. Driving down Church Street, he soon spotted the imposing white bell tower on the Dutch Reformed Church, which he recognized from the photo he'd seen in Annette's album. Checking into a hotel on main street, he began his search for Annette right away by showing the young woman on the front desk the photo of the town he'd taken from Annette's album.

'Ja Meneer,' she said nodding her head, 'that picture's taken from the Viewpoint on the top of a *kopje* just outside town. I can draw you a map on how to get there, but it's a little late to go climbing up there now.'

'Thank you, I'll get that from you in the morning,' he said as he picked up his room key. Acting on a sudden impulse, he returned to the front desk, 'Perhaps you can tell me,' he asked the young woman, 'do you know of anyone going by the name of Hilditch or Deacon who may still living in Prince Albert?'

'*Nee Meneer*, I don't know anyone with either of those names. But, let me ask our Manager, *Meneer* Botha, he's lived here for many years.'

Andre was about to tell her not to bother, when *Meneer* Botha, who had overheard their conversation, emerged from his office. Shaking Andre's hand, he confirmed that he had once heard of a family by the name of Hilditch but had no idea what had become of them. 'It was a very long time ago,' he said apologetically, 'but Deacon I do remember. Unfortunately, old Mrs Deacon passed away a few years ago and to the best of my knowledge, she was the last member of her family still living in this area. I hope this is of some help to you?'

'It certainly is,' Andre confirmed. 'Perhaps you may know the address of the house where Mrs Deacon once lived?'

'Yes, I do; her old house is on Church Street, not far from here. I'll write down the address for you.' As the manager handed the address to him, he asked in a friendly manner whether Andre was in town researching his family tree. 'No, I'm trying to find a friend of mine, a Mrs Annette Fourie. She could be visiting Prince Albert as Mrs Deacon was her grandmother.'

'Now that's quite a coincidence isn't it?' the manager said turning to the young female desk clerk, 'didn't you have two gentlemen in here yesterday also inquiring about a Mrs Fourie? Perhaps they're friends of yours on the same quest?' he asked Andre.

'What did they look like?' Andre asked the young woman, perhaps a little too sharply, but given the implications of the information, understandable.

'Two well-dressed African men; they claimed to be detectives from Johannesburg, but when I asked to see their warrant cards, they turned around and left.'

After a quick breakfast at the hotel, Andre set out to find the house where

Annette had spent much of her time visiting with her favourite grand-mother. Standing on the sidewalk outside the address, he was pleased to see from a prominent sign on the gate that the house was now a bed and breakfast. Pushing open the gate, he walked up the concrete path towards the *stoep* where four elderly women, sitting in wicker chairs, watched his progress with interest.

One of the women got to her feet and smiling pleasantly, introduced herself. '*Goeie more Meneer* - Good morning Mister, I'm *Mevrou* Naude the landlady; I'm sorry *Meneer*, but we are fully booked.'

'If it were up to me, I'd find a room for him any day,' one of the other women remarked, eliciting giggles from her companions.

'Actually *Mevrou*,' Andre said, 'I'm hoping you may be able to help me find a lady friend of mine?'

'And who is this lucky lady?' the bolder of the four women asked.

'Her name is Annette Fourie; her grandmother, a *Mevrou* Deacon, once lived in this house,' Andre said. 'I was hoping my friend may be staying here.'

'I'm sorry *Meneer*, don't recall anyone by that name looking to rent a room,' *Mevrou* Naude replied.

'I've a photo of my friend, if that would help jog anyone's memory,' he said taking out his photo of Annette.

Each woman looked carefully at the photo before the woman sitting at the far end said, 'I think I saw her the other day when I walked up to the Viewpoint, she was with her young daughter!'

Disappointed, Andre remarked that Annette did not have any children of her own. 'Oh, I remember seeing them,' another woman chimed in, 'the young girl she was with, was *Mevrou* Oberholzer's daughter, Ann! I'm sure of it.'

'While I try not to turn business away *Meneer*, *Mevrou* Oberholzer has a bed and breakfast over on De Beer Street. It seems to me your friend may be staying there. Walking with him to the gate, *Mevrou* Naude took him by his arm, 'Young man,' she said in a conspiratorial tone, 'this friend of yours, Annette Fourie, is she in trouble with the police?'

'Good Lord no!' he replied, 'between you and me, she is actually a cap-tain in the police force herself.'

'That's strange; I had two black detectives here yesterday asking if I knew where they could find her. When I told them I'd never heard of her, they left without a word.'

— ◆ —

'Annette has gone for a walk,' Mrs Oberholzer told him. 'I expect you'll find her up at the Viewpoint. It's her favourite place this time of day,' she added. He was halfway down the street when he realized he had no idea which way to go. Having forgotten to pick up the map the desk clerk at his hotel had promised him, he resorted to asking directions from passers-byers on the street. After two or three tries, he eventually found himself climbing an increasingly steep, rocky trail that wound its way up a hill on the outskirts of town.

'More like a bloody mountain than a hill!' he muttered having removed his jacket and loosened his tie as the midmorning sun grew increasingly warm. His leather brogues, smart wear on the pavements of London, were totally unsuitable for a steep climb up what he now believed to be the foothills of the Stormberg Mountains. Pausing frequently, he searched the heights hoping to see the Viewpoint and, hopefully, Annette.

Cresting what he thought would turn out to be yet another false summit, Andre, to his relief, spotted a small sign at the side of the trail confirming that he had finally reached the Viewpoint. Shading his eyes from the intense glare of the sun, he was able to make out the figure of a woman sitting on the ground looking out over the valley. She was cradling her bent knees with one arm and shading her eyes with her other, all the while staring intently in his direction. His casual wave caused her to spring to her feet and start running towards him.

'Andre!' Annette shouted with unrestrained joy as she threw her arms around him. 'I thought it was you! Oh, I'm so glad to see you. How on earth did you know where to find me?'

'I didn't,' he said returning her embrace, 'I just happened to be walking through the Stormberg Mountains when, suddenly, there you were! You forget my darling, you are addressing a Scotland Yard detective; nothing is beyond our capabilities.' Suddenly Annette burst into tears. 'No, this is no time for tears,' he said kissing her and holding her tight. 'All that matters now is that I've found you and you're safe.'

'Yes; but for how long? I can't tell you how desperately sorry and ashamed I am for all the problems I've caused you and Janet. But I was at my wits end; all I could think of was to go someplace where no one could find me; except, perhaps, the finest Scotland Yard detective in the world,' she said smiling through her tears.

'Shall we go back down?' he asked, looking at the town spread out below them.

'Please, let's stay for a while; I've no idea when I may ever come back here again. This was my granny's favourite place to rest and reminisce you know.'

'We can stay here as long as you like,' Andre said spreading out his jacket for them to sit on. They sat close together watching as life bustled about in the town below, his arm around her shoulders holding her close to him.

'Will I ever be free of this accursed drug,' Annette said softly. 'Even now, weeks later, I fear it more than ever. I still have this desperate desire to feel, just once more, the blissful rush of euphoria I got from a single hit of heroin. Trouble is, I know it would never end with just one hit. Andre, I have to fight this awful need every single waking minute of my day and, sometimes it seems, even in my dreams!'

'My darling, I believe that together, we can beat it! I know now you needed far more than what the Blue Horizon Centre could offer. I am guilty of thinking I could shift my responsibility for your wellbeing over to someone else, and I'm desperately sorry for that.'

'I don't think you're being quite fair to yourself or to the Centre. I could have made better use of the rehab programs they offered me. If only I had not been so bloody minded and suspicious of everyone and everything. I've never mentioned this to anyone, but one of the main reasons I checked myself out of the Blue Horizon Centre was because I became convinced I was being watched by men sitting in a car parked outside my bungalow late at night! How's that for paranoia?' she said laughing.

He wrestled with his decision whether or not to tell her that by going into hiding, she almost certainly saved her life. Seeing the expression on his face after telling him of her fears of being paranoid, Annette asked whether her confession bothered him. At that moment, he realized he had to be open and honest with her if they were to fight this thing together.

After telling her of the terrible events at the Blue Horizon Centre and the disturbing fact that others were inquiring about her around town, Annette sat quietly staring out beyond the town and over the vast open spaces of the Karoo.

CHAPTER 41

UITKYK FARM

IT DIDN'T TAKE MUCH TO convince Annette that it was in their best interests to leave Prince Albert as quickly as possible. 'We can be in Bloemfontein by nightfall,' he assured her, as they drove north out of town towards Highway 1. 'Once we get to Bloemfontein, it's an easy day's drive to Jo'burg.'

'Then what do we do?'

'I called Colonel Banerjee shortly before we left; he was all for providing us with a police escort all the way to Johannesburg. However, I managed to persuade him that we're perfectly capable of looking after ourselves, providing we got a little help.'

'And what sort of help would that be?' she asked. He pointed towards the glove box. She opened it and took out two pistols wrapped in a yellow duster cloth. Unwrapping the weapons, she exclaimed with delight, '*Jislaaik!* Beretta P4 Storms with Tritium night sights! Every policeman's dream. How the hell did you manage to organize that?'

'It was the Colonel himself who arranged for me to pick them up at the local police station. Failing that, we would've waited around until a police escort could be organized, and I didn't think that would be a wise thing to do.' Changing the subject, he asked, 'Did he also include two ten-round magazines of ammunition?'

'He certainly did. Loaded with .40 S&W rounds – real manstoppers!' Annette chortled, loading both magazines into the pistols and cocking them. 'One up the spout and safety's on,' she said placing one of the weapons on the seat next to Andre. 'Let's just hope we never have to use them!'

'We're not far from Beaufort West,' Andre said glancing at a roadside sign. 'I suggest we find a public phone and give Janet a call to let her know you're safe with me.'

'Yes, but am I safe with you?' she laughed, digging him in the ribs.

'You're as safe as you want to be!' he smiled squeezing her hand.

'How about I give her a call on my mobile; I've held off using it up until now fearing it may be hacked.'

'And it probably was! The fact that two self-described detectives had managed to track you down to Prince Albert would indicate that's the case. Which is probably why Banerjee insisted we do not use our phones under any circumstances.'

'Well good luck with finding a working public phone,' she joked, 'we're more likely to come across a live dodo!'

———◆———

It was late afternoon when they entered Bloemfontein. 'We should be thinking about getting something to eat and finding a place to stay before it gets too dark,' Annette suggested. 'This is when I would usually do a search on my phone, but that option's no longer available.'

'Then, we'll do it the old fashioned way,' he said. 'Keep your eyes peeled for a bed and breakfast sign. I don't think we should risk a major hotel, just in case those two pseudo detectives think carefully about our likely destination after leaving Prince Albert.'

'How about I enquire at the information centre next to the petrol station. You fill up with petrol, while I see what they can suggest.' Annette got back into the car with a smile on her face. 'I've found just the place! It's a little off the beaten track at a place called *Uitkyk Kopje* and the owner, a *Mevrou* Preller, has a self-contained bungalow on her farm which she rents out to visitors. I called ahead and she's reserved it for us. All we need do now is stop at a grocery store and a liquor outlet and, once we get to the farm, I'll whip up a meal to die for!'

'Well, I hope dying won't be necessary, but otherwise your suggestions sound good to me.'

The bungalow was perched high up on the side of a steep, rocky kopje overlooking the valley below. 'Isn't it beautiful Andre; what a lovely view we have from the *stoep*.'

'I agree it's beautiful; but it's also getting damn cold!'

'OK, let's go inside; I'll start dinner while you get a fire going and pour the wine. Isn't it just as well we've got each other to keep ourselves warm,' she said with a wink?

Clearing the dishes away after dinner, Andre volunteered to look after the washing up. 'Thank you my darling,' Annette said kissing him on the cheek. 'If you don't mind, I'd like to take that hot bath I've been promising myself before slipping into one of those lovely fluffy gowns our hosts thoughtfully provided.'

The washing up completed, Andre stoked up the fire and poured two more glasses of the fine merlot he'd found in the off-sales of a small hotel near the grocery store. He had just settled down on the sofa when Annette emerged from the bathroom wreathed in a cloud of steam and wrapped in a white dressing gown. Curling up on the sofa next to him, she took the glass of wine he handed to her, 'Why didn't you come in and scrub my back?' she asked looking up at him.

'Well, I didn't think...' he said somewhat taken aback.

'Didn't think I wanted you to see me naked?' she continued, 'tell me Andre, what do you think I'm wearing underneath my gown?'

'Perfume,' he suggested, playing along with her.

'Good guess!' she laughed, 'now let me show you,' Annette said opening her gown and taking his hand, placed it firmly on one of her breasts. 'I want you to make love to me my darling, I can't spell it out any clearer than that.'

'Hold that thought, I'll be right back.' He returned in a few minutes wearing the other dressing gown and carrying a couple of pillows and the eiderdown from their bed, which he spread out in front of the fire.

'You can't fool me; you couldn't possibly have got undressed so quickly. Come here, let me check,' she demanded, reaching under his gown. 'Oh! I can feel you have!' she chuckled, 'you're nice and hard and all for little old me. I am impressed!' Annette said getting to her feet and taking off her gown, threw it onto the sofa.

It was the sound of breaking glass that woke him. He lay quite still, slowly remembering where they were and listening for other sounds that may help him work out what had just happened. Pushing himself up on his elbow, he looked about the room. The fire had gone out and the room was cold, but he was aware of Annette's naked body pressed against him. Anxious not to wake her, he carefully slipped out from beneath the eiderdown. He was feeling around for his dressing gown, when the sound of something being broken came from the bedroom and a flickering glow cast red and yellow fingers of light around the room.

'Annette, wake up!' he whispered, 'someone's breaking in! I think they've started a fire!'

As she struggled to wake up, he reached out for the pistol he'd placed beside them the night before. Finding it, he cocked the weapon and eased off the safety catch. Approaching the bedroom, he saw a small fire burning around a broken bottle lying on the floor below the window. 'Fire extinguisher,' he yelled to Annette, 'I saw one next to the front door.' He grabbed a blanket from the bed and was attempting to smother the fire when she appeared, stark naked, carrying a fire extinguisher. Grabbing the extinguisher from her, he used it to put out the fire. 'My God!' he exclaimed staring appreciatively at her, 'you look so beautiful.'

'Men!' she laughed, 'all you ever think about is sex!' Laughing somewhat hysterically, they struggled to make sense of what had just happened.

An instant later, a fusillade of shots punched through the bedroom window and thudded into the wall close behind them, showering them with plaster. 'Get down! Crawl into the lounge; stay down and keep close to the wall,' he yelled as another five or six shots rang out in rapid succession, demolishing what was left of the bedroom windows. 'Sounds like a fucking Skorpion!' he muttered crawling into the lounge. 'Find your pistol, keep it with you. They've got an automatic weapon and they might try to break in.'

Together they heard a car starting up in front of the bungalow, 'Shit! These bastards are not getting away scot-free,' Andre roared as he jumped to his feet and headed towards the front door.

'Andre! Where the hell are you going? Are you fucking mad! Please don't go outside!' Annette pleaded. 'You said yourself they've got a sub-machine gun and you don't know how many of them there are. Besides, you've got no clothes on, you're *kaalgat!*'

Even if he'd heard her, Andre was in no mood for good advice, no matter how sensible. He was just in time to see a man jump into the passenger side of the car as it took off down the steep, winding dirt road headed towards the Preller farmhouse. Ignoring the sharp stones cutting into his feet, he raced across the road and down the side of a small slope, putting him in an ideal position to see the car as it reappeared around the second bend in the road.

Adopting a combat crouch, he levelled his Beretta and twice checked that the safety catch was off. As the car came around the bend, he placed the green aiming point of the Tritium night sight just above the headlights. He squeezed off shot after shot as the car raced by, swerving wildly as the driver struggled to keep control.

The driver was unsuccessful. The car ploughed into the rock wall that ran along the side of the road, catapulted over a steep embankment and crashed headlong down into a ravine.

From his vantage point, Andre could see the lights come on down at *Mevrou* Preller's farmhouse. 'They must've heard the shooting, let's hope they've called the police,' he said running towards the edge of the ravine. 'And the fire station as well,' he added as he saw the flicker of flames coming from the wreck of the car. A high-pitched scream prompted him to make his way down to the rapidly growing fire now engulfing the crumpled remains of the car. 'Anyone still alive in that wreck hasn't a snowball's chance in hell!' he reasoned.

A movement on the ground mere feet from the raging fire, drew his attention. It was a man struggling to crawl away as the clothes he was wearing began to smoulder and burn. Picking up a branch broken off a small tree, he held it out towards the man. 'Grab hold, I'll pull you away,' he shouted, but it was quickly obvious the man was too badly injured to help himself. 'Fuck this!' Andre screamed as he dropped the branch and ignoring every instinct warning him against it, ran to the man and pulled him to safety.

'*Here God!*' *Mevrou* Preller exclaimed as she scrambled down the side of the ravine, only to encounter a stark naked man pulling a body away from the blazing car.

'Sorry *Mevrou* Preller, I had no time to dress,' he apologised holding his burnt hands over his private parts.

'*Moenie worry nie*,' she smiled, 'I used to be a nurse. I've seen many men naked. But not many so well equipped!' she said *sotto voce* as Annette arrived carrying Andre's clothes and a torch.

'Oh My God! Andre,' Annette exclaimed, 'what happened to your hands and your hair?'

'Got a little too close to the fire; nothing that won't heal!' he assured her as she helped him get dressed.

'Your husband is very brave; I saw him pull this man away from the burning car,' *Mevrou* Preller said nodding towards the injured man lying on the ground. 'Don't worry, I called an ambulance as well as the police,' she continued pointing to the red flashing lights turning off onto the farm road with blue police lights not far behind.

'Another farm invasion hey!' the police sergeant said as Annette sat next to Andre on the steps of the ambulance having his hands bandaged.

'Not this time; we believe it was targeted against us,' she replied passing him her warrant card.

'I must ask both of you not to leave *Uitkyk Kopje* farm until we have investigated this matter more thoroughly,' the sergeant said.

'No problem there, Sergeant,' Andre agreed. 'Though I would like to question the man I pulled away from the fire before he goes to hospital under police guard.'

'I'm sorry, *Meneer*, I couldn't allow that without approval from my commanding officer, Major Venter, and he's not available until tomorrow morning.'

'Then, if I may, I would like to accompany you back to your station so I may call the senior officer we're working with, Colonel Banerjee in Johannesburg. The colonel has assured me I could trouble him anytime, day or night.'

'I don't think that would be necessary Detective Chief Inspector Meyer,' the sergeant replied after inspecting Andre's warrant card.

Andre crouched on the floor of the ambulance next to the bandaged man's stretcher. 'Do you speak English,' he asked.

'Was it you who pulled me away from the fire; even after we tried to kill you and the woman,' the injured man replied. 'I do not understand why you did that but thank you from my wife and children!'

'You speak very good English. What should I call you?"

'Phinius. I was a schoolteacher once; but now I cannot find work. What do you want of me?'

'I want to find out who paid you and why you and your friend would be willing to do such a terrible thing.'

'We had no money and there was no work, even for a man like me! We met this man in a *shebeen* who promised us thousands of Rands if we killed the policewoman. When you came to Prince Albert, he promised us more money if we killed you too.'

'Who is this man?'

'I don't know his name, but I heard it said he's Portuguese from Lisbon. We met him at his house in Jeppestown. It's in Johannesburg.'

'Yes, I know where that is. Do you have an address for this house?'

'In my jacket.' Phinius struggled with his handcuffed and bandaged wrists to point towards the clothing the ambulance paramedics had removed to treat his injuries. Andre retrieved the man's jacket which, despite being partly burned, yielded a folded slip of paper from an inside pocket.

'Is this it?' Phinius nodded as Andre slipped the address into his pocket.

'This man will kill me and my family just for talking to you!'

'Not if we catch him. I assure we'll make damn sure he's in no position to kill anyone.'

'Will you be able to help me with the police if I tell you everything I know?'

'I will do what I can. No one died in your attack, except your friend, and even you'd agree, it was largely his own fault.'

CHAPTER 42

JEPPESTOWN

'I'M ANXIOUS TO GET THIS address to Colonel Banerjee in Jo'burg as soon as possible, but I don't want to use our mobiles in case that's how we were followed. For my part, I'm convinced this so called "Portuguese man from Lisbon" is none other than Clive Rylston himself,' Andre said as he and Annette drove into Bloemfontein to present themselves at the police station.

'Didn't that guy you pulled out of the fire tell you how they found us?'

'All he could tell me was that this "Portuguese man from Lisbon" kept in touch with them by phone, directing them where to go and what to do.'

'Yes, but how the hell could they possibly have known we were staying at *Uitkyk Kopje* farm last night?'

'My immediate thoughts were that they had somehow placed a tracking device on the Land Rover. But, despite my best efforts this morning, I couldn't find anything remotely resembling a tracking device. And I would remind you, I've had some experience with them.'

'Could it be that despite turning off our phones, they can still track our movements?'

'I'll put that question to Banerjee when I call him from the police station.

'I've cleared it with Major Venter,' Colonel Banerjee said in response to Andre's call. 'You're both free to go; just get back here as soon as you can. I'll hold off on raiding that address in Jeppestown you gave me, though I will arrange for one of our special task force teams to be placed on standby awaiting your arrival.'

———◆———

The house in Jeppestown was on a dead-end street three blocks away from Jules Street, the main thoroughfare through the community. 'This area of Jo'burg is one of the oldest communities in the city,' Banerjee said to them as they crouched in the back of a police surveillance vehicle disguised as a plumber's repair truck. 'You mentioned you had another address for this Rylston; what can you tell me about that?'

'That address is based on information we extracted under duress, admittedly not a reliable source at the best of times. The subject we questioned, a Nicolau da Silva, is currently in prison and awaiting extradition to Portugal. He gave us the location of a farm in Limpopo Province which, unfortunately, did not check out at all. Also, this man da Silva, made a vague reference to a Johannesburg location but, even when pressed more closely, he was unable to provide further details.'

Troubled by the use of physical abuse to obtain information, Banerjee shifted uncomfortably on his seat in the surveillance vehicle. 'Since no one has entered or left the premises from the time we commenced surveillance last night,' he said breaking the uncomfortable silence, 'I think it's time I authorized the Special Task Force to go in.'

The ear shattering blasts from two stun grenades fired in through the front and rear windows of the house, alerted the neighbourhood that something interesting was taking place, causing a large crowd to gather.

'All clear, Colonel. There's no one home,' the officer, leading the STF team, reported to Banerjee. 'Though watch out for the dozens of used needles, drug paraphernalia and the usual amount of shit we find in derelict houses these days.'

'Thank you, Enoch. Good job as always. Leave a couple of your men behind while detectives Fourie and Meyer take a closer look around. OK you two, it's all yours. I've a string of meetings to go to, so, when you're done, hand the premises over to the Metro Police; they can take it from there.'

'Before you go Colonel, would you please have some of your techies give our Land Rover a thorough going over. I suspect it's had a tracking device fitted, but for the life of me I can't find it.'

'It could also be that one, or both of your phones, has been compromised. I'll take them along with your vehicle back to police headquarters with me. You can get a lift back with the two STF members when you're ready.'

<hr />

'This house was probably built around the 1890s,' Annette remarked as they pushed open the front door, smashed in earlier by the STF's battering ram. The smell of decay and floors littered with rubbish and human faeces, did nothing to make their job any easier. 'For God's sake don't touch anything,' she said handing him a pair of blue forensic gloves while pulling on a pair of her own, 'you wouldn't want to get the burns on your hands infected!'

Leaving Annette to look around the ground-floor rooms, Andre headed towards the rickety flight of stairs leading to the upper floor. As each step creaked and groaned beneath his weight, he carefully avoided steps which looked like they were rotten through. Reaching the upstairs landing, the light from his torch showed three doors. Two stood wide open, revealing empty rooms. The third had obviously been broken open by the special task force team as they searched the house.

Wondering why this door had been kept locked, he pushed the shattered panels aside and entered the room. It was a little cleaner than the rest of the house but, apart from an iron bed, a stained coir mattress and a small table, it was unfurnished. Pulling a black plastic rubbish bag from under the bed, he tipped out dozens of used hypodermic needles, spoons showing signs of burning and small plastic baggies containing a white powder residue.

Also, in the bag were two crumpled Bosco's fried chicken boxes. Careful not to touch anything, he used his folded handkerchief to scoop a few of the hypodermic needles and plastic baggies into one of the fried chicken boxes. Clutching his find, he made his way back down the stairs to see if Annette had found anything of interest.

'Lots of drug paraphernalia, discarded needles and so on,' she reported, 'obviously a shooting gallery for local druggies.'

'Find anything upstairs?'

'More of the same. Though, one of the rooms has all the signs of being a temporary hideout, fitting in nicely with what Phinius told me in the back of the ambulance.'

'OK. So, what's with the fried chicken box and the needles?' Annette asked as they walked out of the house.

'London has samples of Rylston's DNA on file, so I'm hoping Banerjee can put a rush on identifying the DNA on these needles. If I'm right, we may be able to prove, once and for all, that it's Rylston who's pulling the strings around here. Though, if it's him, it would be safe to say that he's taken more than a liking to his own product.'

'It would serve the bastard right if that's the case. But seriously Detective Chief Inspector, what's with the Bosco box, or are you just telling me you're hungry?'

'Very funny Captain! But tell me, are you familiar with Bosco's?'

'To be quite honest, I've never heard of them!'

'My point exactly,' Andre replied, 'neither have I.'

'Andre, your Land Rover is as clean as a whistle, as is your mobile phone. Unfortunately, my dear, our techies can't say the same about your mobile,' Banerjee said to Annette as they arrived back at police headquarters in Johannesburg.

'How the bloody hell could they have got hold of my phone?' Annette asked.

'I'm told it's really quite simple, they only require a few minutes with your phone to install the tracking app. Apparently, parents install them all the time to keep track of their kids' whereabouts. But don't worry, your phone is now clean; just make a point of never leaving it switched on where someone can get hold of it, even for a minute.'

Following Banerjee through to his office, they sat facing his desk while he sorted through reports which had just arrived. 'We've lifted three separate sets of fingerprints off the Bosco fried chicken box you brought in, as well as DNA off the meth pipes and baggies. By the way, the baggies contained traces of heroin, combined with fentanyl and *TIK*. If Rylston's the one using this poison, he'd be a very dangerous man to confront. The DNA will take a while to process, but the fingerprints are already on their way to DI Banerjee at Caledonian Road in London. I told my son to pull his finger out on this one, so we should get a result fairly quickly.'

'Any ideas where this Bosco fried chicken outlet is located?' Andre asked.

'That had us puzzled for a while; we couldn't find any reference to it in the whole of Gauteng Province until some alert officer in Pretoria recognized the name. Apparently, his son works at the Union Mine near Mica, where he remembers there being a Bosco fried chicken outlet in a nearby "informal" settlement called Klipspruit.'

'Klipspruit,' Annette said, concern evident in her voice, 'that's only twenty five miles south-west of Phalaborwa. What the hell is he doing so close to my home?'

'Assuming, of course, this man is Clive Rylston,' Banerjee added.

'Well, we're headed back to Phalaborwa later today. Would you please send me a text as soon as you hear from Caledonian Road,' Annette asked, 'it would set our minds at ease.'

'Of course,' Banerjee said rising from behind his desk shaking their hands and wishing them a safe journey, 'I'll let you know either way.'

CHAPTER 43

BOSCO'S

T HEY HAD JUST PASSED THE turnoff to Middelburg when the call
came through. As Andre was driving, Annette answered. She listened
intently for a few minutes before ending the call. 'Well?' Andre said,
'don't keep me in suspense.'

'The fingerprints are an exact match,' she replied. 'It was definitely Clive
Rylston who bought the fried chicken from Bosco's in Klipspruit. Which
leaves me with the same question, what the hell was he doing in that area?'

'We're going to have try and figure that out. What's the shortest route
to this Klipspruit?'

'OK. When we reach the Belfast turnoff, take the Lydenburg Road
through Ohrigstad and look for the sign to Klipspruit. Once we get there,
what do you suggest we do?' Annette asked.

'I've an idea, but it's a bit of a long shot. I'd like to show Rylston's picture to the staff in Bosco's. Who knows, maybe we'll get lucky!'

The lunchtime rush was in full swing as Annette and Andre weaved their
way through the diners to an empty table at the back of Bosco's Fried
Chicken. Ordering two of Bosco's lunch specials and two soft drinks, they
settled down to wait for the rush to subside. Perhaps, because they were two
new faces amongst his regular customers, the proprietor wandered over to
their table to ask if they had enjoyed their meal. In reality, he was merely

curious and perhaps a little suspicious, about the two newcomers in his community.

'Dimitri Bosco,' he said amiably extending his hand to Andre and bowing gracefully to Annette.

'Annette and Andre,' Andre replied. 'We're on holiday in this part of the country hoping to link up with an old friend of mine from England. It's quite possible he could be living somewhere around here.'

'Well then, today is your lucky day! Not only have you been able to eat at my café, but you have also met Dimitri who knows everyone for fifty miles in any direction. Let me help you, what is your friend's name?'

'In for a penny in for a pound,' Andre muttered to himself as he gave Dimitri the name of the man they least wanted to find living quite so close to Phalaborwa.

'No. I'm sorry, I don't know that name. Perhaps you can describe this friend of yours?'

'I can do better than that,' Andre replied producing a photo of Rylston.

'I may have seen him in here once or twice, but I can't be sure.'

'May I pass this photo around to your staff and the customers still here?'

'Of course. But first you must tell me the truth; are you from the police?'

'Heavens no!' Annette said jumping in quickly, 'we're just trying to contact a friend.'

'Then go ahead; though I'm not sure anyone will be willing to help you.' While wondering what could possibly be behind Dimitri's odd reply, Andre went ahead and passed the photo around the dozen or so customers and staff in the café. Not a single person acknowledged ever having laid eyes on Clive Rylston.

'I've routinely found most locals view the police, or anyone asking questions for that matter, with a great deal of suspicion,' Annette commented as they walked to their Land Rover parked a little way down the road.

As they neared the vehicle, an old woman swathed in a blanket approached them, her hand extended for a handout. Reaching into his pocket Andre pulled out a few coins and a couple of crumpled twenty Rand notes. The woman took the money he offered and in a conspiratorial whisper said, 'I know where you can find the man you are looking for, but first you must pay me five hundred Rand.'

'How do you know the man we are looking for?' Annette asked, expecting to catch the woman in a lie.

'My friend in Bosco's see his picture, it's *Meneer* Rylston. I work in his house for much time.'

'OK,' Andre said, 'I will give you your five hundred Rands, but you must come with us in the car and point out the house yourself.'

'*Aieee*! *Meneer* Rylston is bad man, maybe he will see me?'

'We will make sure he doesn't; all you have to do is show us where he lives, then we will drive you back here.' The old woman climbed into the back seat of the Land Rover and, every few minutes, gave Andre directions on how to find his way through the backstreets of Klipspruit.

Ten minutes after leaving the last of the shanty dwellings behind, she told him to stop on the crest of a low hill. From this vantage point, she pointed out an old house at the bottom of the hill, set back from a gravel road amidst a cluster of bedraggled eucalyptus trees. 'That house where I work for *Meneer* Rylston,' she said, 'now you pay me!'

'Is he still living there?' Annette asked.

'Maybe, maybe not. That is house for *Meneer* Rylston. You pay me if I show you. Now I show you.' Andre handed over the five hundred Rand and turning the Land Rover around, drove the old woman back to the settlement, dropping her off outside Bosco's.

'I'd be feeling a lot better if we hadn't handed the two Beretta pistols back to Banerjee,' Annette said as they drove back to take another look at the house where Rylston might be living.

'All we're going to do is take a look at the place. If he's still living there, we'll call for backup from Baloyi in Phalaborwa before we make any move to arrest him. Is that OK with you?' he asked. Annette nodded in agreement as he pulled off the road into a patch of bush. Getting out of the Land Rover, they made their way through the bush to where they were able to get a closer look at the house.

It was an old, wood and plaster dwelling which had clearly seen better days. Its corrugated iron roof, which had long ago lost its blue colour, now showed large patches of rust. Combined with the broken gutters, detached drainpipes and overgrown garden, everything added to a general air of decay and neglect. 'It looks like he employed the same decorator he used in Jeppestown,' Annette commented dryly.

Making use of the tangled growth of stunted mallees under the eucalyptus trees to cover their approach, they paused for a whispered assessment of what they could see so far. 'It doesn't look as though there's anyone home,' Annette observed. 'And there's no sign of a car anywhere, so it's possible he may be away.'

'Keep a sharp lookout,' Andre said as he rose and ran towards the front of the house, not waiting to hear her angry response.

'Andre, you can be a bloody fool sometimes!' she muttered to herself. Two minutes later, after peering in through the front windows facing the *stoep*, he signalled for her to join him.

'As far as I can see, there's no one home,' he said. 'The inside is almost as dirty and dilapidated as his Jeppestown hovel. Look,' he said using his shoulder to force open the front door, 'if Rylston's actually living here, he is not at all worried about anyone breaking in. I'm going to take a look around inside.'

'Andre! This is breaking and entering!' Annette warned as he stepped over the threshold into the house. The first shot narrowly missed the back of his head as it punched a hole in the wooden panel on the partly open door and buried itself in the wall behind. 'Bloody hell!' Andre shouted as he dropped to the floor and scrambled inside, narrowly avoiding the next two shots which followed him into the house.

'Keep down,' he yelled to Annette as she, ignoring his order, raced through the doorway and dived to the floor next to him.

'There's no way I'm staying outside while we're being shot at!' she shouted in his ear. 'Where do you think the shots are coming from?'

'From the trees across the road. I hate to say it, but I think we've been set up. Whoever's shooting at us fully expected us to arrive by car and park in the front of the house, and not to come creeping in through the trees on the side.'

'You'll get no argument from me. Once this bastard realizes we're not armed,' she said, 'he's going to come over here and finish the job.'

'I can't argue with your logic. In the meantime, we've got to stay out of sight and keep him guessing where we are. Also, may I suggest you break phone silence and call Baloyi; I think we're going to need all the help we can get! While you are doing that, I'll go and see if it's safe for us to get out the backway.'

'Don't you think there could be another gunman out back waiting for us to do just that?' Annette asked as she punched in Baloyi's number. 'Of course,' she said to herself, 'he'd be a pretty useless assassin if that hadn't occurred to him when he was setting this up.'

Major Baloyi answered his phone right away. 'Where the hell have you been?' he shouted. 'We've been trying to get in touch with either of you from the moment we got a call from the owner of Bosco's in Klipspruit. He claims you're in serious trouble.'

'He's right! We were checking out a house where we were told Rylston may be living but, when we arrived someone opened fire on us from some trees across the road.'

'Stay inside the house. A special task force team is already on its way to your location as we speak.'

'Do you know where we are?'

'Of course! We've received at least three phone calls from farmers living in that area all reporting shots being fired. Because of the number of farm invasions around there, you could say they're rather sensitive to such things.'

Keeping below the level of the window, Annette joined Andre in what passed for the kitchen. 'Help is on its way,' she said, 'trouble is it may take some time to get here. Do you think he's got someone out there covering the back?'

'I'm about to find out,' he said draping his jacket over the head of a broom. Lifting it up, he moved his decoy slowly past the window. The glass shattered as a sustained burst of automatic gunfire shredded his jacket, ripping the broom handle from his hands and knocking chunks of plaster off the back wall of the kitchen. Almost simultaneously, the gunman out front opened fire, spraying the front of the house with bullets.

'Bathroom!' Andre yelled as the gunfire continued unabated, 'we've got to get into the bathtub! Pray to God it's made of cast iron.' Throwing caution to the wind, they dashed to the bathroom and, together, climbed in and lay down in the bathtub as round after round punched holes in the wooden walls of the house. 'The bastards are using automatic rifles, AK47's by the sound of it. I hope Baloyi's men are not too far away!'

CHAPTER 44

LUIPERD'S VLEI

SPORADIC BURSTS OF GUNFIRE CONTINUED to threaten the very structure of the house until finally, the sirens of approaching police vehicles caused the two gunmen to consider their now limited options. The silence which followed, was almost as unnerving as the one-sided fire fight which preceded it. 'No, don't get up!' Andre warned Annette, 'it may not be over yet.' A renewed outburst of automatic rifle fire around the front of the house caused them to remain huddled together in the sheltering confines of their cast iron bathtub. They stayed silent until a stentorian bellow announced the arrival of the lead elements of the police special task force, 'Armed police! Drop your weapons! Get down on the ground! Do not move!'

'So, this is what comes of failing to notify your commanding officer of your intention to search a property without his permission and, I've no doubt, without the required search warrant!' Major Baloyi said with a smile as he watched Annette and Andre clamber out of the bathtub.

'Thank you for coming to our rescue so promptly and, if you don't mind me asking, what was the last bit of shooting all about?' Andre asked as he shook hands with Baloyi.

'A man armed with an AK47, ran from the trees across the road out front and foolishly ignored shouted orders to drop his weapon. He's beyond questioning I'm afraid and, before you ask, it wasn't Clive Rylston.'

'Then it must have been Rylston himself firing at us from the trees at the back of the house,' Annette ventured, 'and I don't suppose you've seen any sign of him?'

'We had no idea there was a second gunmen,' Baloyi added. 'That is until we saw the bullet marks on the rear of the house and picked up two empty AK47 magazines amidst a pile of spent cartridges. If indeed it was Rylston, then I'm afraid he's long gone.'

'Oh, I've no doubt it was Rylston,' Andre remarked pointing to the discarded boxes of Bosco's Fried Chicken littering the kitchen. 'And if you look in the bedroom, I expect you'll find dozens of used syringes, meth pipes and other drug paraphernalia he now uses on a regular basis.'

'I can't tell you how pleased I am to be finally going home to Luiperd's Vlei,' Annette said sitting up close to Andre as he drove out onto the R40 headed for Phalaborwa.

'I'm glad you accepted Baloyi's offer of a police car keeping watch on your house in the wildlife estate. I thought you were really going to dig your heels in on that one.'

'I fully intended to! But the look on your face changed my mind,' Annette replied smiling at him. 'Though, you must admit, we've managed to survive all of Clive Rylston's efforts to get rid of us so far.'

'It's the "so far" part that worries me the most,' he said as he stopped at the gate leading into the wildlife estate. Swiping the access card that Annette handed him and while waiting for the barrier to rise, he leant across and kissed her.

'Now that's what I call the perfect start to a long overdue sensual evening at home.'

Andre woke from a deep sleep with a nagging feeling that something was not quite right. He lay listening for any strange sounds but, apart from Annette's gentle breathing, the house was silent. The red glowing numerals on their bedside clock showed it had just gone two in the morning as he gently unwrapped his arms from around her and carefully got out of bed. Their lovemaking, which began on the sofa in the lounge and continued through to the bedroom, meant that he had to search a number of places before he was able to find his shirt and pants.

Padding through to the front door, he checked to make sure the dead-bolts were in place before pulling a curtain aside and looking out of the narrow window towards the road. The reassuring glow of the dome light in the police car parked across the road, gave him some degree of comfort that another pair of eyes was keeping watch on their house. He was about to pull the curtain closed, when he saw the dome light in the police car go out, come back on, then go out again. 'Probably got tired of reading,' he smiled as he pulled the curtain back in place and wandered through to the kitchen to make himself a cup of tea.

As the kettle came to a boil, he brewed two cups, one for himself and the other for the police constable on duty outside. Leaving through the back door, Andre walked down the back path to the side gate and out onto the road. Tapping on the passenger side window of the police car and not receiving any response, he tried the door handle. It was locked and the car was too far from the nearest streetlight to light up its interior. Still carrying the cup of tea, he went around to the driver's door and tried the handle. As the door opened, the dome light came on revealing a scene of horror Andre would not soon forget.

The police constable's body, which was slumped against the driver's door, collapsed into his arms, the unfortunate man's head falling to one side almost completely severed at the neck. Despite Andre's many years of experience as a policeman in London attending far too many brutal mur-ders, the savagery of this man's death shocked him to the core. Lifting the body back into the driver's seat, he carefully closed the car door, hoping to preserve as much evidence as possible for the forensic team which would arrive as soon as he called Baloyi.

Aware that the perpetrator may still be in the area and concerned that he had left Annette alone in the house, he ran towards the back door. At that instant, the floodlights, which illuminated the pool and garden in front of the *stoep,* came on as Annette, wrapped in her dressing gown, appeared on the *stoep.* Clasping her Z88 pistol with both hands, she pointed it at a man, covered in blood, standing on the far side of the pool. He was carrying a bloodied panga, which he waved around in a threatening manner, all the while emitting alarming howls.

'Stay away from him,' Andre shouted as he raced to her side, 'he's just murdered the policeman. I think he's high on *TIK*!'

'Talk to him Andre, maybe he'll listen to you.'

'I doubt that! But I'll give it a try' Andre replied. 'Clive, Clive Rylston, drop the weapon, we can help you.' Rylston stopped waving the panga around and stared straight at them, almost as though he was seeing them for the first time. 'That's the idea, take it easy, no-one is going to hurt you!' Looking down at the blood on his hands and clothes, Rylston raised the panga above his head and with a blood-curdling scream, rushed towards them.

At that same instant, a tawny blur launched itself from the dark shadows of the bush beyond the garden, landing with terrifying force on Rylston's back, slamming him down to the ground. Razor sharp claws gripped his shoulders, as the leopard's powerful jaws sank two-inch long fangs into the back of Rylston's head, crushing his skull like an overripe melon.

'Jesus! It's Xengelela!' Annette shouted, levelling her pistol.

'Don't shoot!' Andre warned, 'you may hit the man!'

'I'm more worried about us!' she replied keeping the huge male leopard squarely in the sights of her pistol. Moving to her side, the two of them watched in horror as the animal licked at the blood pouring from Rylston's head and neck. As if realizing this was not its usual prey, the leopard raised its head, glanced briefly in their direction then, without a sound, bounded off into the darkness.

'Now I've bloody well seen everything!' Andre laughed as the shock and adrenaline rush wore off. 'What will happen now? Do you think the police, or the wildlife people will want to hunt down and kill your leopard?'

'It's quite likely they will. It will be up to us to make sure they never find out how he was killed. Xengelela only attacked Rylston because he was attempting to run away. Any sudden movement like that will trigger a predator's attack response,' Annette said.

'OK, let me get this straight,' Baloyi said watching as the ambulance crews removed both bodies after the forensic teams had completed their initial investigations. 'After murdering Constable Malema in his vehicle, Rylston threatened to attack you both with the same panga. At which point you, Andre, shot him numerous times in the head using Captain Fourie's pistol?'

'Rylston was high on *TIK* and completely out of his mind. I shot him a number of times because that's how I was trained in the army.'

'Ah! Whatever happened to the double tap you people are supposed to use?' he said looking at Andre. 'Your multiple shots shattered Rylston's skull making it almost impossible for our forensic people to establish the exact cause of death.'

'I would have thought a number of .38 calibre bullets to the head would be a reasonable assumption,' Annette said testily.

'Nevertheless, I'm still a little puzzled by all those scratches on his shoulders and back; do you think they may've been caused by some wild animal?'

'Major,' Andre replied, 'this was a man high on *TIK* and God knows what else. He was running around like a madman in the bush, ploughing through *wag 'n bietjie* thorn bushes and slashing himself to ribbons. That's your wild animal accounted for right there!'

'Fair enough,' Baloyi conceded as he turned to leave. 'Andre, on another matter, I'm to tell you that Colonel Banerjee is flying in tomorrow. He wants to meet with you. Can't imagine why though,' he said smiling.

⬦

'Before I left Jo'burg, I received a call from your superior officer at New Scotland Yard, Detective Chief Superintendent Bryson,' Garjan Banerjee said to Andre as they met in the arrivals section at the Phalaborwa Airport. 'He asked me to pass on his congratulations to you and Captain Fourie on the successful conclusion of your investigation into the *Cavalo Marinho* cartel and its leading light, Clive Rylston.'

As they walked out of the terminal to Andre's new car, Garjan turned to him, 'The Detective Chief Superintendent also wanted to know when he could expect your return to London?'

'Earlier this morning,' Andre replied, 'I asked Annette whether she would become my wife. The good news is that she accepted. So, apart from us still having to agree on a date for our wedding, you will understand our future plans are somewhat up in the air!'

OTHER BOOKS BY TONY MAXWELL...

Searching for the Queen's Cowboys
The author's travels in South Africa filming a documentary on Lord Strathcona's Horse, a Canadian regiment that fought in the Anglo-Boer War.

Pacific War Ghosts
A lavishly illustrated book detailing the author's experiences while travelling the World War Two battlefields of the South Pacific, photographing the wrecked aircraft, tanks and guns left behind by that momentous conflict.

The Young Lions
Action, adventure and erotic entanglements play out against the sweeping background of the discovery of gold in South Africa and the Anglo-Boer War.

The Brave Men
In this sequel to the 'Young Lions,' the story continues against the backdrop of a South Africa recovering from the tragedy of the Anglo-Boer War, while the world teeters on the brink of an even greater disaster, the looming Great War.

A Forest of Spears
Derek Hamilton, working as a close protection officer in Somalia, falls in love with Rachel Cavendish, a British Intelligence officer. Kidnapped and held for ransom by the Somali terrorist group al-Shaman, Derek is finally freed only to discover that Rachel has been recalled to London to deal with a new terror threat. The two do not meet again 'til they join forces to hunt down the terrorists behind a deadly threat to airlines around the world.

The Last Wild Rhino

The bleak future the rhino faces in Africa prompts Derek Hamilton to join in the war to save them from extinction. A war that ranges from the bushveld of Southern Africa, to the capitals of Europe, to the cities of South East Asia. Worth more than gold, cocaine or heroin, the rhino's horn, meant for its self-defence, is the root cause behind the relentless struggle to save this species from eventual extinction.

Printed in Great Britain
by Amazon

48314562R00149